JUST
IMAGINE

Also by Barbara Kastelin

THE PARROT TREE

WHEN SNOW FELL

A BAD LOT

HOTEL BELVEDERE

JUST IMAGINE

SHORT STORIES

All the best

Barbara Kastelin

BARBARA KASTELIN

Matador
Unit E2 Airfield Business Park,
Harrison Road, Market Harborough,
Leicestershire. LE16 7UL
Tel: 0116 2792299
Email: books@troubador.co.uk
Web: www.troubador.co.uk/matador
Twitter: @matadorbooks

ISBN 978 1803136 585

British Library Cataloguing in Publication Data.
A catalogue record for this book is available from the British Library.

Printed and bound by CPI Group (UK) Ltd, Croydon, CR0 4YY
Typeset in 11pt Aldine401 BT by Troubador Publishing Ltd, Leicester, UK

Matador is an imprint of Troubador Publishing Ltd

For my daughter, Pascale

CONTENTS

ARABESQUE IN
THE RAIN

'Your past follows you, wherever you go,' Mother used to say. She had been lowered into her grave last February, and Sophie had imagined her, cushioned by memories like polyester packing beans, each one an important moment from her past.

In July, James came home from work and opened a bottle of *for guests* Bordeaux. He insisted on sitting outside on the patio, despite a brisk wind blowing across the fens of Ely: there was something he needed to discuss. He had decided that living in the south of France for a while would do the family a world of good, as well as helping the business. His job was to sell glass verandas, manufactured in Sweden by Klart-Glas, and for some months now he had been struggling, judging from the tossing and groaning in his sleep. Sophie had banished him to the spare room. A year's rent in a farmhouse near Arles, paid for by letting out their English home, was his proposal. He could expand his sales into France, where conveniently he would already be living. And this was the right time to do it; the country could vote for Brexit, after which it would not be possible.

Uplifted by the daring plan, to which she had said

1

neither yes nor no, James spent the next few days preparing his work transition. At first, Sophie put it down as a fantasy. After Alex, their second child, was born, James had tried to convince her they should go and live in Singapore, where nannies and cleaning staff were abundant. Arles was at least reachable by car. In the evenings, when the children were asleep, James spent hours searching on Holiday France Direct, before she heard him going to his bed in the spare room. At the weekends, Alex and his sister, Luna, jumped shrieking through the lawn sprinkler, and Sophie hoped the France idea would pass.

However, she became nervous when James came home in a pair of blue espadrilles and walked around the house to 'get the feel of them'. And then came the moment he shouted out loud, because he had found *their* house. Sitting next to him at the computer, she looked at an estate agent's description of *Les Hirondelles,* a converted farmhouse with a Mediterranean-style interior, a spacious kitchen, and a straw-covered pergola. The garden was described as easily manageable. The four bedrooms were done up in rustic style, one in a round tower at a corner of the house.

When she asked if he could show her any other possibilities, he admitted they were already committed to *Les Hirondelles*. He had made an international bank transfer.

Was there any other information which he thought he might share with her?

James squirmed and wiped his forehead with the sleeve of his shirt. 'The rental starts on the first of August.'

'Less than two weeks!'

'There is another thing,' he said, and rolled his desk chair further away from her. 'I am off to Sweden tomorrow, the factory in Gothenburg. I won't make it back in time to drive us to Arles.'

'You mean, I have to…?'

'I'll be able to join you in *Les Hirondelles* two or three days after your arrival, hopefully.'

'Hopefully?' Sophie was aghast. *I can't do that on my own*, she thought. *None of it.*

'Remember our estate agent's instructions,' continued James. 'Apart from the furniture on the inventory, our house has to look as if nobody ever lived in it. At least half of our clutter will have to go, you are aware of that? I mean go, bye-bye for good.'

'Clutter?'

'I have rented a six cubic-metre space in a storage warehouse. They'll bring you boxes, and will come and pick up the packed-up stuff when you tell them to.' James stuck a pink post-it on the computer rim. On it was written the warehouse contact number.

'You *have* been busy,' Sophie said, patting his hot hand which cupped the computer mouse. He was too far into cyber-land to hear the sarcasm in her voice.

All the preparations for the move would be her responsibility: the arrangements with the school, letters to banks, insurance companies and close friends, not to forget the clearing of the *clutter* from the home in which they had lived since they got married eleven years ago, when she had been thirty one – a nest in which two children, now nine and seven, had started their lives.

3

A secure place, in which old-fashioned items from Mother's house were only beginning to adjust to IKEA.

'Go room by room,' James suggested. 'I'm sorry to load this on you, but you have ten days.'

'God created the world in six, didn't He?' said Sophie. 'But then He didn't have clutter.'

'That's my girl.' His arms reached out to capture her. She ducked.

'*Les Hirondelles* is only two miles from the sea,' said James, 'fifteen minutes from a supermarket, on foot.'

She said nothing, just sat there, eyes closed. When she opened them, his tongue was moving around on the inside of his cheek, something he did when he felt cornered or embarrassed. He went on to suggest they slept together on this last night. That surprised, but pleased, her.

When the time came for their rare coupling, he tried, but it felt half-hearted. She responded as best she could, but he rolled off her, mumbling he was sorry, and fell into a deep sleep, snoring away. Nothing would be different in France. Klart-Glas, even online, his endless customer calls and factory trips, would demand his energy to the last. She realised that, over time, it had come to suit her; she did not enjoy sex with him. For her not to have to fake it, she had to replay the worn-out memory of her uni love – an afternoon in a woodland clearing on an orange mohair rug, with a relentless woodpecker knocking against a tree.

Early the next day, she made fresh orange juice while James got ready upstairs. The children appeared and didn't want toast, didn't want cereal, didn't want orange juice. They could feel the tension. In the hall stood James's packed silver aluminium suitcase, to be driven to France for him. On top of it was a Panama hat she had not seen before.

When he came down the stairs ready to leave for Gothenburg, he was dressed with his usual care in an eggshell linen suit and a dark-blue silk shirt. His hair, wet from the shower, was parted neatly along the side of his head. His failure last night pushed from his mind, his sperm untapped, he was ready to compensate by dispensing advice.

'Don't forget to service the Volvo before you leave. Book it today. And here, a map of France.' He unfolded it. The children approached and looked at the camouflage-coloured expanse, through which ran a fat yellow highlighted line. 'That's where you are going to drive with your mother.'

'What's the red cross?' asked Alex.

'That,' James checked the map, 'is where you will spend the night. A routier motel called Première Classe.'

'What room number?' Sophie asked.

He sensed her hostility. 'It is a drive up and crash out for a few hours motel. I thought you would like the simplicity of it. All you need is a Visa debit card. Don't forget to take it.'

'Dad, please don't go,' pleaded Luna. 'Mum can't drive all that way. We want you to do it.'

'Sure she can,' said James. 'Now, listen you two. You're already on holiday, so you can help your mother pack up the house. Be good. I'll see you in *Les Hirondelles*. How exciting is that?' He showed his teeth in a grimace.

5

'Hirondelle means swallow,' said Sophie, who had downloaded *Google translate*.

'My taxi is waiting.' James picked up the Panama, bent and kissed her. With two hands, he set the hat on his drying hair as one places the plastic bride and groom onto a freshly iced cake. Stiffly, he walked out of the door and down the sun-filled garden path.

She closed the door with a bang.

★

The next morning, while the children were making a mess in the kitchen with cereals and milk, Sophie attacked the garage. It was so full that the car had not fitted in it for some years. How could intelligent people amass so many useless items? She backed the Volvo Estate up to the open garage door and folded down the back seats. When the car was full, she asked the children to tidy their rooms while she was out, and drove off to the Milton recycling centre, south of Ely.

The site was busy. An employee in a hi-vis jacket made her reverse into a tight space against a row of massive skips. After a spell of hot, dry weather, the concrete looked parched. Pebbles and debris showed stark against the bleached surface.

At the open door of a converted trailer stood what must have been the gang-master, judging from his hard face and the bodycam fixed to his chest. To the trailer walls either side of him were stuck notices, one clearly a time chart with a pen dangling from a string.

Feeling the man's concentration on her, like being

singled out in class by the teacher, she reached into the back of the car and began tugging at the metal legs of an old workbench. She needed help. She looked around and the staff she could see were all young and athletic; but, if there was a pattern to how they operated, it was not evident. Each man was busy doing his own thing and yet there seemed to be a bond between them – a pack of large, strong dogs in their own territory, communicating by instinct rather than words. No music was being played, despite the piles of boom boxes and CD players in the *small electric goods* space. The gang-master presumably would not tolerate it; he was the type to thump them if they stepped out of line, or otherwise leave them to get on with things. She saw him jerk his chin at two workers who were carrying a flowery sofa. They interpreted the gesture and nodded their consent.

James would belittle her imaginative interpretation of the site. For him, it would be a well-run, no-nonsense county council work-yard. Making more of it would only hamper her efficient use of it. She had to believe that she could manage this decluttering by herself, despite the heat and dust.

In the distance, on a new landfill mound, a bulldozer crawled up the hill. At the top, earth was poured out of the front loader to cover the sin of human wastefulness. A row of crows sat on the flattened-out ridge of a covered fill, like black clothes pegs clipped to the horizon, where cloudless blue sky met red earth.

A shrill whistle made her jump. The gang-master shouted to one of his workers, who was balancing in a skip on a high pile of cardboard.

She yanked at the legs of the workbench wedged in the back of the Volvo. When the bench gave, it came out with two flower pots, which broke at her feet. A hot beam of guilt shot through her. How could she pack up a whole house if she failed at the first trip to the dump? The gang-master must surely have seen and photographed it. His *dogs* would be sent her way, snarling, and when given the chin signal, they would attack. *I mustn't show my fear*, she told herself. The sun burnt on her shoulders; the metal of the Volvo was searing. Nothing happened, but she heard a repeated scratching. She looked down, and the stiff bristles of a platform broom on the bone-dry ground swept away the pot shards, and her clumsiness with them. She hopped aside, as one of the gang with two reflective silver bands around the bottom of his black trousers continued sweeping.

She relaxed and took out her phone and messaged the children that she would be home soon. The broom sweeper shouted something to a colleague. To Sophie, he said, 'Polish', with a broad grin. Sophie remembered a programme she had seen about families living near a huge pile of refuse in Nicaragua. Their livelihood depended entirely on what they found and could sell. All day long, even the small children rooted around the stinking rubbish like scavenging animals, fighting each other for finds. Did these Poles hope to salvage something valuable and hide it from the gang-master, to supplement their minimum wage?

The man stopped brushing.

'Thank you for…' She waved vaguely at the ground where the flower pots had lain.

He said nothing and did not move. His hands at the broom handle were beautiful, elongated fingers wrapped around the wooden stick; the oval nails had a silk sheen. She decided not to ask him to help her with the bench, but instead smiled at him tentatively.

The broom did not move.

'It has been hot for a long time,' she heard herself say to him.

He glanced at the smartphone in her hand, as if it were similar to his gang-master's camera. She slipped it back into her skirt pocket.

'My children,' she said, 'at home.' She should not give personal information away, she reminded herself. 'A heatwave, as we English probably call it erroneously, now happens every summer. We're not used to it. It has to do with polluting our planet, probably.'

He lifted the broom and banged its head against the ground. His biceps strained against the sleeves of his black T-shirt. The fuzz on his forearms shone gold-filigree against a deep tan. She sighed.

He stopped the banging. She sensed a growing impatience, a tension, in him. Suddenly, he looked directly at her. The flecks in his amber eyes took her by surprise. She was standing intimidatingly close to a Polish member of a work-gang, whose eyes offered her an intimate glimpse into his soul; she felt absurdly nervous, emotionally and sexually. Ridiculous. Of course she could handle bringing clutter to the dump by herself. Had she, at forty-two, not handled many human situations?

'On the continent,' she persisted, 'summers are normally hot. In Poland...' Words dried up.

'Poland,' he repeated, bent and picked up a silver bottle top as if it were a sovereign. She felt the urge to take it from him and give him real money instead.

All of a sudden, the gang-master was standing next to them. Her instinct was to run away. She overcame it. Also, she was wearing the wrong shoes.

'No chit-chatting with customers,' the boss snapped at her young Pole. 'Watch it, Pavel. You're still on parole and will go back inside if I don't sign you off. Lots can still go wrong.'

Pavel looked uncomfortable to have so much revealed about him. The gang-master got the message.

'Are we done here, lady?' he asked aggressively.

'Not quite.' Sophie opened the car door and pulled out a large blue vase in the shape of an open-mouthed dolphin.

Pavel took the vase from her. 'Rubble and glass,' he said. The gang-master walked back to his trailer office.

'Is beautiful,' said Pavel, holding the dolphin in the crux of his arm.

She laughed. 'It was a joke gift for Aunt Dot gone wrong. She always makes us fish pie.'

He did not understand. At a skip, he eased the dolphin gently down amid the other detritus.

'Our Aunt Dorothy has no sense of humour,' she continued. 'None at all. It's fish pie every time.'

Pavel rubbed his hands against his council trouser legs.

'Not to worry,' she added. 'Not your fault. Thank you for your help. There are more things to bring. I'll be back.' And then, with a glance in the direction of the trailer office, 'No chit-chatting. My fault. Sorry.'

Driving the empty car away, she mulled over the incident. It certainly had taken her mind off the challenges she was facing at home. James had only left the previous day. 'See you in the south of France' sounded more romantic than it was.

In fairness, he had a demanding job. She didn't. He needed a change. Hard work had earned him forty-five per cent of Klart-Glas. It was their livelihood. What married woman with children would argue with that? All that was expected of her was to drive along the yellow highlighter on the French map. What more direction did a woman need?

She ambled through the house. At the bookshelf she pulled out *A Year in Provence*, which James had brought home and read avidly. Peter Mayle had a lot to answer for. She went to the kitchen and threw the book into the pedal bin.

'Mum,' objected Luna, 'that belongs in recyclables.'

Her daughter was right, of course. A book was paper, soiled by words. It would be washed and stonked, to make cardboard or doormats or something.

Their father gone, the children increasingly dared to express their feelings about what was happening. She showed them pictures of *Les Hirondelles*, emphasising the joys of the nearby sea and the covered pergola with barbeque.

'We can sit outside to eat.'

'Eat what? Onions and baguettes?' said Alex.

'We won't know anyone,' fretted Luna. 'Won't have, like, friends.'

'There will be neighbours, with children your age,' said Sophie.

'Yeah,' replied Alex. 'Frère Jacques who sleeps all day long.'

'We will be happy,' she said, looking at her son fondly. He was a funny boy. Adorably so.

'We don't speak French.'

'Your dad says, the point of going is to learn a new language.'

'He can speak it. That's cheating.'

'I wouldn't say he can speak it. He took French A level yonks ago.' *He can order a bottle of Bordeaux in the Coach and Horses without much of an accent, showing off to the waitress.* That, she did not say. Her own French was restricted to *hors'd'oeuvre, ambiance, flambé, futon* and *sauce marie-rose.*

The real panic in the children, of course, was the thought of having to go to a French school.

'It will be the real thing,' she said. 'When we come back, you'll sail through French GCSE and A levels.'

'*Merde!*' said Alex, making her laugh and forget that time was ticking and that she would not be ready in time. Perhaps she was short of a normal person's stamina. Perhaps she was not bright enough. She needed a lot of sleep, soft sweaters, a temperate climate. Her ideal was gentle rain and nothing urgent to do.

That evening, Luna had a melt-down. She was a nine-year-old, who took friendship seriously; a child who cared about people, sensed what they needed. She was generous, a giver. It was important that James's adventure did not harm her. Only when Sophie suggested they invite Luna's best friend to France, did her daughter calm down.

12

'That would be special for her,' Luna concluded.

The next day, Sophie dared tackle the children's bedrooms. As she entered Alex's room with an empty box, he pretended to shoot her with his Nerf gun, not happy that everything would have to go into storage, including the entire space rocket and launch pad set. He did, though, willingly hand over the electronic guitar, an instrument Alex never practised, despite James yelling at him, and only air-played in front of the hall mirror.

She would leave sorting out her own clothes for last. For that, James had planned on each taking only one suitcase. They would buy clothes in Sunday markets, clothes which suited their new climate.

What about her peacock party dress, bought in London but never actually seen on her? Luna had prevented the tenth wedding anniversary party, by falling off her bicycle and needing stitches. In the dress under a raincoat, Sophie had sat in A&E. Arles would not offer an opportunity to make it up to Versace.

*

And then, far too quickly, the last day in England arrived. The estate agent came to check the house. After his departure, Sophie drove the full Volvo Estate back to the recycling centre, going slightly over the speed limit, spurred on by anticipation. Perhaps her accelerated heartbeat was caused by eagerness to see Pavel again – or, more likely, sheer nerves, because the next day she would have to drive off at six in the morning, catch the nine o'clock ferry from Dover, and then drive all the way through France, a trip she was dreading.

At first, Pavel was not in sight. The gang-master stood at the door of his office, his sharp features scanning the scene. Only after taking an armful of duvets to the textile container did Sophie see the fleck-eyed Pole pulling a bedframe, the metal squealing as it scraped along the concrete. Her eyes on him met his on her. She had to control her trembling and looked away. Up on the landfill, the bulldozer was labouring. There were no crows, but white cumuli bulged over the horizon. She sensed danger.

At her feet, a clump of groundsel deprived of water lay limp and brown. She realised that she was so emotionally raw that she felt sorry for it.

She carried a sack with wooden building blocks up to the *natural wood* container. As she started down, her shoes ringing on the metal stairs, she noticed Pavel standing nearby.

'Take care, lady.' His smile was generous and personal.

'You, too,' she said, which meant nothing. Curiously, it did not matter. She had entered a world in which communication was cryptically monosyllabic at its most expansive – a world with values which existed outside her routine existence, but one into which, with a thrill, she felt she fitted. She hesitated halfway down, because he was lingering at the bottom. What did she expect could happen? Hundreds of women came to this yard every week to discard unwanted things. It was ridiculous to imagine that he, a low-paid rough worker, might think of her as special.

She rumbled to the bottom of the steps, and he went with her back to the Volvo.

'A sad last thing the charity shop did not want,' she said, and pulled the electric guitar from the passenger seat. 'My son's. We bought it because his teacher said he had musical talent. He wanted it, but then never practised – metal?'

Pavel shook his head. A lot of unsaid things happened between them. With a rash move, she pushed the instrument against his chest, wondering whether she had just forced a gift on him. He carried it away, and it seemed natural that she followed.

A steel-grey shipping container stood at ground level, its side open. The random items inside in the musty heat looked sadly abandoned, but they had survived by being too valuable to discard. Perhaps the gang-master hoped to sell them. There was the flowery sofa. Several paintings leant against each other. An Afghan carpet was loosely folded. A wood-carved fire surround was propped against the ribbed metal wall. A mantel clock ticked on a random round table. A drinks cabinet, the top doors open, displayed a mirrored interior. Two large, dark-blue porcelain seats in the shape of elephants stared at each other. A brown upright piano, the lid open, displayed its keyboard. Pavel put the guitar on the sofa.

A crackling and prolonged growling outside changed the mood in the metal enclosure. It became a cave.

'Rain. Strong rain,' Pavel said.

A loud thunderclap. The first heavy raindrops started to knock on the roof of the container. Pavel carried one of the elephants to the piano and hitched up his trousers a notch, before sitting on the porcelain saddle. A sharp shower now drummed over their heads. Outside, it had gone dark in the middle of the day. They were separated from it by a cascading silver-bead curtain. Still the force of the downpour increased. In the greyness outside their shelter, voices shouted with urgency, car horns hooted, figures ran past as if something sinister was happening. Safe in their private, oddly furnished sanctuary, Sophie edged herself closer to him at the piano. He started to play a classical piece, the sounds pearling against the resonant metal walls, while on the roof the rain tapped its own rhythm.

How could one play such intricate music on a honkytonk? Was this a delirium? The contrary, actually; she felt an eagerly engaged sense of reality. She saw the unevenness of his hair cut at the nape, with a clarity and closeness she had never experienced before. She even perceived individual hairs growing through his suntanned skin. She felt, more than saw, everything with clear outline: the young man at the piano, one of his heavy work shoes working the brass pedal, the painted bottom of the elephant sticking out under the backside of a man, a young criminal, who played romantic music undisturbed by the thunderstorm overhead.

'Debussy,' he said, without turning round. 'The first Arabesque.'

Tremolos followed. She watched his rapidly moving fingers. In the grey world beyond, men still shouted; something heavy was being dragged along the ground. Pavel and she seemed to be forgotten. There came a passage of infinite beauty, despite the slightly tinny sound of the instrument. Pavel's fingers indulged an arabesque dance on the keys and then, after a sprint, slowed to a soothing melody. She sat on the second elephant. The pianist did not stop; he had turned the confined space into a universe of pleasure. He ceased to be a council employee. He was beyond the gang-master and had entered a realm in which creatures like him were rewarded by angels.

At the open container side, the silver curtain still fell. He played with abandon, lifting her as in a dream to another world; he could invent any world, anything she wished for. Love. A most ordinary wish everyone harboured. She did not desire so much to be loved as to be able to love.

A gust of trapped moist air brushed along her, as the rain stopped and the pressure lifted. He came to the end of the arabesque, and his fingers, without creative purpose any longer, slowly lowered the lid over the keys. It was a sad move.

'You liked?'

Her tender smile thanked him for the escape he had shared with her.

The gang-master came through the thinning rain curtain. He grabbed Pavel's arm and pulled him off the elephant.

'He plays beautifully,' she remonstrated.

'Madam, don't meddle. He's not here to show off.'

Once Pavel had been marched out of the container, the magic was destroyed. It was her turn to leave. The rain was banal now that the storm had moved on.

Against neon lights in the trailer office, Sophie saw

17

Pavel being talked to by the boss. And then the young Pole emerged, pushing a folded piece of paper into his trouser pocket. He was not wearing the hi-vis jacket any longer. Head down, he walked past her without caring. Why should she matter to him? She was at least ten years older and knew nothing of his life.

She went back to the Volvo and drove out and along the lane which led to the traffic lights and the A10, carefully and slowly to avoid large, rain-filled potholes.

The figure trudging along the grass verge was Pavel. He carried a small black bag over one shoulder. Heavy wet hair dangled deep over his forehead. She slowed to walking speed. He did not engage. She drove on, stopped and reached over to pop open the passenger door. He ignored her. She drove a little further and opened the door again.

'Get in,' she shouted.

Reluctantly, he climbed into the car. He smelled like a wet dog.

'Where to?' she asked. 'Where are you going?' She made it clearer for him.

'Don't know.'

'Where do you live?'

'Don't know.'

She drove off. He dug into the pocket of his council trousers and pulled out the folded paper. He pointed an imaginary pistol at his temple and said, 'Pang!'

'Fired? Because you played the piano? What about your parole?'

He offered her a sideways glance. 'Finished now.' He did not really want to talk.

When she turned into the close in which their house

was located, she realised she had driven him to her home. In some panic, she asked, 'Tell me quickly, please. Have you murdered someone? Have you hurt children? Why were you in prison?'

'Just stealing. Only three months.'

'Ah.' She felt relief. 'Diamonds? Robbed a bank?'

'Armagnac bottles.'

'That's brandy, isn't it?'

'Better than brandy.'

'Are you an alcoholic?'

'I don't drink spirits.'

'You steal Armagnac, but don't drink it?' Now they had arrived in front of her house.

'I did not steal them. They disappeared.'

'Really?' the word escaped her.

'Is a long story.'

*

The children were in the living room, watching television.

'That took a long time,' complained Alex.

'There was a storm. Did you close the windows in your rooms?'

'Who is this?' asked Luna.

'He helped me unload the Volvo at the dump.'

They did not like this answer. 'So you invited him to our house?' said Luna. 'Dad would not like it.'

'I go,' said Pavel.

'You stay. My husband is in Sweden. We'll work something out.'

19

'Mum?'

'He can sleep in the guest room for this one night. Tomorrow, we drive off early.'

'He doesn't even speak English.'

'Pavel is a musician. Plays the piano like a pro.'

'Probably plays the guitar, too,' said Alex grumpily.

'Practice,' said Pavel. 'Only practice.'

The children eyed him with suspicion.

'Hey, it's almost dinner time,' Sophie said, louder than necessary. 'We need to heat up what we have in the freezer. Who wants to help me?'

The children turned away from her.

'I help,' offered Pavel.

Over a family-size Italian meatball bake, Sophie asked Pavel how come he could play the piano so well.

'Is a long story, too,' he replied. He explained that his mother had been a cleaner in the Conservatory in Warsaw. His father was not in the picture. As a child, he listened, played when nobody was there, was taught over the years by bored piano teachers, who appreciated his passion to learn.

Sophie showed him to the guest room, gave him a towel, and demonstrated the small shower. Before she left him to it, he took her hand and kissed the back of it. The little warm puff on her skin from his nostrils felt immodestly intimate.

*

The alarm clock woke her at five-thirty in the morning. The bags were packed. Pavel helped the kids get organised and then loaded up the car. He helped her wrap and pack the lunch into the cool box.

'Mum,' complained the children. 'Pavel is still here. Is he coming with us to France?'

She looked at the young man as he pushed James's silver suitcase into the back of the Volvo. Just then, a small red Skoda drove up.

'Aunt Dot!' the children greeted Dorothy.

'My brother pinged me to say you were off to France today,' she said, getting out of the car. 'I came to make sure you're all right.'

'Vive la France,' Alex proclaimed.

'Who's the bloke packing up your car?'

No-one answered this question.

'I get it,' said Dot. 'You're taking an au pair with you. Sensible – but, a man? James didn't say anything about this.' Dot put her hands on her hips to evaluate this male au pair.

'He is more than an au pair,' replied Sophie. She sounded defensive. 'He is also handyman and music teacher.'

'Oh, no.' Alex waved the idea away from him.

'Where did you find him?' asked Dot quietly. 'He looks more like a nightclub bouncer than a nanny who reads Cinderella to kids in their bedrooms, if you ask me.'

'I didn't ask you, and we need to go.'

To Sophie's surprise, the kids, without further complicating things, took their places on the back seat, Pavel between them. She slipped behind the wheel.

As they backed out of the drive, Luna shouted,

'Goodbye, door. Goodbye, garden. Goodbye, Aunt Dot.' Turning to Pavel, she asked, 'Are you really going to be our au pair?'

'Maybe.'

The girl decided. 'It's cool to have a boy au pair – man au pair, I mean.'

What have I done? wondered Sophie, driving south on the M11. Dorothy would now text her brother and James, hopefully, would not believe it.

As they boarded the P&O ferry, to her relief the immigration officer saw nothing wrong with Pavel's passport. They sailed away from the white cliffs of Dover, and the children explored the different decks, bent over the railings to watch the waves wash up on the hull, and felt exhilarated by the feel of hair flying free.

Sophie sat with Pavel at a table. He insisted on buying her a diet Coke. She watched him order it at the bar. The barman's body language, the matey pat on the shoulder across the bar counter, showed they had recognised each other as Poles, spoke the same language and were instantly connected. In prison, there must have been a lot of male ganging up, or fighting each other, or worse.

And now she was harbouring this criminal, trusting her children into his care. Just because he could play Arabesque by Debussy did not mean he was innocent or mentally stable. And yet, she wrote him an employment contract on a sheet of paper that she asked the steward for.

Grateful for her trust in him, he started to talk, while she stared out of the window at the waves.

Three Polish mates of his had been working in an

Armagnac vineyard in France, while he was employed as a gardener on an estate near Sandringham in Norfolk. The vineyard had released hundred-year-old brandy in hand-blown crystal decanters and presented in a velvet-lined wooden box. Each sold for two thousand five hundred pounds. His Polish friends had stolen twenty-five of the bottles and driven them to England, rolled in turf which was being delivered to Pavel for his gardening.

Pavel's job had been to bury the precious bottles in the park and roll the turf over them. He then had to sell the Armagnac by impersonating his well-connected Russian employer, who was spending time in his Caribbean property. Pavel wore the man's clothes, his aftershave and pretended to be a friend of the royals next door. Handsome as Pavel was, with hurriedly learnt wine jargon, he pulled it off and sold ten bottles. But then he discovered that the rest had been dug up and stolen. The other Poles accused Pavel of going behind their backs.

'Did you?' she asked. 'Did you cheat them?'

'Not me. The owner came back from the Caribbean, and I got arrested and sent to prison for three months.'

'How about the others?'

'They are still out there.'

'Maybe this is a good moment for you to tell me more about yourself,' she began. 'Are you married? Have you been married? Do you have children? Parents?'

'Woah, woah, lady.' He held his arms up in surrender. 'I am willing to tell you more about me, if you like. All you have to do is ask.'

'I guess,' she said, 'if you were married you would be wearing a ring.'

'I sold it in prison.'

'See, that's what I mean. I cannot trust you.'

'You picked me up, remember? I never guaranteed anything, nor promised.'

She realised that she had bungled this conversation from the very start. 'You sold your wedding ring because you and your wife were not together any longer?'

'She slept with my brother, Borys.'

'Ah, there is a brother. Good. Now we're getting somewhere.'

'Not good. I punished my wife. She broke ribs and called the police.'

'Were the police strict in Warsaw where you lived?'

'We did not live in Warsaw. My brother and I had already moved to… I know what you are doing, lady. It's clever, but it will not work.'

'Don't call me lady or madam. My name is Sophie.'

'Sophie,' he repeated. 'A nice name for a pretty woman.'

'I know what you are doing, too. It's clever, but it will not work.'

*

Immigration was no problem in France, either. The employment letter she had written on the ferry was not needed, and any suspicion would have been dispelled by the way the three of them in the backseat were getting on.

24

'Why are you driving on the wrong side of the road?' asked Luna.

'That's how they drive in France,' replied Sophie.

Alex shouted out of the open window, 'Bonjour Monsieur, bonjour Madame', at random until Pavel pulled him back.

Sophie maintained the same speed on the near-empty motorway. From the map, Pavel read out the towns they passed.

'They have a lot of saints in France,' observed Luna.

Saint-Omer? thought Sophie. *An Arab saint?*

After a couple of hours, her eyes felt dry and itchy. She drove into a large service area and gave the children and Pavel twenty pounds each to spend as they pleased.

Luna and Alex disappeared into the mall. Pavel hesitated and then strode away. *Have I done something illegal, smuggling a criminal out of England?* she wondered.

The children returned, Luna having bought a dinosaur egg. 'If I put it into water, a baby dinosaur will hatch.'

When Sophie asked what Alex had bought, he twisted about a bit before saying, 'Pavel asked for my twenty pounds.'

'Did he now?' Pavel had let her down.

'Mum, one egg is enough. Dinosaurs are really big,' her son defended Pavel.

With her generous children, she waited for Pavel to return, but he did not. He had forty pounds from her. She had helped him get to France and now he was gone. She ached with disappointment. Swaying, she was unable to get rid of the voice inside her. *Pavel is not a person for you. He has dangerous depths of which you know nothing. Now you've lost him, lost him.* Weirdly, something incomprehensible in her regretted not having caressed the hair at his nape, when he had played the piano. Too late.

She caught sight of Pavel in conversation with a lorry driver who was leaning out of his cab. *Polski Transport* was on the side of the vehicle. Pavel spoke vehemently and struck the cab door with a spread hand. The driver jumped down and, head to head, they started to shout at each other. What would James think? He would never understand how a man like Pavel had got involved with his family, even though, Sophie reasoned, her straying from the normal was the result of his rash idea to live in another country. Anyway, James was not here. The safety of her children was paramount; that was clear.

'Come along, children. We're leaving.' She began to walk back to the Volvo.

'But,' objected Alex, 'that man from the truck has just punched our au pair.'

Glancing back, she saw Pavel reacting violently. He pushed the driver against the side of the lorry, drew back his fist and landed a punch in the driver's face. The older man buckled at the knees and crumpled against the wheel cap.

Sophie trembled from the brutality, as if it were her being attacked. That same hand had played Debussy and moved her to tears. Pavel, unaware that he was observed, lit a cigarette and blew the smoke down at the beaten man.

That morning, putting the rubbish bag from the

kitchen into the black bin, she had noticed several cigarette butts. It had been too late to figure out what she could or should do about it; he smoked. He also delivered violent punches. What more was there to discover? The smart thing would be to just drive off and leave him behind.

'Mum, are you listening?' insisted Alex. 'Are we going back to the car?'

'We might have to make a rash decision here,' she said, mostly to herself.

Pavel caught up with them and reached his hand out to Sophie's arm. 'You OK?'

'Yes,' she lied.

The children dissolved the tension by babbling about the dinosaur baby they would soon have. Sophie had no idea what to say to Pavel as they walked to the Volvo.

'You don't have to worry about anything,' he said softly. 'I am here.'

'Smoking is bad for you,' was the best she could do.

'Sorry.'

'Never in the house. Promise?'

He did, and offered to drive them to Rheims.

'Do you have a valid driver's licence?'

'I drove tanks in military service.' He laughed. 'Eleven ton heavy.'

'No way,' admired Alex.

'I bought you this in the shop back there.' Pavel gave Alex a small paper bag. It was a CD: *J.S. Bach Piano Music*.

Once they were all installed in the car, he handled the heavy Volvo with confidence and drove evenly, respecting the speed limit, overtaking calmly. Sophie pushed the CD into the slot; the car was filled with piano music.

'You'll be able to play that,' Pavel shouted back to Alex who sat there, both hands over his ears.

It was nearly six o'clock when they saw the luminous Première Classe motel sign. She was glad she had a man with her who dealt with getting rooms, three next to each other along a narrow balcony which wrapped around the two-storey hotel cube.

'Look at the shower,' enthused the children. 'It's all plastic. We're in a plastic hotel.' At a picnic table on the grass in front of the building, they ate the sandwiches and shared the salad she had prepared.

*

When she woke in the morning, she heard the children laughing and playing with Pavel, a game which involved door-slamming and running along the balcony.

She drove them south towards Dijon. They made a stop for a late-morning coffee and croissants on the way. Pavel took over and, passing Valence, they entered Provence. Two hours later, they reached Orange.

'Is that like an orange?' asked Alex. When Sophie said 'Yes', he shouted, 'Hey, I can speak French.'

After another hour they came to Arles. Sophie read the directions to *Les Hirondelles* from the printout of the website. 'A droite, à gauche,' aped the children. *Gosh* for left amused them again and again.

Les Hirondelles. Here it was, just like in the picture. Pavel stopped the Volvo. The motor ticked as it cooled down.

28

The large hallway had uneven, white-washed walls, a bench, a worn carpet and a bizarre lamp on the ceiling. In a recess stood a suit of armour.

'This is good.' Pavel stroked over the helmet. 'Is a valuable antique.' He admired the ironwork. 'The owner leaves it here for people he does not know.' He tisked. 'At least three thousand pounds.'

'Some people are trusting,' said Sophie. 'Perhaps you have not come across many of those.'

They explored further. An arch to the left led into a large room with a pool table and two massive sofas and television, the room in which the kids would probably spend most of their time. The arch to the right led into a study area and, from there, into a sparsely furnished living room. Wide, glass doors opened up onto the pergola-covered patio with a table and ten chairs.

She walked straight ahead through the kitchen and utility room into the garden, which could hardly be called easy-care. The herb and vegetable patch alone demanded expert care. Beyond, she noticed a woman hanging what looked like cushion covers onto a line strung between metal posts. She came over, wiping her hands on her apron.

'Bonjour. Je suis Madame Roblon,' she said and immediately inundated Sophie in French, about the cushions not being ready but soon, and she would come once a week to clean for thirty euros. 'D'accord?'

It sounded helpful. 'Yes, d'accord.'

'Mum,' the children reported breathlessly, 'we found a statue of a naked woman with a pot under her arm at the end of the garden. There is a large snail on her bottom.' They giggled.

In the meantime, Pavel had unloaded the car and was upstairs on the landing with all the cases. He fidgeted nervously, not knowing how to go from there. A quick look around showed her a master bedroom with balcony and en suite. The family bathroom was spacious, and there were three more bedrooms. The most attractive of them was in the round tower on the east corner of the house with separate toilet and sink. She had embarked on this adventure with Pavel without explaining it to herself. Now, she was confronted by the practicalities of the situation. There were beds and pillows and bathrooms.

Waiting for instructions from her, in the light slanting onto the landing, he resembled a Polish prince – an image of beauty, power and mystery. He had shown violence, but towards them only patience and kindness. He had made no sexual move towards her. Analysing it would not offer clarity or peace, and she was incredibly tired. She just had to hang on to the memory of his playing of the Arabesque in the storm.

As if the sky read her thoughts, it sent rain. The children, driven out of the garden, came upstairs to choose their bedrooms. She expected them to fight over the round tower room, but Luna wanted the yellow one and Alex the dark-blue one. Together, they decided that Pavel had to sleep in the tower – it was special: all the walls were curved and the bed had a baldachin. A wrought-iron candlestick and two lead-encased windows gave the illusion of a medieval castle.

Sophie walked up to Pavel. 'Your room,' she said.

They entered. He turned towards her. 'You are a beautiful woman, generous.'

30

She seemed suddenly devoid of strength and had to go in and sit on his bed, fighting tears. 'Rain,' she said. 'We don't have a piano.'

He looked into her eyes. 'No, we don't. You can rent one. I can search on the internet.'

'In the silver suitcase is a laptop. My husband's. Can you set it up? In the study?'

'For you and music, I can do things.' He left her to go downstairs, carrying James's case. His strong, tanned hand on the handle gave her a feeling of guilt mixed with excitement.

Left alone, she felt a fierce regret at the lost opportunity to detain him, but it passed, and guilt at having to do her duty replaced it. She took her phone out and texted James that they had arrived at *Les Hirondelles* and that all was well. James did not respond right away; she presumed he was busy at Klart-Glas.

In the round room, she unhooked the brass lock of one of the lancet windows and opened it. The rain had petered out; already the sky was brighter. Pavel would sleep in this room, in the baldachin bed. Nude, probably, as he had no change of clothes. Had she not hijacked him from the side of the road? There were pyjamas in the silver suitcase, she thought, expensive ones from Hugo Boss. She shook her head. That would be like stealing boots from a dead soldier.

Pavel reappeared. 'You are connected to the internet. I have also found a place for renting pianos. I sent them a message.'

'Thank you. Now you can let your family and friends know where you are.'

'I don't want anybody to know where I am,' he stated rather firmly.

Perhaps the gang-master had given him a damning report and parole had been extended. Perhaps the Armagnac thieves… She stopped her thoughts wandering in that direction.

'Family and friends make life complicated,' he added, to soften his first reaction.

★

An hour later, they were all under the pergola preparing a welcome drink.

Madame Roblon had provided them with survival essentials, as she probably did for all renters. The French essentials being: baguettes, potato chips, three types of cheese, full cream, butter, eggs, cured ham, jars of paté, pasta and, best of all, bottles of chardonnay and grenadine for children. The country kitchen was equipped with appliances for serious gourmet cooking. Instead of time-saving tools, there was a rotary whisk, a mouli grater for cheese, a set of canvas icing-bags with metal nozzles, a very long steel knife-sharpener and a set of good-quality knives, including one for fish filleting.

Pavel readied a tray with the drinks. Before installing themselves, they had to move the table because Madame Roblon had hung drying cushion covers right over it. A high-pitched twittering came from a swallow's nest in the corner under the straw roof, which explained the name of the house and the small stalagmite of white bird droppings on the patio floor. That was a problem James did not have with his Klart-Glas verandas.

They lifted their glasses to toast their safe arrival. They were eager to tell each other how perfect the house was and how much they liked France so far.

Two hens waddled up and dived under the table, clucking gutturally.

'We have chickens!' exclaimed Alex. It was a big deal for Luna when she was able to stroke one of them. Alex looked under the table for eggs.

Pavel sang a Polish song for them, a campfire song with many tra-la-las they could join in with. Apparently, it had to do with a cockerel.

When Madame Roblon came to say goodbye for the day, Sophie asked about the poultry.

'My husband's chickens. He is doing the garden,' she explained.

'Any more animals?'

'The pig is dead. Eaten long ago. The guard dog ran away.'

'Oh no,' exclaimed Luna. 'I love dogs.'

Pavel generously offered to make spaghetti carbonara for supper with whatever was at hand. He hired Luna as his sous-chef. She glowed with pleasure.

Alex insisted on laying the table. 'It's the lamest thing ever, but I'll do it.'

'Only real men have a go at lame things,' said Pavel.

'How come?'

'If a real man does a lame thing, it is not lame any more, is it?'

Pavel showed Luna how to add the beaten egg yolks

to the sauce without letting them solidify. He grated mature parmesan over it all and let her shred basil leaves from the herb garden.

The sun started to set, and Sophie went to fetch her angora cardigan and brought down the wrought-iron candlestick. The smoker among them had a lighter.

The indulgent creamy pasta dish was much appreciated. Pavel and Sophie shared the bottle of wine. The children stretched their tongues out to each other, tongues tinted red from grenadine.

It was not dark enough for full candle effect, but the twilight mood worked. The air was fragrant. A zealous cricket began to chirp, though it was not quite night time. Her children's eager faces shone in the dancing candlelight. Pavel found a tub of vanilla ice cream in the freezer. She and Pavel sat opposite each other, the large expanse of a farm table between them. While the children ate the ice cream, the adults had oven-heated baguettes with Alex's runny *come on bear*. And tomorrow, she thought with gratitude, would be another day of the same.

★

The next day, the piano store replied to say they rented out pianos up to six months at a time and suggested they come to choose one. First, however, Sophie and Pavel had to go shopping in the nearby Champion supermarket. He had made a list covering their needs for the next three days, obviously planning on doing all the cooking. She added clothes on the list for him.

When they returned, a sack of chicken grain had

been delivered in the meantime. Alex had dealt with it. '*Pour poulet,* I said, and *Ma mere et ami in supermarché,*' he recounted proudly.

Once the shopping was put away, Sophie and Pavel set out again, this time to the piano store in Nimes, leaving the children in the care of Madame and Monsieur Roblon, who promised to teach them about looking after chickens.

The piano store was in a barn on a farm. Fixing up old pianos was the farmer's father's hobby, and he watched them look around, Pavel playing some of the instruments. Eventually, they decided on a simple lacquered black-wood upright, made by a reputable piano manufacturer in Paris.

Sophie paid for the first month in cash, after signing a six-month contract. The piano would be delivered that evening. Pavel seemed delighted. It was difficult to get him out of the barn.

'Tomorrow morning, I will teach Alex his first lesson.'

'You might find the boy not entirely co-operative.'

'He will love it. Let's drive home, my beautiful.'

⋆

In the family room, they found Alex curled up on the sofa, weeping.

Luna was on her knees in front of the sofa. 'I have tried everything. He won't stop crying.'

'What happened?' Sophie put her hand on the feverish brow of her son.

'At first I cried a lot, too,' Luna admitted. 'Monsieur Roblon came and…'

'He is a murderer. I hate him!' Alex sat up.

Sophie exchanged glances with Pavel.

'Did he kill someone?' Pavel asked. 'Not just punched, killed?'

'You can't punch a chicken.' Alex rubbed his puffy eyes.

'Monsieur Roblon murdered a chicken. Is that it?' said Sophie.

'First, he showed us how to feed it and how to carry it,' said Alex. 'And then, with an axe, he cut the head off.'

'I know a bloke who did that to his wife,' said Pavel.

'Did the wife still run around, flapping her arms, without her head?' asked Luna.

'I don't know. I wasn't there.'

'I am sorry to have left you in the care of the Roblons. Animals should not be treated like that.' Sophie helped her son get off the sofa.

Alex further explained that Monsieur Roblon only killed the hen because Pavel had asked him to.

'Is that correct?' Sophie realised she sounded like her mother.

'Chicken in cream tonight,' Pavel said and gave Alex a wink.

Later that afternoon, the piano was delivered. It came on a horse-drawn cart, strapped down. Two men installed it in the family room and left.

Once Sophie was in bed, after the chicken dish which the children found difficult to eat, she heard Pavel playing the piano downstairs. The night breeze danced with the gauze curtains over the open balcony, and he played so long that she fell asleep. Her last thought was how peaceful life could be with a man sensitive enough to play an instrument as well as he did, one who could feel art, and stir yearnings in her.

Early morning, however, she was rudely woken by a loud altercation downstairs. Confused at first, she slowly shed the layers of well-being the night had wrapped her in. At the top of the stairs, she leant forward to see who was destroying the peace in *Les Hirondelles*.

Pavel, a bath towel wrapped around his waist, must have let someone into the house, for the entrance door was still open. The stranger had red hair and the same strong build as Pavel. They were arguing in Polish. She could almost smell the hatred they had for each other. The stranger reached out, and his large hands grabbed Pavel's arms. Overpowered, Pavel spewed invective at his opponent. His outrage made him spit in the attacker's face. This did not help the volatile situation. The stranger marched Pavel backwards over the worn carpet and, with a final shove, threw him against the suit of armour, so roughly that the antique fell sideways into the corner. The arm came off, clattering on the floor.

'Mum,' Alex tugged at her bathrobe belt. 'What is going on?'

'I'm not sure. But it has nothing to do with us. Go back to bed. Don't wake Luna.'

'Pavel said that I must always keep my back to a wall so that I can't be killed by surprise. He's not really our au pair, is he?'

No, he isn't. Sophie watched as he drove the redhead

37

back to the entrance door, bashing him with the metal arm. The door closed behind the undesirable visitor with a thud. Pavel slid the bolt.

Nothing was said at breakfast in front of the children about the fight. Luna asked Pavel to make Polish egg toast again, and he engaged in the task at once. Alex, reserved, said he was not hungry. Pavel noticed.

Smiling at the boy, he announced, 'Today, Alex will get his first piano lesson.'

'Not so fast,' Sophie spoke up. 'There are things to sort out.'

'There are,' Pavel acquiesced. 'The piano stool is too low for Alex.'

When the children had gone upstairs and Pavel was at the kitchen sink washing the breakfast dishes, she approached him.

'Who was the man you were fighting with in the hall this morning? How dare you invite someone into my home without consulting me?'

'It's a place for holidays, not home,' he reminded her annoyingly.

'Pavel!' she snapped at him, while he dried his hands on a kitchen towel. 'Who were you fighting with? I have a right to know.'

'Is private.' He folded the towel in two and then four, before placing it on the kitchen worktop.

She shook her head, her eyes pinned on him.

Almost smugly, he added, 'You don't wear a wedding ring, because you don't love your husband?'

'Now, that *is* private.'

'Same thing.'

Annoyed, she spluttered, 'You have to leave. I cannot trust you. You are dangerous, and a bad example for my innocent children.'

'My brother,' he finally said. 'My brother, Borys. He did things with my wife I cannot forgive. I told you on the ferry.'

She remembered. 'How does he know you are here?'

'Some people keep track of me.'

'Because of the Armagnac story?'

'Maybe.' He did not want to continue this interrogation and walked out under the pergola.

She felt so angry and frustrated that her hands were trembling. On impulse, she ran up the stairs.

'I do have a right to know,' she said, as she burst into his bedroom to look for clues about him. In the drawer of the bedside table was his passport. His first name really was Pavel, and his family name, the one he had helped her write on the au pair contract, was Przezinski, not that she could pronounce it. He was twenty-nine years old.

In an open envelope was wedged a gold cross on a chain and a thin wad of euros, as well as a photograph of him dressed grandly in front of an English manor house. There was also the au pair contract. None of this pointed to a criminal. She felt more let down than relieved.

As she gave the room a last glance, she noticed a little black object in the corner under the dressing table: the charger for a mobile phone. Pavel was a liar. He was in contact with other criminals. What should she do? What could she do, a woman alone with two young children? She had got herself into this situation all by herself. And it dawned on her that the redhead was probably not Pavel's brother.

In the hallway, the suit of armour had been reassembled. She had to get a grip on herself. Pavel may not have done anything wrong; he was the victim, and as vulnerable as she and the children were. She would calmly ask him to move on in his life and let them wait for James to join them at *Les Hirondelles*.

Sophie settled down, but the 'same thing, not loving her husband' was bothering her. The ring James had slipped on her finger at their wedding had been lost while she was making sandcastles during a family holiday in Norfolk.

She heard the first piano lesson start, and watched discreetly from the hallway.

Pavel asked Alex to open the lid. 'What do you see?'

'White teeth. Many of them. Some have gone black.'

'Imaginative, but wrong.'

Pavel got Alex to stand on the piano stool and look into the sound box while he played some notes.

'They are like hammers,' said Alex.

'Exactly. They hit the wires and make them sing.'

Sophie was called away by Luna and had to miss the unfolding of this lesson.

A girl about the same age as Luna had arrived unannounced, a black poodle high-stepping next to her.

'Minette has come to play with me,' Luna enthused. 'Madame Roblon asked her to. When the poodle has babies, can I have one, please?'

'Bijou is a boy dog,' said Minette.

'Oh,' moaned Luna.

The girls went into the garden. Sophie smiled. Luna would have a friend to play with, a girl who spoke some English and who obviously had a dream dog. She sneaked back to listen to the piano lesson.

Pavel was playing a short, simple piece ending with a flourish. 'Boring?'

'Pshaw,' was Alex's reaction.

'Correct. It is magic. Listen to the birds outside the window. They twitter just like the notes I played.'

Alex nodded.

'Birds fly away, they sleep at night. You can play this any time you like.'

'I can't play that.'

'You can learn to play. I'll help you.'

Sophie's mobile beeped and she moved away. 'James,' she exclaimed. He was tidying up loose ends and hoped to be there soon. 'Things are fine here.' She sounded reassuring. 'It is warm and the sun is shining.'

'Love you,' they said to each other, and the connection was cut.

For the rest of the day, things really were as fine as she had said they were.

When Sophie returned to the piano lesson, she saw the grown man's hand on her son's shoulder, Alex looking up trustingly at Pavel, his anxiety overcome. From the open window behind them, came the happy twittering of birds in the bushes.

That evening, Pavel boiled artichokes and made a vinaigrette to go with it. The children thought at first it was a joke. Once they had learnt to pull off the scale-like leaves, dip them into the sauce and nibble the flesh at the narrow end, they loved it. Alex fixed some leaves behind his lips, pretending to have large, green teeth. Luna arranged the leaves to form a flower.

'I've just eaten my first cactus,' said Sophie, and Pavel responded by throwing a leaf at her. They all threw leaves at each other. After that, Pavel served up fish fillets in a creamy sauce.

After supper, Minette reappeared with the poodle, out for their evening walk. She encouraged Alex, generally not comfortable with dogs, to stroke Bijou. The dog pulled away from him, though, and retched several times before throwing up. Alex watched with interest as the dog ate it all up again.

'France,' the boy said, shrugging philosophically. 'I love this country.'

'When I passed your house earlier,' said Minette, 'someone was playing the piano. Played really beautifully.'

'My piano teacher,' explained Alex, pointing to Pavel. 'I'm learning to play Bach.'

'Good for you. Will you play for me?'

'Give me three weeks to practise and I will be able to.'

'D'accord. Three weeks.' The girl blushed.

Sophie smiled.

'We will be living here for a year. Can you bring Bijou again?' Luna asked.

'A whole year? Absolument. Every day, if you like. In the autumn, you will have to go to school. My class, probably. The school is down there.' The girl pointed. 'Madame Luron, the English teacher, she sneezes all the time.' Minette demonstrated dramatically. 'She has polyps in her nose, that's why.'

After Minette had left, Luna and Alex were sent upstairs to bed. Alone under the pergola, the adults finished a second bottle of wine. They smiled at each other self-consciously. Now was her opportunity to say what she had to say: *Thank you, Pavel, and goodbye forever.*

He did not read her mood. He left the table and returned with 'something I bought when shopping you might like.' On the plate he proffered were sugar-coated puff-pastry hearts. 'Coeurs de France,' he said. 'Much liked in France.'

'How do you know so much about France?' Before he could say anything, she went on, 'The internet, isn't it? A mobile phone?'

Still he said nothing.

'I discovered your charger under the dresser in your room.'

He pushed the plate of cookie hearts close to her again. She declined. 'I thought you were… I don't know what I thought you were. I made a mistake.'

'Sophie, you like the mistake.'

His use of her name for the first time undermined her decision to be firm.

'I like your mistake, also,' he continued, seeking her eyes while working his chair closer to hers. It was an intimate move. With a hurried gesture, half-impulsive but half-anxious, she wrapped her arms around his neck and pressed her face awkwardly against his.

Then, shocked by her own behaviour, she moved her chair back with a scraping noise. 'Let's think about what to do about this tomorrow,' she said into the cold space between them. He bent to pick up the paper napkin which had floated from her lap.

'Goodnight,' she said over her shoulder, walking away.

★

Sophie lay in bed, unable to sleep. Pavel had seen right into her. What troubled her was that she felt no shame. Had her commitment to her husband been buried in the Norfolk beach, along with the ring? Infidelity was known to end in disaster. She turned on the pillow to face the other way. She had not done anything that could be called unfaithful. Surely sleep would come now. The loose curtains over the open balcony door hung straight, as there was no breeze outside. A sudden flash of light caught in them, and then again.

Intrigued, she got out of bed and padded onto the balcony. The garden below was dark and silent, the moon above half its full size. There was nothing to worry about. Yet, something did not fit in with the breathless nocturnal setting.

Renewed flashes of light from a torch played on the bushes near the stone wall to the side of the garden. In the sparse light, she thought she could see a dark, sack-like object being lobbed over the wall to a car parked in the road. The car drove off. She saw the rear lights like two red eyes, disappearing down the country lane.

Puzzled, but too tired to investigate, she slipped back into bed.

In the morning, the children were waiting for Pavel to make them breakfast, but he was nowhere to be found.

Sophie went outside, stepping out from under the pergola onto the flagstones which crossed the lawn. On one was a puddle of red paint. The word *blood* sprang unbidden to her mind. A trail of it led her to the stone wall. Perhaps it was not Pavel's? This hope seeped away, however, when she stooped and picked up a blood-covered object – the little gold cross with its chain broken. Now she knew: the blood dripping onto her blouse was his. With growing dread, she remembered the heavy sack being lobbed over the stone wall last night.

'They took him,' she gasped. 'He was killed last night.' Perhaps he wore the cross to protect himself, because he had guessed. Her mother was right: *Your past follows you, wherever you go.*

The crunching noise she heard was a car driving up to the house. Sophie rushed back to the kitchen, a flicker of hope in her heart. In the hallway, Madame Roblon was already unlocking the door to whoever was knocking.

James, in a new suit and tie, walked in. 'Hi,' he said. 'Change of plan. Klart-Glas can't get safety approval in France. We can go home to England.'

She stared at him as if he were a ghost. He took in his surroundings. 'I say, this house looked a lot better online.'

He stepped further into the hallway. 'Armour. How tacky.' He then peeked into the playroom. 'A cheap old upright. Who needs a piano in a rental property?'

They ended up in the kitchen in which, thankfully, he found nothing to belittle.

Madame Roblon came to say that the taxi driver wanted to know whether he could leave now.

'Not yet,' James said to Madame Roblon and turned to Sophie. 'I got the news about the bloody-minded Frogs just before I left Gothenburg. I've got to fly straight to Paris to sort out the mess. If you and the kids drive off early tomorrow, you'll make it back by late afternoon Thursday. I've got to go. See you in Ely.'

Sophie began to knock her forehead against the tiled worktop. 'They came to kill him,' she whispered between bouts of sobs.

'What's wrong with her?' James asked of Madame Roblon. 'And why is there ketchup on her clothes? Or is it paint?'

Madame Roblon moved the knife stand out of Sophie's reach.

'I loved him,' Sophie sobbed. 'I did not know that I did, and now it is too late. He is gone forever, forever.'

'Is my wife drunk?'

'I don't think so.'

IN SLIPPERS

Ethel Sinclair, after seventy-nine years, still hated her given name. She was wearing the knee strap insisted on by her assertive daughter, Aurora – who, thanks to her mother, could take pride in her name. Disappointingly, Aurora was now driving her to an old people's home. Aurora parked in the forecourt of Riverview Residence, after speeding down Kimbolton Road and running an amber light in her white Alfa Romeo Giulia. The sky above them was overcast and as grey as the pebbles they crunched on towards the entrance. All the downstairs windows had stout bars on them.

After Aurora had shouted into the intercom, they were buzzed in. They entered the stale, heated air of an over-carpeted Edwardian building in Bedford, situated close to the town park. Aurora pulled her mother's suitcase silently behind her, while, over her shoulder, a leather tote-bag clattered with framed photographs.

'Someone will be with you shortly,' said the receptionist. They were invited to sit in waterproof-covered armchairs in the reception area. Aurora yanked the case close to the armrest and pushed down the handle.

Ethel cradled the tote-bag on her lap. 'How do I look?' she asked, letting go of the bag to touch the top of her head.

'Mum,' Aurora said cheerfully, 'you look good. Nobody can tell you're wearing a wig. Besides, you won't be the only one here.'

'Did you pack the special shampoo?'

'Of course. And the spare wig. They have a visiting hairdresser. Use it. You can afford it.'

It was the beginning of February and raindrops splattered against the window, fat drops which ran down the glass in dribbles.

The mother and daughter's attention was drawn to a young woman who emerged from the lift carrying a kick-step stool. She put it down in front of a noticeboard, on which remained drawing pins holding the corners of carelessly torn-away papers. She pulled a card from the patch pocket of her tabard and fixed it to the green felt, reusing a pin. On the card was a large red heart with a strong shadow which made it appear three dimensional. Next came a cut-out ladybird, stuck onto a cloth with daisies and a tulip.

'Have we got more drawing pins?' she called over to the receptionist. The receptionist's landline phone rang. The fake blonde answered by saying, 'Riverview Residence' in a high-pitched robotic voice.

At the noticeboard, the woman in the tabard had recourse to Blu-Tack but, despite considerable softening, it wouldn't stick and fell down almost immediately. Annoyed, she stepped down from the stool.

Mother and daughter were wondering what she

48

would do next, when a mature woman appeared in their field of vision.

'Hello, I am Pamela.' A pause. 'Pam, the manager of Riverview.'

She was thin, tall on heels and wearing a tailored skirt because she could. A lightweight beige angora sweater set off a fashion jewel on a gold chain around her neck. The butterfly-shaped pendant had moved askew between her breasts. It probably pinched, because she straightened it. Her narrow nose looked sharp, and her eyes were light grey, as if starving herself had robbed the iris of colour. The manageress managed a pinched smile. She nodded at the noticeboard. 'We are preparing for Valentine's Day. There is always something going on with us here.'

The woman struggling with the Blu-Tack was heard to curse.

'Well then,' said Pam easily. 'I understand you are Mrs Sinclair – or may I call you Ethel? And you will be joining us today. A grizzly day, I am afraid,' she added, as if this had anything to do with anything. 'But soon it will be spring. This will be your new home. My staff and I hope you will be very happy here.'

'Unlikely,' muttered Ethel.

'Thank you for coming so early.'

'Sadly, we didn't have an accident en route. Should have, the way my daughter drives.'

'This will give us time to settle you in before lunch,' Pam went on undisturbed.

A bent old man appeared from somewhere, shuffling behind his Zimmer frame as if in a creepy film which depended heavily on slow motion. A foot slide, then a stop to measure his progress, before building up to the next slide, in which his slipper slipped off, as the name of the footwear promised. Pam swiftly crossed reception and helped him put it on again without toppling over, which was a complicated manoeuvre.

When she returned to the newcomers, she was almost happily out of breath. 'The gentleman I've just helped is Sir Philbert, a lifetime cameraman for BBC News. One of our more accomplished residents.'

Aurora said to her mother, 'You'll make friends here.'

'He's a war relic,' said Ethel. 'His fly is open, and he hasn't got a clue. Don't push me onto him. I'd rather rub myself on a pillow thinking of...'

'Yeah, yeah. I know who you're thinking of. Don't be so gross.'

Pam listened to the conversation, her lips pursed. 'In old age, inhibitions are let go. We're used to it. I will personally show you to your room.' Pam presided over them. 'Do we need a wheelchair?' she asked Ethel.

'I don't know about you,' said Ethel. 'I, for my part, walk fine.'

'We've prepared you a room on the second floor.' Regrouping, Pam offered, 'Apart from handicrafts, we offer yoga classes on Tuesday mornings for the fitter of our residents. It's much appreciated. You might well be one of them.'

'I'm not into Chinese things. I hope you don't serve chopstick meals on Tuesday.'

Pam imitated a short laugh and tapped in a code at the lift.

Getting out of the lift on the second floor, a lift in which not only a wheelchair but a single bed would have fitted, Pam marched in front of them along the baby-blue carpet, chin up, stiff right arm swinging. She stopped in front of one of many doors: *Begonia*. And begonias were painted on a label.

'Before we go in, I need to tell you that the doors you see at either end of this corridor are locked. Our residents are not allowed off their assigned floors or out of the building without a specific reason, which has to be approved by me or my deputy.'

Ethel's shoulders sagged. She reached up and made sure her wig sat tight. Pam tried the doorknob, but it didn't turn. Impatiently, she wriggled it and rattled the door, before taking a phone out of her skirt pocket.

'Kate, I need the spare key for code blue, Begonia.'

In the awkward wait in the corridor, Pam felt the need to explain. 'Normally, room doors aren't locked, but your room was made up this morning, and the cleaner must have locked it by mistake. They are often temps. Rules are so important when running a residence like this.' The lift chimed. 'Here she comes. Our receptionist has copies of every key. Can't be too careful.'

Kate, the fake blonde, shook a key out of a brown envelope. It fitted the lock.

'Have a copy made immediately and try to find the other one,' said Pam to the receptionist.

'Will do.'

Pam pushed the door open all the way. 'Here we are,' she announced grandly, as if disclosing to them the palace chamber of Tutankhamun.

Ethel looked glum. 'I hate begonias,' she grumbled, and went into the room as enthusiastically as a dog is dragged to the vet's.

'It's one of our friendliest rooms.' Pam had recovered her sunshine attitude.

Ethel walked past the single bed and an easy chair with footstool. An incontinence pad lay on the seat. At the window, she asked, 'Why do you call this Riverview? There is no view of any river.'

'When the house was built, the Ouse River meandered all over Bedford, river arms, lakes,' explained Pam. 'Much has been filled in and built over. However, in St Neots and Huntingdon, the Ouse still runs freely all over the place. Beyond the lawn and the shrubbery, a brook still flows.'

'Well then, someone can carry a chair there for me.'

Pam sucked in her breath. 'I am afraid residents are not allowed beyond the lawn on days out.'

To Aurora's surprise, her mother said, 'I understand.' But then she spoilt the effect by adding, 'We don't want corpses piling up under the bridge in the centre of town, do we?'

'If you feel faint or need anything, use the red-toggled pull-cords,' continued Pam. 'You have one near the easy chair and one in the shower room, to which the water has been cut as you will be given assisted showering. And remember, the cords are there to be used, not abused.'

A thump came from above them. 'Not to worry,' Pam smiled. 'The top floor is our A floor. Alzheimer's.'

'Anemones and azaleas all over the place,' Ethel mumbled.

Pam glanced at Aurora. 'Your mother will value

conversations with Sir Philbert. He is said to have filmed in every war zone.' She checked the position of her butterfly pendant and then her wristwatch. 'I was hoping Sunita, my deputy, could join us, but she must be busy elsewhere. I will have to leave you to it, I'm afraid. If you brought pictures you wish to hang on the wall, our handyman is on standby Monday afternoons. Let Sunita know.'

'Hardly worth it for the short time I'll be staying here,' mumbled Ethel.

'Oh, no,' exclaimed Pam. 'You still have life to live.'

'Which I don't plan to use up in Riverview Residence.'

The door closed slowly behind Pam, before it clicked.

'See?' Aurora flung the suitcase onto the flowery duvet. 'You've already caused trouble with your corpses floating down the river. There's a waiting list. It took me months to get you accepted.'

'Good. Give my place to someone who wants to be in prison. It won't take me months to tunnel myself out.' Ethel imitated her daughter's voice.

'Mum, let's have no talk of escape. Try out the easy chair and we'll have *real speak*.'

Ethel sat on the chair without removing the incontinence pad. 'What's real?'

'I'll start.' Aurora took control. 'You are widowed and cannot stay in your house any longer. I am married and live in too small a place to take you in. Riverview is highly regarded by older adults who led middle-class lives like yours. I realise that you will feel closed in, but then you have not exactly roamed the world, have you?'

'I went to Paris. And can speak French.'

53

'Maybe. I did pack your silly Eiffel Tower. It's in the outer zip pocket of your case.'

'He adored me.'

'The French adore mature Camembert riddled with maggots. Dad loved you realistically enough to marry you. Jean-Jacques is a dream, nothing more. I need to get home.'

'So, I am left to do *real speak* to myself.'

'You have a lot to assimilate in this new place,' said Aurora. 'I'll be back tomorrow to see how you're doing, OK?' She went up to the chair, which smelled of disinfectant, and kissed her mother on the rice-paper skin of her forehead.

Ethel felt tears sting her eyes, a lump in her throat. She looked down and away from Aurora.

'We will take care of you here,' said an unfamiliar voice. 'My name is Sunita. Don't be embarrassed for crying. We all cry here from time to time. I cry watching sad films. I cry when someone leaves Riverview.'

'Because they are in a box and can't tip you any more.'

'Mother, I've got to leave now,' Aurora insisted. 'Try to be kinder to people. Some politeness would also not come amiss.'

Ethel's interest was entirely consumed by the exotic young woman. After the rain, the room was flooded with late morning light which bathed Sunita. Her hair, contained in a solid thick tress reaching down to the middle of her back, seemed to shimmer, and her full-length silk wrap-around, ending in a handkerchief hemline, revealed shapely ankles, and feet in trainers.

'Could you bring me another pillow, now that you are here?'

'I will pass on your request,' affirmed Sunita. 'I am Pam's deputy and her accountant.'

With a claw-like grab, Ethel held Aurora back. 'Take me home, please,' she whined like an abandoned dog.

'You know I can't.'

'What was so wrong with my old home?'

'You fell. Three times.'

'Only two and a half.' Addressing Sunita, she added, 'The last time, it was more like a stumble, but my daughter needs to make a big thing of it.'

'The little stumble tore the cartilage in your knee,' said Aurora. 'Have you ever thought about me and Bobby, fretting all the time about something happening to you, flinching every time the phone rings?'

'Usually, it's from a call centre in India, probably one of Sunita's cousins.'

'Mother! You have never been unkind to people before.'

'Before, I wasn't talked to with a patronising *we*. Anyway, I hope they hate the stink out of me here.'

'Mum, you have to let me go. You can't return to your house.'

'You burnt it down?'

'No. We are going to rent it out to pay for the cost of Riverview Residence. Sunita might as well hear this, as I will have to deal with her about finances. It costs almost three thousand pounds a month and, using your pension and Dad's half-pension, plus the rental income,

55

we can afford for you to be here, safe, well fed and in the company of people your age.'

'Behind my back, you're going to invite strangers to live in my house, sleep in my bed and eat off of my Wedgwood plates?'

'You sound like a fairy tale princess – and you ate beans out of a *tin*.'

'It's not my fault if they package them like that. And, say again, what have you done with my pensions?'

'You remember, when a man from NatWest came to your house,' said Aurora.

'The one whose shoelace was undone?'

'The paper he got you to sign was a power of attorney. I am legally allowed to make decisions about your finances. I'll make sure that you still receive bank statements, so you can see what comes in and goes out. If you are not happy, we can talk about it.'

'That figures,' said Ethel. 'Bobby is making you steal all my money. I have to sit in this place without a penny to my name, when I worked my bones off all my life. Never went anywhere, always had to look after you and your brother who…'

'Who what?'

'Where is he? Why isn't he here to gloat about my incarceration? He'd love this.'

'You know he is in Brussels, very busy at work.'

'If they were less busy in Brussels, we English could have a better quality of life.'

'Let's not get into politics. I must go. Bobby is waiting for me.'

'To do what?'

'Meet up with a gardener to sort out your garden. We can't expect the tenants to undertake such a challenge.'

'You leave my garden alone. I never gave you permission to mess with my garden. And nor should a banker, whose mother never taught him how to lace his shoes.'

'About money, I will make an arrangement with Sunita for you to have a monthly cash allowance for a hairdresser and other personal needs.'

'I can't be bothered.'

'You must make an effort. Remember the BBC reporter.'

'Englishmen make lousy lovers.'

'I was thinking more of scintillating conversation,' said Aurora. 'Many, I am afraid, will not be up to it any longer, unlike you.'

'In a place like this, they're all away with the fairies.'

'Mum, please remember, you are not in prison, and I will come and see you often, like tomorrow to see how your first night went.'

'You don't need to check on me. They've already hired an army of employees to say *no* to everything I need and like. Go now, go.'

'I love you, Mum.' Aurora hugged her mother briefly.

A bell rang somewhere, and Sunita opened the door to leave. She was replaced by a young man in a see-through plastic apron.

'It is lunchtime,' he announced, walked up to Ethel and offered her his arm. 'I am Gino, your escort for today, and here to look after you.'

'Heavens above!' Ethel exclaimed, refusing the elbow. 'Aurora, don't leave me here. Tell this man not to touch me and to never, ever, take my clothes off.'

'We can have a shower with you wearing a loose shift, if that makes you more comfortable.' He smiled at her.

Ethel could not think of anything to say to that.

'Let's go. We don't want the food to get cold.' He held out his hand, and she took it to help her out of the chair.

Aurora, about to follow Sunita, turned and asked, 'Could you please arrange for my mother to sit next to Sir Philbert?'

'I will try,' said Gino. 'We always try. We bend over backwards to please.'

'I hope Gino's smarm battery runs out soon,' muttered Ethel.

Aurora gave her a tough last look, before hurrying along the blue-carpeted corridor and down the staircase, from which a carer had just emerged. Downstairs, she punched in the number Kate, the receptionist, gave her and stood in the forecourt, stunned. She looked up at the beautifully bricked building and tried to work out which window was her mother's, but couldn't.

'Hi, baby,' she said to her wet, white Alfa Romeo, and squipped to unlock it.

★

Up in *Begonia*, finally alone, Ethel forced the knee strap over her knee and down her leg. There were grooves in her flesh from the tight, tough seams of the pink medical

58

support. She considered the waste basket in the corner, but the first person back in the room would retrieve it and tell her off. Ethel put the footstool under the window. It was locked, of course, but the narrow window above it could be pushed open a tad, if one reached that far up. Using the stool, Ethel reached up, opened the window and pushed the knee support through the gap. As it fell, it took in air and resumed its tubular shape, resembling her bent leg. Ethel banged her forehead against the glass, trying to see where it landed. Perfect! It lay half-hidden in a bush, and could have been thrown out of a window above her or, even more credibly, any resident allowed on the lawn could have shoved it into the greenery. No doubt many among them wore leg or arm straps, and even corsets, each one a discomfort to the wearer.

★

In a room above a launderette near Bedford station, the windows blinded by white paint, three men sat at a scratched metal table. The eldest of them got up to pace the room. In the diffused light stood an industrial-sized tumble-dryer, its disconnected paper vent-hose trembling in the faintest movement of air. In the smoked glass door of the dryer, the man's movements were dimly reflected. He was known in the cocaine business as CT, which he claimed stood for *Cut-Throat*, and he acted mid-forties but, in fact, was just thirty-two, a man from the Balkans. Huddled into a worn leather jacket with a shiny grease ring on the collar, dark hair a bit too long and combed straight back over his head, he sported a deliberately unkempt appearance. However, in contrast, he permitted some personality to show in an American college ring on his finger and a Texan bolo tie of gold coin and leather strip – affectations from his boyhood fantasies. If, in his mind, it showed American icon coolness, in reality it gave away a poor upbringing in which only television had formed his tastes.

CT stopped in his pacing. He looked down and stepped over a triangle of light on the boarded floor, as if it were a physical object. Some hooligan had thrown a stone at one of the windows and knocked out a triangular shard.

'How low does a loser have to sink before starting to break windows? I hate mindless vandalism.' With his fist, CT thumped the top of the tumble-dryer. Loose bits in the broken machine clattered.

He returned to the two young men at the table and said, in a controlled voice, 'What we're about is a business. Management, legal and accounting departments are wherever they need to be. Factories in Colombia, transportation worldwide, local warehousing, distribution, sales.'

Tarik tossed his dark corkscrew curls, his teeth brace clamps glinting. Now that he had some money, he could afford an orthodontist, but his nickname 'Rat', the start of Tarik in reverse, could not be fixed. Next to his corpulence, Viktor was sinuously thin with deep-sunken, dark eyes which glittered even in the shadows. His brown hair was gathered in a short, measly ponytail at his nape.

'Apparently, we've been losing market share to the

Somalis in Bedford,' CT continued, 'and I've been sent up here to get you back on track. They say you two have done your time as checkout girls. Now, I need you in local distribution. I've bought this busted laundrette as our hub. The goods have shipped in, cleared Felixstowe, and our tranche is downstairs in Bold washing powder boxes, mega size, with Lenor softener, advertised as two-in-one.' He snorted a laugh. 'We have a client who'll be in Bedford next Friday. You have to get 500 grams safely into his hands. The stuff is going for 48.50 a gram. It's ninety per cent pure. Buy Bold with the scent of lavender.' He snorted again. Tarik and Viktor smirked politely. 'And you need to collect the twenty-five thou. But it's going to be tougher than before, and not just because of the Somalis. They knifed Nico last week, and now the cops are all over the place. We will get our payback but can't afford to stir things up any more, until we've got this deal through. So,' he rubbed his hands, 'you have to work out where and how to organise the drop-off and pick-up, safe from the Somalis and the cops.'

Viktor grimaced. 'We can't use a backpack in left luggage any more, not since somebody called Nico lost the ticket.'

'And hollowed-out loaves in bread delivery wasn't great, either. That dog must have been as high as a kite when it died,' Rat contributed. 'I'm thinking Bedford Park,' he said nasally. 'Medium pedestrian traffic, innocent people, lots of cover.'

'Explain innocent people. I don't know any of those,' said CT.

'There are a lot of trees, a bandstand and a caff.'

'How about policing?'

'Not unless they are called in for a specific reason.'

'How well do you know this park?'

'After Dad left, the council put Mum, me and my brother, who has cerebral palsy, in a park lodge. It's just for temporary accommodation till a flat is available. I practised football on the grass. It's a really large, old park with a big duck pond.'

'Go on. It's fascinating.'

'Actually…' Tarik missed the sarcasm. 'There are swans in the pond as well.'

'Lots of people on a Friday morning?' asked CT.

'Oh, yes. Joggers, old men on mobility carts, hordes of guys with dogs, kids in prams, on scooters, tricycles. Arabs, blacks, Chinese, Sikhs – you name it.'

Downstairs in the launderette, the telephone started ringing. On his way out, CT turned. 'If you value your life, come up with something that works. In principle, I like the idea of the park, because it is so pathetic it might be outside the narco-fuzz's thinking box. Don't use children or animals, you understand? I'm off now. After ten minutes you can leave; carry one of the small laundry baskets from downstairs. Pretend you came here to wash clothes. Lock the front door. You should know I have hired a useless woman called Lydia who will wash her mother's B&B sheets here. The launderette has to look legit. She'll start two days after Friday, by which time the extra white powder pouch will have gone from the laundry box.'

'The phone has stopped,' said Viktor.

'It'll ring again,' replied CT. 'It will always ring again. People can't live without the white powder. Washing powder, I mean! We are helping them. Let me know the plan, so that I can pass on the info, and the client can get the dough together in time.'

CT clattered down the stairs in his cowboy boots.

★

Ethel sat in her room in Riverview Residence. She listened to the rumbling above her head and wondered how Alzheimer patients could make that noise. Her back was supported by the extra pillow which Sunita had brought her. It was round and small.

'It's the best we can do,' she said. 'We are full at the moment, and have no spare bedding.'

The position of Ethel's chair forced her to look into the shower room, more precisely into the mirror above the sink, low for wheelchair access. Where was the face of the woman who, after the death of her husband, Hugh, twenty-eight years ago, had picked herself up and gone to Paris on her own? The daring one, who had read the menu displayed outside a restaurant on the Champs-Elysées and been accosted by a Frenchman.

'Don't eat here,' he'd said. 'It's not a good restaurant.'

She had thought it rude, but challenged him. 'Do you know a good enough restaurant?'

'I do. It's called Chez Pierette, and I own it.' He was so unnerving with his charm and his cologne that she forgot all about eating. They went to a brasserie for coffee, where he smoked and said little while she blabbered about herself. Hugh had died of pneumonia and, after his funeral, smoke had also curled out of the crematorium chimney.

Jean-Jacques, as he had introduced himself, got up and drained his tiny coffee cup. 'I was actually on my way to the fishmonger.'

She decided to accompany him, because it was spring and she felt energised by the encounter. Hugh, who had made it through winter, had not found the energy which spring requires. On the small headstone in the churchyard was his name, and dates of birth and death revealing, to those who can add fast, how long he had lived.

Her interest in Jean-Jacques had not been an act of defiance against a husband who had neglected her; it was more like being enthralled. Perhaps, he could achieve the same effect with gourmet food. She went to the fishmonger with him, where he bought cod for *morue au Muscadet*.

They had coffee again the next day, and she went to the charcutier with him, again as an onlooker. Afterwards, he took her to the principal tourist sites because, on Monday, his restaurant was closed. At the Arc de Triomphe, he tapped her bottom in view of everyone and crushed her against him. He gave her a gift after going up the Eiffel Tower, a wrought-iron miniature.

The romance ended at the Gare du Nord, which had regular trains to Orly. He kissed her on the lips. It was, however, his words which had stayed with her, more than the sensual kiss – words like *desirable* and *exciting*.

'The next time,' he offered, looking soulfully into her eyes, 'when you come back to Paris… D'accord?'

She had been totally infatuated when she turned round a last time to wave adieu.

Tears welled up in Ethel's eyes remembering the goodbye scene in Paris. The old woman, reflected in the mirror above the low sink, could not be her. Not yet, and hopefully never. She had to find a way out of here.

She turned in the seat and ungracefully swung her legs over the armrest to face a wall instead. On it, the Monday afternoon handyman had hung the painting she had brought. The picture was of pink peonies in a simple jar on a tabletop. There was no signature on the canvas. Ethel had bought the picture from a painter on the Rive Gauche, despite Jean-Jacques' objections that it wasn't worth the price she paid.

Ethel made the effort to get up and straighten the picture on its hook. 'Better,' she said and returned to the chair.

Shortly after that, the now-familiar buzzer sounded from the corridor. Her door opened, and Gino in his plastic apron leant into the room.

'Hello, Ethel. Supper time. You want me to escort you downstairs?'

'More food,' she sighed. 'Where am I going to put it all?'

He came all the way into the room and stood close to her. 'You look pale. Do you feel all right?' He picked up her limp arm to check her pulse. 'I am not just your carer; I am also a qualified nurse, assisting if need be in our sick bay. It's fully equipped. If you want, I can show it to you sometime.'

'I hope I'm not going to get sick. I am quite capable of getting out of a chair without help. It just takes a while.'

Gino picked up the model of the Eiffel Tower by its tip. 'Paris,' he said. 'I am from North Italy, not far from France.'

She needed to spend a penny and asked him to wait in the corridor, because she didn't have the courage to piddle with him in earshot. Then, he took her arm, escorted her to the lift and tapped in the code. On the ground floor, he went with her through the reception area. The Valentine's Day display had been taken down, but one thin red ribbon still dangled from a brass pin. She nudged Gino.

'Valentine's Day – the day for lovers,' she said. 'Did you declare your love to your sweetheart?'

Gino put his hand over his heart. 'I heart you, lovey dovey. Such rubbish! The heart is a pump and nothing more.'

'And I thought Italians were romantic,' said Ethel. 'Perhaps not in the north, where you come from. The cold winds of Austria and Germany must have blown out the flames of passion.'

'Sunita told me…'

'Aha. Sunita is the one your heart desires.'

'No,' said Gino. 'Sunita is bossing people around all day long. What I'm trying to say is that Sunita asked me to try harder to get you seated next to Sir Philbert. Often, the man eats in his room and he is fussy, but I am optimistic about tonight.'

★

66

'You're the new one,' Sir Philbert said, and a bowl of soup was put in front of Ethel.

'Your fame thickens the air in this home,' Ethel replied.

'Residence,' he corrected her.

'It's still an old people's home, and they don't let anyone out.' She gently tapped his shoulder.

'Ouch,' he objected, and snapped his upper body sideways to face her. 'Never, ever, touch me again, especially not on my shoulder.'

'Sorry.' She was surprised. 'Did the Queen drop her sword on you in the ceremony? She is getting frail, and the sword is heavy.'

He slurped his soup, identified on the menu as 'hearty winter vegetable soup'. The other two residents sharing the table were Jane, only just seventy but a stroke victim, and a man called Len who collected clocks. The ticking and chiming in his room were resented by his neighbours.

'Pork chops with apple stew coming next,' Len said.

Ethel picked up the menu. 'You're right.'

'It's Thursday,' said Len. 'Every other Thursday, it's pork chops with apple, a fourteen-day rota. They think we're too doddery to notice. I have been in here for five years now. I don't need a menu. Tomorrow, there will be *saumon poché a la française*. Why it has to be in frog language, I've asked myself all these years.'

'Because France is the home of *haute cuisine*. I know, because...' Ethel looked coquettishly about her, 'I know the owner of a restaurant in Paris. It's called Chez Pierette.'

'Michelin stars?' asked Sir Philbert.

'I don't know. He hasn't taken me there yet, but we went to Montmartre, Sacré-Coeur and everywhere else. I can speak French, too.' She added hastily, 'I have forgotten most of it, though.'

Sir Philbert gave her a slow handclap. 'All the way to Paris, wow.' And then he did his unnerving twist to face her again. 'I have been lowered onto the Himalayas from a helicopter. I have ridden through the Sahara on a camel for a month. I have sailed on a merchant ship pirated in the Straits of Hormuz. I have filmed in Korea and Afghanistan. Khrushchev gave me the shoe with which he banged on the desk in the UN.' He drew breath. 'Why do you think my shoulder is crushed? The camera and tripod weigh sixty pounds. You are just as old and lost as all the other dames here. I don't know why they made it such a thing to seat you next to me. Sophia Loren in the Georges Cinq dropped her napkin just so that I could pick it up and admire her legs.'

'This isn't pork chops with apple stew,' complained Jane. 'How dare they change the routine? Pears don't go with pork.'

Philbert crossed his cutlery over the remaining food. 'In Ecuador,' he said, 'they enhance the meat of guinea pigs with pineapple.'

Jane shrieked. She simultaneously shoved her plate away from her, while pushing her chair away from the table.

'Since her stroke, Jane has hallucinations and often sees things still alive in her food,' explained Len, the clock collector.

Undeterred, Sir Philbert sought Ethel's attention again. 'Did I tell you that I met Mother Theresa?'

'And I,' said Ethel, straightening up, 'have just met the biggest show-off in all of Britain.'

'Ethel, what an unpleasant name,' said Philbert. 'You haven't been anywhere in your sad little life, and are trapped here now. There is no reason for you to play up with me.'

'I am interested in only one thing,' Ethel said, aware that she had coped maturely with her sensitivity about her name, 'escaping from River-no-view Residence. I've been here now for three days and can't stand it any longer. Are you game?'

'Silly woman.'

'We could inflate catheter bags pinched from the sick bay and float down into town when the brook's swollen after heavy rain.'

Sir Philbert laughed, showing his worn upper denture. 'I am ninety-one.' His concentration was on catching the eye of a carer to help him get up. Eventually, Gino came forward.

'How did that go?' Gino sounded as if he was about to add 'nudge, nudge' to his question.

'Philbert is a show-off,' complained Ethel.

'The woman with the ugly name is a pain in the ass,' reported Sir Philbert.

'I'm glad you two hit it off.' Gino grinned. 'I thought you would.' He pulled Philbert's chair away from the table and advanced the walking frame. 'Get hold of the rail and hold tight, old boy. We're going for a spin.'

Philbert mastered the abyss between chair and walking frame.

'Off we go,' warbled Gino cheerfully, and Philbert slid one foot forward, leaning so hard onto the frame that it shook.

★

One evening a fortnight later, in her room, Ethel was ready for the last routine check. She lay in bed, her wig off, light out, on her side with balled fists like a newborn. The door was gently pulled shut again, the light taken with it.

She got out of bed, switched on the light and said to herself, 'I have much to do in a short time.'

Each day, Ethel had collected something to assist her escape. Little Orphan Annie had escaped in a laundry trolley. Lassie jumped over a high gate. Papillon caught the seventh wave. Ethel had to find her own way.

From beneath her underwear in the chest of drawers, she pulled out the round, extra pillow she had asked for. On it, she had already drawn a face with a permanent marker picked up from fake-blonde Kate's desk. Beetroot smuggled out of the dining room had provided the dark lip colour. It wasn't bad and could work at a distance, but a face was not a face unless it had a nose. She had cut through the pillow seam with scissors stolen from the handicraft class that she had attended only the once, and sacrificed her Eiffel Tower, pushing it into the cushion stuffing to where the nose ought to be.

Taking a wooden hanger from the wardrobe, she threaded her purple pullover onto it, before wriggling the metal hook into the cushion stuffing. Now she had a head which stuck up as if on a neck over shoulders. Fixing her spare wig on the cushion improved the illusion. Ethel had made a human effigy once before, one which had successfully duped her mother into believing that she was studying at her desk, when in fact she had been out with friends. It was the trickery which her mind still treasured.

Tearing up newspaper pages, she crunched them tight and stuffed the balls into the arms of the pullover. A smile spread on her face. She had heard Sir Philbert complain to the staff that copies of *The Telegraph* he ordered and paid for kept disappearing from in front of his door.

Next, a dress was needed. She had found a way into the downstairs laundry room on the excuse of having left a necklace in the pocket of a skirt, and had pinched someone's tulip-print dress. Now, she cut away the sleeves of the dress and enlarged the collar opening, before threading it over the pillow head and onto the hanger. The filled arms of the pullover stuck out realistically, while the skirt of the dress hung straight. She stood back and liked what she saw.

Moving onto the next body part, Ethel fetched the two 'hands'. It had been easy to find see-through latex gloves; dispensing boxes of them were fixed to the wall on every floor. It had taken longer to get carrots not cooked so much as to lose all rigidity. Stuffed into the gloves, the fingers worked. The red carrot colour showed through the plastic as flesh.

It was getting late, and Ethel realised that she had not prepared feet. The head defined a person at one end, and the feet at the other. She had to think fast because she was starting to wilt.

She tried stapling her slippers to the hem of the dress, with the stapler she had cleverly removed from on top of the photocopier in the alcove next to Kate's desk. But the staples could not cope with the thickness.

'Feet. Feet.' Ethel looked around the room, but there was nothing usable. Perhaps in the room of the man across the corridor? Without knocking, she entered *Bluebell*. Mr Miller lay in bed sleeping, each intake of breath producing a gurgling noise. She looked around. There was a vase, but only one and breakable. She glanced into his shower room and then she saw them – her feet.

With two pulp-cardboard male urine bottles stapled to the hem of the dress, the doll Ethel had put together could trick the mind for a short time, at least from a distance. She rubbed her hands. As a final step, she checked her tote-bag: spare underwear and blouse, passport, photograph of her and Jean-Jacques, her purse with the last twelve pounds of her pocket money – not much, but freedom had no price.

Worn out by the hard work, initial sleep took over, the twin-bell retro alarm clock Len had given her as a present set to six-thirty in the morning.

*

The alarm clock did not have to ring; Ethel had woken well before that. Sleep deprived and dry eyed, she opened the narrow upper window, which was not locked because no human body, no matter how thin, could fit through. The fading dark of night was being taken over by a hint of light purple.

After dragging the large-footed effigy across the room, she forced its feet through the window gap, twisted the hanger shoulders and, after a few gentle pushes, the 'woman' fell out of the window and down to the ground. 'She' landed, the skirt of her dress entangled in the bushes, arms outstretched. By now, it was a quarter past seven.

Ethel ran into the corridor, yelling at the top of her voice. 'Help! Help!'

Several doors opened. Residents in night clothes approached, fear distorting their faces. 'What happened? What's going on?'

Ethel flapped her arms and hopped up and down. 'A resident has just fallen out of an upstairs window! Help us all!' She bent her head back and emitted a blood-curdling scream.

'Oh, my God. Not possible. Our windows are locked.'

'Desperate, she must have smashed the glass and jumped to her death.'

Jane came running, flapping her arms. 'Yes, yes. The poor soul fell head first, screaming. Upside down she fell. I saw the teeth in her open mouth.'

Appreciating Jane's imaginative support, Ethel shouted at the onlookers. 'Don't just stand around. Pull the emergency cords, run about, call for help.'

'Help! Help!' Emergency alarms rang out, which stirred things up on the A floor, where a separate pandemonium erupted. Demented howling could clearly be heard.

'We don't believe you.' Some of them pushed their way into Ethel's bedroom, rushed to the window and looked down. 'It is true. Help us all. Her body has landed in the garden, broken. Dead, destroyed. She is dead, dead. Down in the bushes, dead.'

'Isn't that Dora in her tulip dress?'

More checked the window. They all came away, distraught and agitated.

Mr Miller from *Bluebell* appeared at his door, pale and disoriented. 'Why are you all shouting? Who is dead?'

'There!' Jane took everyone's focus from the man by pointing excitedly into Ethel's room. 'Another woman has just fallen past the window. She only wore undies. She was bleeding,' she shrieked. 'There is blood everywhere. Look. You're standing in it.' Jane's fixed gaze was on things others could not see.

Mr Miller lost his balance and slid down the door frame to land on the blue carpet, his upper body in a twist. He was shivering and rasping. 'I've just broken my hip again.'

'We are all doomed,' Len the clock collector contributed. 'They push us out of the windows when they decide it's our time.'

Gino and Sunita finally appeared.

'What on earth…?' said Sunita.

They were surrounded by hysterical residents. Gino knelt by Mr Miller on the floor. Sunita kept her calm.

'Nothing is wrong,' she tried to appease the crowd. 'Residents cannot fall out of the windows.'

Ethel hid her smile. Her throat hurt from the constant yelling.

'Ambulance!' Gino shouted into the ongoing chaos. He had covered Mr Miller with a blanket. Sunita took out her phone and dialled.

Ethel yelled at her to call the police, the fire service, the air ambulance. 'The woman who fell from the window might still be alive.'

'Hush.' Sunita pushed Ethel rather roughly from her.

Pam came out of the elevator. She tried her best to assess the situation she was presented with. The man on the ground was clearly the priority.

'The ambulance is on its way,' Sunita said quickly. 'Mr Miller will be taken care of. There is no need for a grand-scale panic. Please, all go to your rooms and stop pulling the alarm cords.'

'What about the woman down in the garden?' asked Len. 'She might still be alive.'

'What is all this about?' said Pam.

'Two women fell out of the window,' Jane informed her.

'Suicide,' stated Len. 'It gets to all of us. We're here to die. At least the second one decided for herself.'

'There is blood everywhere.' Jane threw her arms around.

'Mr Miller is stable,' said Gino. 'And Jane, you are hallucinating. I'll go and help the women in the garden.'

Sir Philbert, on his Zimmer frame, appeared from the lift and crossed painfully over to Pam. 'This is a crisis. You're the commander of this lot and you have no clue what to do. First, you line them up and take a head count, making allowance for those who have been declared dead.'

'They might still be alive,' said Ethel. 'You can see them from my window.'

Pam went into Ethel's room and looked down from the window. A strange, strangled sound escaped her chest, while her spread hands landed against the window pane.

Ethel decided it was time. Picking up her tote-bag, she made her way to the open door to the staircase and trotted down the stairs. In reception, the desk was unmanned. Many red lights flickered on a board. Ethel headed for the kitchen, where two chefs were working with eggs and bacon for breakfast.

When they saw her, they stopped all activity.

'You are not allowed in here,' said one. 'What floor are you from?'

'Residents are falling out of windows,' Ethel exclaimed. 'The bodies have landed in the garden. The ambulance and police are on their way. We are in a state of emergency.'

The cooks looked at each other, shaking their white-hat-topped heads. At this moment, the fire alarm started up. It was painful to the ear, a continuous high-pitched ringing.

'Stone the crows, the old woman is right,' said the other chef.

Ethel thanked her angels for the alarm bell. 'We're supposed to assemble on the lawn.' She threaded herself between kitchen equipment to the outside door.

'Not unsupervised, not at your age and still wearing slippers,' said the first chef. 'You stay where you are. Don't move. We have to turn down our ovens.' The alarm kept ringing; the whole house seemed to vibrate with it.

The cooks busied themselves securing fire hazards, and Ethel slipped through the back door into the garden. Being close to the tulip-dress doll, she had to move away fast. She worked herself along the back of the house between brickwork and bushes until she reached the corner. Then, she scuttled to the next corner, which brought her to the front car park.

She dodged behind Pam's SUV, just as a police car drove in. Checking around, she left the property.

'I'm out,' she said to herself, pleased.

The street ran north, she knew. Not far away was the large Bedford Park, with its imposing gates, to which Aurora had taken her once for a walk and tea in the pavilion.

At the end of the road, Ethel turned right and was out of sight of Riverview. A left turn, and the park should now be in sight. She remembered what Hugh had said to her in his last hour at the hospital. 'Once I am gone, I hope you can have a fresh start.' She had gratefully taken his ice-cold hand, and he had slipped into the comfort of permanent death, while she now had to fend for herself.

She had come to a wide, busy road. A car stopped to let her cross. She found herself at the periphery of the park in which magnificent trees had been planted by the Victorians, who had designed for the future. Her shoulders sank with relief. Avoiding the formal entrance and pathways, Ethel followed a trodden track through dense shrubbery. A vast laurel bush stood, unyielding, in front of her.

'Let me through,' she begged. 'I am free. I can go to the coffee pavilion and order anything I want. I have twelve pounds to spend.'

She battled onward. Wearing slippers did not help. She started to feel cold. It was early March, and she had become used to overheated premises. The bushes were now twice her height. She heard the sound of water splattering on water. The pond – the fountain on the large pond. She was heading straight for it. That was not a good thing. Ethel had not planned her escape further than reaching the outside of Riverview. From now on, she had to make it up as she went along.

Voices made her turn round. Through the bushes, she caught glimpses of colourfully dressed children. She was still too close to the path. She had to push further into the undergrowth for, if she could see them, they could see her, and she wasn't about to be dragged back to Riverview by anyone.

A thin tree in front of her had broken and fallen against another tree, thus barring her way. On the one side was a long branch in the shape of a bow, blocking that way. On the other side, a voluminous bush sported thorns, mean pointy needles. The exhaustion after a night working on a decoy and then fuelling a pandemonium caught up with her. She felt dizzy and needed to sit down. However, pressing on, she knocked her forehead against a low branch. Touching her skin, her finger came away with blood on it. She felt close to swooning.

Ethel sank to the soft ground at the foot of a large tree, its leaves just about to unfurl. Lying on her back, she closed her eyes and listened to the world around her. The sound of the fountain was faint; she was safely away from water. A crow croaked. She wrapped the dressing gown closer over her body. Above crisscrossing branches, she saw little fractions of blue sky and sunlight. A strange, 'tisking' noise nearby alarmed her. There was a squirrel on a branch looking down at her, making that noise while whipping its bent tail.

'Shoo!' she hissed, and the rodent leapt away.

Nature did not offer the serene silence one often imagined; an approaching snuffling made her even more uneasy. She closed her eyes, trying to ignore it. The cold, wet nose that touched her hand was that of a brown dog. The owner kept shouting 'Rufus!', but the dog remained. Ethel feigned deep sleep. Rufus started to bark, but finally he obeyed his master and left. Vulnerable and prostrated on the ground, she remained. She had to crawl away, but must first find her calm. Head on the soft earth, she decided to stay just a tiny bit longer. Now a bird twittered pleasingly.

In front of her was an imposing tree. Unusually, the trunk split at shoulder height and, in the crook of the branches, was something which did not go with the natural scene. Intrigued by this misfit, Ethel got up to investigate and pulled from the cavity a large sunglasses case. It was hard to prise open at first, but, once she had succeeded, she gasped. Inside were tightly packed rolls of money. She tugged one out and had a better look. Fifty pound notes – many of them; probably a thousand pounds. And there were lots of rolls in the case, tens of thousands of pounds. Who said money didn't grow on trees? She was rich. She could do many more things now. She could go to Paris.

*

The taxi driver was rewarded with a fifty-pound tip at St Pancras station. She bought a ham and cheese sandwich and paid with another new, slightly curled, fifty-pound note. The man behind the counter shook his head with annoyance.

'That's all I've got. So sorry,' she said.

He decided not to argue with an eighty-year-old who had pine needles in the curls of her wig and pink slippers on her feet.

It was not difficult to find Paris on the departure board. The Eurostar left in fifty minutes and she bought a ticket, still with time to shop for clothes. She started by purchasing a holdall. In the first boutique, she remembered that it was Friday and wondered what Sir Philbert would have for supper. She giggled and selected a red dress that came with a black-rimmed matching red blazer. She bought a trouser suit and a frilled blouse. Browsing through clothes in a shop called Ted Baker, she found a darling handbag on a silver shoulder chain. She could afford it, as well as the black loafers she chose. And she added a red beret.

It had to be her love for Jean-Jacques which had produced the money miracle.

In Boots, she bought a bottle of Opium from Yves

Saint Laurent, after having sprayed herself liberally with sample bottles. She now smelled like a scent cacophony.

Soon it would be time to board the train. The queue at passport control was unpleasant, because standing for a long time was painful. She ground her teeth. *Paris, Paris, Jean-Jacques*, she chanted.

Finally, in the comfortable train seat, she dozed off and on. In between, she read the free magazine she had picked up about owning property abroad. She read an ad for a high-ceilinged apartment with fireplaces in every room and view over sugary Sacré-Coeur. Two large bedrooms in case Jean Jacques had not given up smoking.

Through the tunnel, she slept solidly and woke up in France with a wet patch on the front of her red blazer, where she had dribbled from her slack mouth while asleep.

When she arrived at the Gare du Nord, it was four-thirty in the afternoon. She had to press on. A hailed taxi brought her to the restaurant Chez Pierette. She felt dizzy with excitement. Perhaps it was partly the femme fatale perfume she had finally settled for.

*

The houses in the old part of Paris were elegant and tall, the back roads still cobbled. The taxi driver dropped her in front of the restaurant and had a dry coughing fit as he took the fifty-pound note she gave him as a tip.

She put her trembling hand on the old-fashioned door handle. The name Chez Pierette was painted on the

81

entrance in gold letters. Ethel stepped into the panelled room with square tables covered in white tablecloths, and wooden chairs. On the walls were many photographs of celebrities who had dined in the establishment. On a drum table was an impressive display of silk flowers.

From a swing-door at the back materialised not Jean-Jacques but a waitress, young, perhaps only seventeen years old. Her wavy blond hair was held back from her pretty face by a gingham cloth band, matching her dress. She spoke rapidly and tapped her wristwatch. 'Six', she kept saying, trying to send Ethel away.

Ethel produced the little French she knew. 'Amie,' she started. 'Amie de Jean-Jacques.'

The girl hesitated, an unreadable expression on her face. It could only mean that the waitress knew about Jean-Jacques and her. It revealed that Jean-Jacques had been missing her all those years, and talked to his staff about it.

'Grandpapa!' the waitress shouted, before starting to lay cutlery on a table. Ethel, standing there ignored, could feel his presence. She turned to look behind her. The old man in her focus had short-cut, grey hair. He looked back at her through rectangular spectacles on a wire frame. He wore a white apron over trousers, a shirt and a waistcoat. There was nothing familiar about him.

'Bonjour,' she ventured, having practised this word.

'Bonsoir,' he responded with a slither of a smile on his lips.

And this made her let go of her reticence. 'I am Ethel, remember? You loved me. You said such lovely things to me. I came with you to the fishmonger and we had coffees.' Her words failed before her courage did.

He looked blank.

She pulled the photograph of them from her bag and approached him. The scent of his cologne gave her a déjà vu high. 'It is you,' she warbled. 'You've grown so old.'

'I remember,' he said, thankfully in English. 'You are the American tourist I showed around Paris.'

Disappointed, she shook her head. 'English tourist. Remember? I bought the painting with the peonies from an artist along the Seine. It is hanging in my – my living room.'

An ugly, scraping noise was caused by the waitress pushing a table to join up with another. Instantly, the old Jean-Jacques went to assist her. While grandpapa and his granddaughter worked, they whispered to each other and laughed. Perhaps at her expense.

'Sorry,' he said, returning to Ethel and touching her shoulder fleetingly. 'Sorry I forgot you. It is a long time ago.'

'I have kept you warmed by my heart all these years.' She sought his eyes, hidden behind the spectacles. Her lips trembled in disappointment.

'Céline,' he shouted right past her. Ethel flinched. What he then instructed his granddaughter to do was too French to make out. Céline gave up laying the cutlery and disappeared through the door at the back.

Left alone with Jean-Jacques, Ethel felt shy and nervous.

'Céline is the daughter of my son. She helps in the restaurant now that my wife is unable to. Pierette has cancer, you see. We started this business together, over thirty years ago.'

'Ah,' Ethel managed. 'Your wife.' And it became clear to her that, when she had been in Paris, Jean-Jacques had just started this restaurant with his wife, after whom he had named it. It was a blow. Ethel felt her knees go weak.

He pulled out a chair and offered it to her. They had absolutely nothing to say to each other.

Luckily, the awkwardness was interrupted by two men coming into the establishment. Jean-Jacques made arm moves to invite them to come in and sit down at a table. It was by now a quarter to six. 'Céline! Deux cafés!' he called out.

'Do you still cook *morue au Muscadet*?' she tried, and it worked.

'Non, non.' He laughed. 'You came with me to choose the fish. When I gave you one of the fish to hold, you couldn't bring yourself to do it. I remember now.'

Only something negative had jolted his memory.

Noticing her disappointment, he said more gently, 'When I was younger, I loved showing attractive foreign women the city. You are the first one to come back and remember me. I am touched.'

'Jean-Jacques,' she said, emphasising the Frenchness of the name, 'you promised to do so many more things with me.'

He looked uncomfortable. 'Ah well. It was the nineties then.'

'That has nothing to do with anything,' said Ethel. 'I made it back here now and can treat you to anything in Paris you like. I won't interfere in your life or be a burden. Let's just sneak away for one day, like Audrey Hepburn in *Roman Holiday*. You won't have to pay for anything, either. I brought a lot of money.'

'I can't,' replied Jean-Jacques. 'I have my family to consider, my professional reputation. It is all delicate. I can't afford a blemish to my name. The restaurant business in Paris is competitive. Why don't you go and do what you want by yourself? Many little old ladies enjoy the city on their own. For a generous tip, our taxi drivers are patient.'

'Oh, Jean-Jacques,' she cried out in pain. 'You don't believe me. I'll show you the money. We can have fun with it.'

He squirmed, and a woman's voice was heard shouting 'Chéri!' from the back.

'You have to see this,' Ethel insisted and eagerly produced the sunglasses case, which she opened carefully in front of his face.

His eyes grew large and he reached out to ascertain that the rolls he saw were real money. 'Where did you get that?'

A hand grabbed his arm. 'You are under arrest for the handling and laundering of the proceeds from the traffic of illegal narcotics. Both of you, come down to the police station.'

The two men having coffee must have been plain-clothes policemen. One confiscated the sunglasses case and started to fiddle with it. 'I have de-activated the beacon. Inform our British friends that the operation is completed.'

Being marched out of the restaurant, Ethel noticed that the policemen had not finished their coffee.

HOT STEAM

Mother was late. Louise kept checking her watch. Any intrusion into her solitary life caused her anxiety, even when it had been agreed on and was just her mother bringing cooked food. Mona, living not far away, still thought it her duty to feed her thirty-two-year-old daughter. Louise fetched yesterday's empty gratin dish and checked it for cleanliness. It would be a swap for more food in a different dish.

Coping with everyday chores was not easy for Louise because she lacked practicality. She had an aptitude for accurate academic thinking. 'Brainy', they had called her at school. Not surprisingly, she had chosen to become a proof-reader and editor, and to live alone in the small flat over the double garage of her grandparents' home. The house was named *Tourbillon,* meaning water turbulence. That name was chosen for an obvious reason; the property was constructed lengthwise along the Swiss side of a wild, glacier torrent, which ran straight through the border town of St Gingolph, separating Switzerland and France before gushing into Lake Geneva.

St Gingolph, on the south bank of Lake Geneva, was a small town nestling against the lake as, right behind it, the steep mountains barred expansion. It was unique in that half of it was French, the other half being Swiss. Two different legal systems, two different social structures, and difficult policing. Every year, two national days were celebrated; the Swiss franc and the Euro were both accepted everywhere, and people got on. At least the language was French for everyone, and tolerance was widespread.

From the window of her flat, Louise could see the small piece of land her grandfather owned across the river on the French side, accessible by a private wooden footbridge, where he kept his six chickens. He paid taxes in France to keep livestock and taxes in Switzerland for their feed. Near the lake, the watercourse of the torrent broadened to flow more tamely under the wide bridge of the lake trunk road. Two border guard huts stood on the bridge with two sets of border police, the French in dark blue uniforms, the Swiss in green. Drivers had to show their passports and were often searched, especially unmarked vans and large lorries. From her window, Louise watched the border control activities.

Louise heard footsteps and opened the door. Mona Picard came in; she was tall and trim. She had fading brown hair, cut short, and looked her fifty-five years, with a worn face which was still handsome. She looked at her daughter for a second.

'You look pale,' she said. 'It's June. You should be outside more.'

'I'm busy editing a fat novel.'

'Another Philippe Turpin?'

'That one is promised to me in two months' time.

Right now, I am doing a Marielle Lambert. Her new story plays on a Caribbean island. A lot of replacing ellipses. While she wrote, she must have been guzzling piña coladas to identify with her heroine.'

'Look,' said Mona, forcing a smile, trying to sound bright and in charge of things. 'I cannot understand why you have to practically rewrite Turpin and Marielle Lambert. Without your help, they would not be published and make heaps of royalties. You deserve both of those things. Write a novel. Yours, at least, would be grammatically correct.'

'I can only be a proof-reader,' said Louise. 'Imagining a whole novel is beyond me. You know that.'

'I came to force you off your chair and out of the house. The sun's out.'

'The sun is never in or out. It's covered or not covered.'

'Whatever makes you happy, darling. Normal young people immerse themselves in nature, exercise, enjoy the suppleness of their bodies. You sit hunched at that old desk. I know, I know, it was Grandma's, and she gave it to you. All your grandmother ever used it for was scribbling shopping lists, no doubt full of spelling mistakes. Her back is still straight at the age of eighty. For you, with lumbago problems beckoning, decide now. Either write a novel to be remembered by, or go out there and do something for your health.'

'I like what I am doing. I abhor mistakes in books.'

'To be honest, I came here to tell you to take a holiday,' said Mona. 'A short holiday next month, away from semicolons, to a place with an emphasis on outdoor activities. Don't give me that old-fashioned look. Aren't you yearning to get away from St Gingolph for a bit?'

'I went to Lyon in spring.'

'That was a three-day copy-editors' forum in a large town with a pollution problem. I would not have to harp on, if you at least swam in the lake from time to time. Swimming tones muscles and builds strength.'

'It's often choppy,' replied Louise, 'and I hate swallowing dirty water.'

'Close your mouth, then. The lake water is as clean as it has been for a hundred years. I know, I pay taxes as a resident of a lakeside house.'

'I am grateful that you let me stay in the annex over the garage, and that you pay for all the costs.' Louise went into the small galley kitchen. 'Let me give you back your dish.'

Mona did not follow, as the space was too narrow for two. She reached into the bag she had brought and lifted out a brown oven dish with a lid. 'Leeks with ham in béchamel sauce. It only needs heating up.'

'Ah.' Louise looked pleased and pushed the dish into the fridge before handing back the empty one.

'Once your grandparents are gone, you will have the whole house to yourself,' said Mona. 'Did you know they've found out your grandfather has arrhythmia?'

'Can the doctors help?'

'I don't know. He is old.'

'What would Grandma do without him?'

'She could move into your flat, while you live in the rest of the house. One day, your father and I will be gone, too, and you can decide to sell *Tourbillon*. It is worth more than two million with its location, the large terrace overlooking the torrent and down to the lake, plus five double bedrooms, three with en suite, and your flat. St Gingolph is an international hotspot, with its large sandy beach, the lakeside restaurants, the hiking in the land of Mont Blanc, proximity to Geneva, Lausanne and the Valais, not to mention the skiing season. As a resident, and used to it, one takes it for granted.'

'Foreigners sure pour money into St Gingolph,' replied Louise. 'The Hotel Swan is being entirely refurbished.' She stopped talking to watch her mother's fastidious scraping at a tiny remnant of food on the inside rim of the empty dish.

Mona continued wiping the spotless rim. 'Right, I have searched and found Club Vivendus to be the best healthy holiday for a single young woman like you. There is an inviting three-star resort in Turkey. The pictures look lovely. The calm, mesmerising Aegean, early morning walks, gymnastics, water aerobics twice a day, healthy food, lots of fish. If I were still young... Now, before you launch into objections, I want you to know that your father agrees with me. Here...' She held out an oblong envelope. 'This is his contribution.' On the envelope was written in her father's hand, *Bar money – have fun*.

Louise lowered her eyes, as if this could hide her smile.

'Promise me you'll go,' said Mona. 'One short, healthy week. Cobwebs cleaned out of your clever brain, right?'

'I'm waiting.'

'Why? What for?'

'For you to mention that there I would meet a suitable young man, who pumps iron before breakfast and who would find me irresistible, despite my fat legs, my soft belly and my thin hair.'

'I wasn't going to, but why not? The Turkish coast is popular with the Swiss.'

'So, the muscle hulk you envisage for me should be Swiss. What's wrong with the French?'

'Nothing. The French just have less of an image of outdoor gymnastics, whereas the Swiss with their rolling cheese down the hill… As long as you don't plan to be available to a Turk,' Mona continued. 'Or a German, for that matter. And steer away from a Catholic, right?'

'Any other restrictions?'

'Not a motorcyclist.'

'Would a Mercedes do?'

'For your age, you are quite naïve about men. And you are too old now to make a major mistake again.'

'What does "again" mean?'

'Remy, the border guard.'

'I can see him working on the bridge from upstairs, Mother. We were friends at school, and in our twenties went to the cinema in Geneva a couple of times, had a few coffees in the *confiserie*. Hopefully, he'll ask me again. I need to ask him about the new Swiss duty-free import allowances.'

'Why is that important?'

'I've agreed to edit a leaflet on the subject and want to show that I am up to date with information.'

'You have an over-inflated sense of responsibility,'

said Mona. 'The contents are for the writers to get right, not you. You will be sprawling on a sun lounger under a palm tree, eating figs and waiting for the gym teacher to pull you up and drag you to aerobics.'

'I don't like figs. Gritty grains get stuck between teeth.'

'You're booking, right? Don't let us down.'

Louise took the envelope with the money.

'One tiny week in your long life, Turkey, Club Vivendus. And your laptop stays in St Gingolph. Promise?'

Louise watched her mother tackle the stairs with her platform shoes.

'You win. I could do with some relaxation.'

'Love you,' shouted Mona upwards.

*

Ten days later, having worked late nights to finish editing Marielle Lambert's novel, which ended inevitably with the heroine running on soft, virgin sand towards her beau, Louise packed her summer clothes, two bathing suits on top, the load tidied by a red Polynesian pareo. Suitcase ready, she went to the window.

Grandfather, carrying his metal bucket, was testing his way across the rickety bridge, the water broiling underneath. In spring time, when the snow melted, the swollen waters brought boulders tumbling down dangerously. Her grandfather, on the other side, fiddled with the wire door and then pushed into the pen, in which the few chickens were not too bothered about the intrusion. He had given them names. Sometimes he picked one up, clamped it under his arm and stroked it. Two years ago, a fox had managed to bite through the wire mesh, and Grandfather was short of two chickens the next morning, but could have filled a pillowcase with feathers.

Turning her head to look down towards the lake, Louise saw several lorries on the bridge, waiting to be cleared by her sweetheart. Remy, who had sat behind her in primary school. Remy, who had dared to brush her long hair with his sister's brush. Remy, who had held her steady when she learnt to ride his bicycle. Nowadays, he got around on a Vespa, which was far enough remote from a motorcycle to be tolerated by her mother. The big *but* was that Remy was newly married to Anne-Marie from the Co-op.

Louise pushed down on the suitcase lid and closed both clasps, reciting, 'No Turk, no German, no Catholic, no muscle-less indoor man. Ideally, a Mercedes limousine. Right, Mother?'

★

Louise Picard took deep breaths on the tiny balcony of her Club Vivendus cabin in the pine-tree wooded area of the club grounds. The scent of pine sap perfumed the air, while sun-warmed air caressed Louise's naked shoulders. She felt exposed, wearing only a swimsuit and the pareo knotted around her waist. Her pale, shaven legs, showing from under the cotton wrap, seemed to be made of cheese. She had to give her body some attention, but right now she needed to take a nap to recover from the flight and airport transfer, in a coach with a driver who was the proud owner of a powerful stereo system. It had blasted out Arabic-style music, with its maqam undulations, throughout the drive, music which made one start to waggle one's head and feel good about it for no identifiable reason, until a headache set in. Later, according to the programme, dinner would be served, followed thankfully by a load more sleeping.

Sticky pine needles, fallen from a gnarled branch over her balcony, worked themselves into her new flipflops and between her toes. She went back into the room and kicked off the flipflops, tossed the towel swan, with the hibiscus flower pushed into it, onto the occasional chair and lay on the newly made bed.

Escape map in the emergency case she read on the back of the door. It should be *Escape route in case of an emergency*. Having corrected this in her mind, she dozed off.

Rising when her mobile's alarm tooted, she groped around in her suitcase for a light summer dress, the small white clutch bag, and slipped her feet into moccasins. She then left her cabin in search of the bar.

A trio was playing on a felt-covered podium, a young woman singing in soothing alto. Guests had gathered and sat at nests of low, imitation-wicker seats and tables. Some of them circulated at the large display of appetisers, while a few still swam in the underwater-lit pool. A gentle evening breeze teased tablecloths. Insects danced in front of spotlights, celebrating the end of an easy day.

At the bar, it turned out she did not need money. In

Club Vivendus, everything was included and accessible, as long as one wore the rubber bracelet the receptionist gave one on arrival. Dad's bar money was superfluous. She decided to buy her father a nice gift to make up for it. Then she ordered a gin and tonic from the barman, who wore a black polo shirt with a large white CV printed on it.

Someone snatched away the tall glass the moment it was put in front of her. She did not object once she turned round. The handsome young man who had appropriated her drink offered her a mega smile, good teeth showing.

'Where do you want it to go?' he asked with a foreign accent.

'Into my stomach,' she said.

He put the glass back onto the bar to laugh freely. 'You are a funny lady,' he managed to splutter.

She noticed then that he, too, wore a CV polo shirt. 'You work here?'

He nodded, sobering.

'Is your accent Turkish?'

He shook his head. 'Catalan and French. Heard of Andorra?'

'Small, independent European principality situated in the Pyrenees on the border of France with Spain. Mainly tourism, some export of locally grown tobacco.'

'You're good. Good and funny,' he admired, looking her up and down.

She tucked one leg behind the other.

And then he turned and walked briskly away. She had failed herself. It was not a good feeling.

'I just wanted to say…'

He kept walking.

She stood watching the broad back of a good-looking man, whom she had kept interested in her for a short while, before he decided that she was not good enough for him. She now read the signs of her rejection in his alpha male assured composure: chin consciously up, hips sinuously jutting his pelvis forward with each step.

She had taken a risk sitting on a bar stool. Had she chosen a cane chair at a low table, less of her would have shown, but then he would not have come her way. The game was over. She had been rejected before. From now on, he would avoid her, and she would smile until her face hurt, to indicate that she didn't mind not being liked, didn't need to be liked, already had a bagful of people who liked her. Had she not almost married her school sweetheart? Well, she was at his wedding with Anne-Marie, sitting right at the back of the chapel and struggling with the sequinned comb which kept slipping out of her too thin hair.

The sudden impact of the vernal scent of his aftershave took her by surprise. Magic had brought him back.

'I found you a seat near the pool. Over there,' he pointed. 'The one reserved with my cap. You'll be more comfortable.'

'Thank you.' She gave him a smile, feeling its stiffness. He escorted her to a table next to the lit blue water, carrying her drink, and a plate of nuts and fresh coconut pieces he had swiped off the apéritif display on the way. She returned his cap and plunged into the cane seat while he lingered, half-committed, half-perched on the armrest of the other seat, as if there might be more to come.

'I'm not supposed to mix with members during apéritif time,' he explained. 'We can't get drinks from the bar. My name is Hasan.'

'Louise,' she said. 'What is your role here?'

'Land sports. Soon, I'll be made director of sports, which comes right after the holiday village boss.' Pride glinted on the enamel of his teeth.

'Do you have a motorcycle?'

After a hesitation due to the surprise of her question, he answered, 'No, I don't. I'm saving up for a small Porsche.'

'Not something larger and flashier like a Mercedes, perhaps?'

'We only ever buy compact cars.'

'Who is we?' she asked, her voice giving away her fear of his answer.

'My parents own the Hotel des Sports in Andorra la Vella. Roads are narrow and bendy. Small cars are practical.'

'A hotel,' she said admiringly. 'What is your role in that?'

'Sport, apart from being the son of my parents. In the winter, I coach skiing to guests and, in the summer, tennis, gymnastics and hiking. Sport hotel – sport offered.'

'We are in high season. Shouldn't you be back there now?'

'I've taken a year's job with Club Vivendus to learn about hospitality etiquette, and so on.'

'Can I ask you a few more questions?'

He frowned, but said, 'If it's that important to you.'

'Are you Catholic?'

'What?'

'It's best to establish the basics early. Such things matter to my mother.'

'I have no time for religion,' said Hasan. 'My father is French and has no religion. My mother is Turkish, and her family comes from a village near here. She is not a practising Muslim any longer. And me, I play Buddha Bar tapes for the cooling down after a gym class. That's as far as I commit to religion.'

'My mother will be pleased. Her name is Mona Picard, and she is back in St Gingolph, where I come from – a town which straddles the Franco-Swiss border.'

Hasan slid himself into the seat to sit properly, as if the mention of her mother commanded it. Louise pushed her drink towards him on the glass top.

'Help yourself, if you like.'

He offered her the sight of his perfect teeth again.

He made it easy to trust him. She told him about her life in St Gingolph, her small flat over the garage, her grandparents. She talked about the chickens, the wild river. She told him that, one day, she would own the house, which was worth over two million Swiss francs. She even mentioned Remy, now working at the border, when Hasan interrupted her.

'You now live with Remy?'

'No,' she said, almost too vehemently. 'He was not attentive or romantic enough for me.'

'Romantic. I know lady tourists like that.' Hasan

started to dig around in his trouser pocket and pulled out a keyring to which was attached a blue *eye* in glass. 'For you.' He put it into her hand, saying, 'It is an amulet to protect you from harm always. If you put your house key on it, you will remember me every time you come home and turn the key in the lock.'

'That is romantic,' she admitted, 'a bit clumsy, but well meant. Thank you.' Then she went on, telling him about her father, who liked fishing in the lake. Finally, she spoke a little bit about her editing work, which she realised he did not entirely understand. 'People write books and brochures with mistakes in them, and I put it right.'

He had never thought that could be a job. He kept sipping at her glass until nothing was left, and she got up to return to the bar to ask for two more of the same. The barman, craning his neck to get their table into sight, knew what was going on. On the way back to their table, she swiped a small bowl of almond-sliver-filled olives from the display. She felt daring and up to anything. Everything around her seemed to cajole her. The evening was so velvet blue, so balmy. Perfume trailed through the air, and romantic music lightened her steps on her way to a table at which one of the best-looking men present was expecting her.

Instantly, Hasan, who had had time to think, took the conversation up again. 'You were right. It's helpful to learn about a new person.'

'Except that I seem to be doing all the talking,' she complained playfully.

'Maybe,' he admitted. 'But first, one more for you.'

She made a gesture of surrender.

'With a border between two countries right through your town, isn't there much smuggling going on?'

'St Gingolph's history is almost entirely about smuggling, goods and people,' she replied. 'During many years, cigarette smuggling was big.'

'You said your boyfriend is a border guard, and you watch him work from your house.'

'That's not exactly what I said. He is not my boyfriend, but a married man and a senior border policeman.'

'But you are still good friends? He would do you favours if you asked him, wouldn't he?'

'Yes, he would.'

'Now these are valuable details,' Hasan beamed. 'But I don't understand why your mother did not force him to marry you?'

'She couldn't do such a thing.'

'She is a weak woman.'

'I don't think so.'

'Does your house have a cellar?'

'A very large, chill one, sort of carved into rocks at one end. That is not interesting.'

'It is good to know.'

'Now your turn again.' Louise moved her seat closer to him. 'Tell me about your family, especially your weak or strong mother. Whether you are married should have come first.'

He laughed shortly. Perhaps coconut flesh kept teeth white.

She got out of her seat. 'I'll get us two more drinks while you prepare to lay bare your life in front of me.'

He frowned, and she swept away.

On her return, he appeared apprehensive. 'He saw us sitting here. The barman is a pain in the,' he hesitated, 'neck. We all do it with guests, but he still runs to the Boss to rat.'

'Are you engaged, perhaps?' asked Louise. 'Many pretty girls work in Vivendus.'

He shook his head. 'My parents want me to marry someone local, because we are now Andorrans, and one day I will own the hotel and it keeps things authentic.'

'There are about sixty thousand inhabitants in Andorra. If half of them are female, you're down to thirty. If most of them are over the age of sixty, there is not much choice left.'

'You are like a computer lady,' he said. 'You know everything, just like that.' He flicked his thumb against his finger. 'I only need one wife to start with.'

'True.' She laughed at his joke.

'Now I will tell you about my mother.' He made it sound a conspiracy. Deepening his voice, he confessed, 'She was incredibly beautiful when she was young. Her mother let her marry my father, even though he was a foreigner and turned out to be irresponsible. She was happy, because she was weak and liked to cook and stay inside the house.'

'You've just set your mother into medieval Turkey.'

'My father was not good to her. He left my mother and me when I was seven.'

'I am sorry.'

'It was a bad time. The judge asked my father to pay my mother, but he had no money. He was getting

102

together with dangerous men and did illegal things. One day, he met another weak woman and got engaged to her. Her parents had a large property and money, but the two sisters of the woman took everything and the weak woman got nothing. My father had to leave her and return to making money with his criminal friends. When I was already seventeen, he finally managed to marry a strong woman called Selma who had money for all of us, but she gave my father away saying he was a criminal. The police arrested him, and a judge put him into prison for ten years. After five, he was let out. Angry with Selma, he mixed anti-freeze with her drink. It made her ill.'

'This is a story which goes from bad to worse,' said Louise. 'We have just reached the feudal era.'

'It will end well,' Hasan replied. 'Selma was so ill that she became weak and let him have her house and money. That's when my mother and father got together again, and we moved to Andorra and started a life there. Selma is dead now; the poison had damaged her insides. I knew her when she was strong, and then when she was weak. I learnt a lot from my father. After that, we had enough money from Selma to buy the hotel in Andorra.'

'Do you think I am a strong woman or a weak one?'

Without hesitating he said, 'Strong. Your mother is probably even stronger. It will be a problem.'

For a moment, she tried to figure out what he meant with that. However, the Boss passed their table, and Hasan sat up straight and pushed his cocktail glass surreptitiously across the table closer to her.

'This charming lady asked me to explain what a

103

hammam was, and here I am explaining,' Hasan invented on the spot.

The Boss, also in a black CV polo shirt, greeted Louise in a civilised manner. To Hasan, he hissed out of the side of his mouth, 'How about the gym? Ayeleen was forced to cover for you.'

Hasan got to his feet and sprinted away without even looking back.

The company gone, Louise picked up her clutch bag and went to supper. She had to eat at a table alone, and felt exposed.

On her way back to her room, she passed the indoor gym. Through the wide glass door, she saw Hasan piling weights back onto their brackets, while a cleaning lady with a ponytail that reached down to her bum vacuumed the carpet-covered floor.

'Good night, beautiful man,' she whispered, but Hasan did not look up and therefore did not notice her.

★

The bed was comfortable, but her anxieties produced worry dreams. When she woke up, she felt up to doing very little. She had already missed the early walk and could not bring herself to go to the morning gym class. Breakfast was all she managed and, after that, she changed into her swimming costume and walked down to the beach. She found a sun-lounger under a palm tree, and spent time enjoying the effect of the shadow-and-sun stripes the moving palm leaves printed on her pale body. She dozed off.

A little later, she was woken by loud voices. The source was a game of volleyball further along the beach. She turned on her side to watch. Hasan was a key player, the instructor. He was wearing only swimming trunks. When he jumped up, whacking the ball across the net, the white sand was kicked up and the muscles on his thighs stood out hard. He had so many hard muscles on his body that it would probably hurt him to sit in an office chair for any length of time.

Several volleyball-playing women fancied him. This was clear from their body language. One, in a tiny pink bikini, with long blonde hair, happened to bump into him with calculated regularity. He grabbed her thin waist, lifted her up and put her down like a Barbie doll a little further away from him, wagging his finger playfully at her.

Louise closed her eyes and thought of the annoying new rules concerning italics, which she did not like but had no choice but to accept, as she had now to accept tough female competition as far as Hasan was concerned.

When the ball game was over and the participants dispersed, to her panic Hasan came her way. Had he seen her watching him all this time? Did he think she was uselessly infatuated with him?

'Hi there,' he said nonchalantly, and pulled an empty chaise longue through the sand closer to hers. She covered her body with her pareo, while he crashed out on the taut plastic cover with a noisy 'pouff'. In the glow of his sweat, he shone like an oiled bronze sculpture of the perfect young man.

'You should have joined us,' he said. 'Volleyball looks

like child's play, but every muscle of the body is engaged, and the breathing is strong, which brings oxygen to the blood more than in most other fancier sports.' After a short pause, he continued, 'Sorry,' and pushed his strong, straight hair away from his glistening forehead. 'I talk too much about me, but it is thanks to me that the Club offers volleyball in this village.' Suddenly, he smacked the side of his head forcefully.

Louise gulped.

'Rude,' he said. 'I am rude. It's the main problem I have to work on.'

She relaxed her shoulders and eased her grip on the wrap. 'You are natural and direct. Direct is good.'

'Thank you.' He sighed with a touch of drama.

She felt like kissing his shapely lips. She did not, of course. Their conversation had run out. The fanned leaves distributed zebra shadows.

*

That night after dinner, Louise heard scraping at her door. She sat up. It scraped again. She left the bed and opened the door a crack.

Hasan pushed himself into the room.

'You can't just...'

'There is only one way to get to know someone well, and you know what that is.'

'I can't.' She winced. 'It is wrong. A holiday romance is cheap. I'm not that sort of woman, girl, person. I don't know you.'

'In one hour, you'll know me a lot more.'

'It's not funny, Hasan. Please leave.'

'You're right. It is not funny. I take any sport seriously.'

'Could we meet at the bar again tomorrow and talk some more before…?'

'You can't even say it. Look, I dig you. I want to have sex with you. Let's start by sitting on the bed.'

'No,' she almost yelled. 'I don't like digging, whatever it means.'

'It's not written down,' he said. 'You don't have to edit it. Just relax and let me touch you. You are an attractive woman.'

'No, I'm not. You are.'

He strode right in, pushing her gently but firmly in front of him towards the bed. She twisted round to object, but a last, decisive push brought her to sit on the duvet.

'What I mean,' she continued, 'is that you are the attractive one, but rudely you don't listen to me.'

'I don't want to listen. I want to touch.' He leant over her and nuzzled his head close to hers, kissing her neck.

'I'd rather go back to the bar and talk,' she objected, her hair tousled, her upper body propped up on bent elbows.

'Finish talking for today. The bar is closed. Everyone went back to their rooms to have sex.' He put his weight over hers and sought her mouth with his lips. Her elbows sank into the softness of the bed.

'I would call this sexual imposition,' she protested.

'You invited me in. You chatted me up. You bought me drinks against Club rules. I could call this open invitation.'

'Technically…' she started.

'Shush. Stop your clever talking. Admit you want me. Look at your nipples; listen to your breathing.'

'It's because I am angry. I want to be wooed by a man, understood?'

'This is going to be a short story, lacking the romance you are after.' With his mouth he tried to find hers again.

She fought him. Their foreheads knocked against each other. 'Sorry,' she said, 'you have to understand…'

He sealed her lips, which pushed her head deep into the pillow. She could not protest any longer; her body went slack while his became more active.

He concentrated his eyes on hers. 'You're what I have been looking for,' he said intently. 'Can be made to be what I need. You are warm, soft and will be generous. Try to engage a little. I can't make love to a corpse.'

'The word is necrophilia.'

'I'll call you Ophelia if that turns you on. Come on, open your legs, sweet Ophelia.'

'No, no, I can't! Not yet. Not now.' She panicked. Outside the room, the wind must have risen, for the branch of the old conifer started to knock against the roof tiles, as if it was the finger of some higher authority trying to thwart wrongdoing.

'I'm not letting you go. It took me a long time to find you,' he continued, undisturbed. 'You'll be helpful to me,' he breathed hotly against her ear. 'You'll be mine, and I always take care of what is mine.'

'I hear you, Hasan. Men don't own women, ever.' The branch knocked against the roof sinisterly.

'Ignore it,' he panted. 'Move with me. Let me.'

Twisting her mouth away from his, she was able to say, 'It's a stone pine specimen.'

'Who gives a shit? Oh no, I'm coming. Look what you've done to me.'

After sliding off her, he lay on his back, his thorax rising and falling. A man in her bed, one whom she had caused to breathe heavily. She examined him closely, as if he were her prey. A pleasing profile, high forehead, straight nose, shapely full lips she already knew and remembered pressing on her body everywhere. The strands of strong, dark hair falling over his right eye; others darkening the white pillow. Although her fingers itched to touch him, she held back, contenting herself with admiring the rest of his nude body next to her. How amazing. A sun-kissed Adonis in the chill bed of a pale, cellulitic tourist, a woman without allure or sex appeal – him, with her, and in her bed.

'You're thinking so intensively, I can hear the noise coming from your head,' the trophy male next to her whispered. 'Are you that uncomfortable with yourself, or with me? Don't worry.' He took her hand and put it on his flat belly. 'It was still good for me. Next time, I'll do everything to make it good for you, I promise.'

'Next time,' she squeaked.

'Yes, my beautiful friend from the border town. You'll learn to be more relaxed. I suggest you go to the hammam tomorrow afternoon. This will cleanse your body the way I should have explained to you, and relax you so that you feel as if you are floating in thin air, before we even meet up.'

'I'm sorry to be difficult. It's just…'

He cupped his hand over her mouth. 'You're not difficult. You are special and a serious young woman, the best I've ever met. And you are beautiful. Sadly, you don't even know it. I will show you. I care enough for you to do that.'

He said nothing more, but kissed the tip of her nose. 'Smile, little lady, smile.'

He knows what I think, pounded in her head, *knows how women feel*. For a man to get to that point, he must have been with many of them. Could it be that he was sensitive and attentive towards her in particular? Most unlikely. This handsome, full of testosterone, male was temporarily short of females to practise on, and she had got here just in time. Tomorrow, he would not even remember the shape of her belly button. Was that written in two words or with a hyphen?

'Better,' he said, resting his large hand on her forehead. 'You appear to be more relaxed. The games men and women play with each other should be fun. They can be fun, believe me.'

Angry, Remy had once called her a dried-up old maid after she had put a stop to some of his fondling on *their* park bench. At least Hasan had chosen her, had taken the trouble to walk to her room, remember her name. Furthermore, which always had a comma after it, he was not just a randy Turkish local. His parents owned a hotel.

'Stop being far away. I am here. Talk to me.'

'I'm sure men and women can have fun with each other,' she replied. 'My authors write about it in their books. I personally just don't have much experience.

Always been busy with other things: pressure from publishers, authors, deadlines. What Remy and I had, I now realise, was just kids' play. I've never seen him naked.'

'You are a virgin,' Hasan said, as if he had just found a famous diamond in the bed.

'Ah, ah, I sort of guess... I am,' she waffled, deeply embarrassed.

'In Turkey, every single young woman, and less than young single woman, says she is a virgin. Men treasure that, as if it were true.'

'Why?'

'Untouched, women can be shaped to men's desires.'

'Male possessiveness,' she said. 'Women all over the world have gone into battle to combat this, although the word *possessiveness* does uniquely contain the letter *s* six times. And why did you choose Turkey to do your tourist training in? Why not Switzerland, with the best-run hotels in Europe?'

'My best friend Ali is Turkish, and I learn many things from him,' said Hasan. 'He is one of the Club's odd-job men. Early in the morning, he fumigates against mosquitoes and bugs. He cleans out drains and catches snakes, which screaming guests see, and spiders in their rooms. He is like a brother to me.'

Hasan pulled at the duvet and covered the lower part of his body with a corner of it. 'You don't want sex. You are already a strong woman all by yourself.'

'Perhaps you are wrong about me.' She smiled weakly and reached out bravely to trail over the ball of his shoulder and down his firm arm.

111

'What does that mean? Is that a come-on? Are you ready to try it for real?'

'Can I touch you where it is safe?'

'There is no safe on me.' Masculine pride came through. 'Given half a chance, I'll ravish you.'

'As you have done so many others.'

'My past is my past. You, on the other hand, come without a past. That is helpful in my planning.'

After he left the cabin, from the balcony she watched his now familiar figure walk away and was surprised that she felt little more than relief.

Mother could not say that she was naïve with men any longer, was the first thought that came to her mind, when she stepped into her shower to wash the sticky stuff off her body.

*

The next morning, their paths crossed in front of the breakfast buffet. She told him that she had put down her name for the Bodrum city tour and, on return, would try out the experience of a hammam. If the coach returned too close to dinnertime, she would skip the meal in favour of the steam room experience.

'Very good,' he approved. 'You'll see.' To her relief, he made no suggestion of sex between them following the hammam. His plan for the day was to get off duty after the afternoon volleyball lesson and pop straight over to Ali's village to have a drink with him.

'Have fun with Ali,' she said light-heartedly. 'You'll have to introduce us.'

With a plate, she walked over to the cook who made scrambled eggs in a large pan over a live fire. Hasan went in the other direction towards the espresso machine.

★

On the coach returning from town, Louise just could not help having another look at the shirt she had bought in the Hilfiger shop. It was beautifully tailored, good cotton, mother-of-pearl buttons with a motif of stylised fish against a soft steel-blue – and medium size: her father was proud of his slim body. He would love it. *A fat man is an old man*, was his saying. The Belgian woman called Brigit, with whom Louise had spent the day and who now sat next to her in the bus, commented on the purchase.

'The man for whom the shirt is meant must be close to your heart.'

'Very close,' Louise said smiling, and lifted the shirt up against her face to nuzzle in it.

Shortly after that, the coach slowed down because of roadworks. From then on, they advanced in bumps and starts. When they finally reached the Club, people were already at dinner.

Louise headed straight to the square, concrete building in the gardens in which was the hammam. In the changing room, she hung the gift bag containing the shirt on a peg, took off her summer dress, sandals and underwear, and wrapped herself into the pareo she had taken with her to town in the hope of finding a matching red bathing suit. She knotted two of its fringed corners over her left shoulder.

113

Barefoot, she went to the thickly padded door. Behind it, she found herself in a steam-filled room that was entirely clad in blue and white tiles. Clammy heat plastered itself against her face. Fog clouds obscured clear vision, as if one wore someone else's spectacles. There were no windows; a tiled bench ran around the room to sit on, feet in a water-draining runnel. In the centre of the room was an heptagonal platform, also tiled, providing more spaces to sit or laze on, even lie flat. In several places on the wall were bronze taps. Under each was a bronze-coloured bowl. She turned a tap. It squeaked before cold water started to prattle into the metal bowl.

Nobody else was present, which was not surprising as it was dinnertime.

She raised herself onto the platform and flinched when she heard a prolonged, sharp, hissing noise. Up on the ceiling, in two places, thick hot steam was being pumped into the room. When the moisture hit her, she gasped. The vapour was so hot, it smarted on her skin, burnt the tips of her ears, stronger than she had anticipated. As per instructions in the changing room, she put the bowl on her lap and scooped cold water from it over her face with both hands. It soothed the steam burn.

She refilled the bowl. Spilled water gurgled as it went down through the draining slits on the floor near her feet. Slithering on her backside on the tiles, she found a comfortable position. By now, the drenched wrap was stuck to her body. Hasan had been right; this was a strong, physical experience. It felt sexy to be so naked and get slowly soaked, but warm at the same time, and to feel the glaze of tiles against her private place, while vapours

114

beckoned her to let go and swirl with them through the room. She closed her eyes; sweat poured down her face, and condensation pearls rolled down between her breasts. Her hair was plastered against her head. Renewed heat pumped into the steam room, obscuring the already weak light from the small lamps on the walls.

She thought she heard faint noises from the changing room and expected someone else to join her, but the padded door remained closed. There was no way to know what time it was. Time had lost importance. Intense heat took her into its clutches, squeezing her breathless, and then released her as it expanded to the rest of the dream-like room.

She filled her bowl at the tap again, and saw herself as a female figure performing a biblical gesture. Slowly, she poured the cold water down her heaving chest. The darkened cotton cloth outlined her physical shape. She felt as she had never before. She sprawled on her back, arms out, letting new steam heat roll over her. A quote from a poem in *Arabian Nights* came to mind: *hammam of delicious bathing* – written by humans who lived amid gritty dry sand, yearning for water.

New, hot vapour wrapped her into a scalding cloud. She cooled her heated face by dipping it into the battered brass bowl. She started to hum a tune, only the refrain, again and again. She felt as if she were melting into wellness. The repeated hot and cold sensations brought out hidden, untapped sensuality. Now she would like Hasan to come through that door to be with her, naked ideally. How could water heated to boiling point make her wanton?

New puffs melted her some more. She patted the cloth against her. It made smacking noises. Nothing else. Nobody else would be coming. It had to be the time the hammam was officially closed. That did, of course, not apply to her as she was already in it. Condensation ran from her belly down into her crotch. It tickled. She used her hand to stop it, as she lay in abandon, legs apart. Hasan was with Ali. She could take her time, had no-one to answer to.

Would Hasan talk to Ali about her? If so, what would he say?

*

Yonca watched Ali walk into her restaurant, accompanied by the athletic friend she remembered him bringing before. Ali's hand was on the young man's shoulder. They would order raki. She stood up out of the plastic chair next to her gleaming new chest freezer, and gathered her ample serge skirt which reached to her ankles. She would encourage several rounds, until they needed to fill their stomachs to avoid drunkenness. Inside the large trunk were the frozen portions of bulgar and vegetable pilaf with ground lamb meat she had prepared precisely for an occasion like this.

The premises were modest. *Local charm* was printed on the hand-out cards. Guests would eat outside on the patted mud terrace, covered by rafters of conifer wood and jute blankets. In a loop-strung garland of lights, several bulbs were dead.

She made the effort to cover the rough-hewn wood table with cloth for these guests, and put down a pewter plate with bread. The young men watched her with detached interest, eye contact between them showing their impatience for her to be done and leave.

The restaurant made most of its money from men who dropped in after sunset, stood at the bar and sucked raki from the small glasses which her husband filled. A bit of money was made on the side selling keyrings to customers. The ring attachments were blue, eye-shaped amulets protecting against evil.

This evening, Ali and his friend clearly intended to talk in private. She tapped with her flat hand on the lid of the freezer. Ali looked her way. She smiled and tapped once more. He lifted both shoulders. They might go on to ordering her bulgar stew later.

Ali sipped raki, put the glass down and licked over his upper lip. 'This lion's milk isn't bad,' he said, and then asked Hasan to change places with him, so that Ali was more hidden from the road.

'Your mother?' asked Hasan.

'She's OK with alcohol, but old time-like,' said Ali. 'I don't want to disappoint her. Turkish boys respect their mothers. Let's forget about Islam. Tell me about that woman you met.'

Hasan drained his glass. 'She fits.'

Ali made a grimace.

'Not that way, idiot.'

Yonca was already there, ready to refill their glasses. She heard *idiot* and looked worried.

'Not him,' Ali reassured her. 'He's my friend.'

'Good to hear,' she said, and held the bottle against her chest as one would a puny baby.

117

'Just bantering.'

When Yonka was out of earshot, Ali said, 'It is surprising she is pouring us raki. Normally, her husband does. She wants our business. Needs our business. We'll have her stew later. It is good. I mean good. Now, back to the one who fits you.'

Hasan grinned. 'Louise is from Switzerland. Lives in a border town with France. First-class smuggling place. Switzerland offers bank accounts with guaranteed discretion, and often has to turn a blind eye to smuggling, because it is in the middle of Europe and needs to please many adjoining countries. I know that from my father.'

'You're not still into that synthetic drugs shit? Wasn't your father caught years ago and put in prison?'

'My father, I was told, now lives somewhere in South America.'

'The international crime agency, the drug-ring buster squads,' said Ali. 'Even the FBI must be checking every move you make, son of a drug criminal as you are.'

'That's why Louise is so perfect for me. Manufacturing synthetic stuff can be done in small, hidden places. The tricky bit is the distribution of it: how to store it and transport it across borders, to get it into the hands of the thousands who can pay for it and keep their mouths shut. In my father's time, it was disguised as bath salts, sold in cloth bags in health stores – small fry.'

'Louise has no clue that you plan to exploit her, does she?'

'She'll benefit from helping. I'll give her sex in return.'

'You plan to completely ignore the Koran advocating sexual restraint?' said Ali. 'It's haram, you must know that. We'd better get Yonka over here for more lion's milk. I need courage to listen to your ideas.'

When their glasses were full again, Hasan continued. 'Calm down. Louise is over thirty and still a virgin. She is naïve, you wouldn't believe. Sexual excess is not part of the plan.'

'Be aware, my crazy dangerous friend,' said Ali, 'naïve women are not automatically weak, or stupid. She will find out very soon that you are the son of a drug smuggler, and that the hotel in Andorra is made-up shit. Or did you come up with your Bulgarian hospital story this time?'

'Andorra. Nobody knows what a Catalan accent sounds like, do they?'

'Bulgarian wasn't so bad, either, but then that dame turned out to be a lesbian.'

'And offered only a large, unused garage and nothing else.'

'Why do you keep doing this?'

'My father never cared about me,' said Hasan. 'Never took me anywhere. Never talked to me man to man. He looked down on me as if I were his punishment in life. When I choked on my first cigarette, he called me a pathetic little girl. It has to be put right. I don't know where he lives, but if I make a name for myself in his mates' circle, he will hear about it sooner or later.'

'Revenge,' said Ali. 'Revenge only increases the problem. You must be familiar with that saying in the Koran. Your mother has largely given up the Islamic faith after marriage to your French father, and therefore you were badly taught. Even so, good sense must rule humans, and I don't want to hear any more about tough-to-conquer Louise from you.'

'You've just put your finger on the problem,' replied Hasan. 'I need to make her weaker to be any use to me. I'm already working on that. Also, if you care to listen, I came up with a brilliant idea.'

'I am frightened to hear it.'

'Do you take aspirin?'

'Drinking more now, tomorrow I will have to take a handful.'

'It's a drug,' explained Hasan. 'Manufactured somewhere. A sect in the States is not allowed to use it. Aspirin in Europe is weaker than that produced in the States. What is inevitable about that?'

'You tell me.'

'Business transactions where people along the line make money. And, where people get what they want. The same goes for synthetic methamphetamine, LSD or Ecstasy.'

'These are illicit chemicals, dangerous.' Ali waved his hands as he spoke vehemently. 'We are talking illegal trafficking.'

'You don't get it. I'm a shrewd businessman. I came up with a top idea on how to store, shift and sell man-made drugs, with the help of Louise. Don't panic. Just listen. Cattle, horses, sheep and goats need calcium sodium for their well-being. They crave it. The modern farmer throws large blocks of that salt into meadows for the animals to lick. Hidden in that can be thousands of fixes. Farm tractors on rural borders are not stopped, are they? Louise has a large cellar, a large valuable house, a family of naïve yokels who fish and bake and count their pile of gold in the bank. Louise's mummy wants her blue stocking daughter to marry a man with a large Mercedes. Boy, I'm gonna afford a fleet of those, just for shopping in Monte Carlo.'

'I really don't want to hear this,' said Ali. 'You frighten me. I can't get myself and my family into trouble. There are good people out there. You probably don't know. Some of it, I understand. Your father went away when you were seven, and your mother was left without security.'

'Your family shared everything with us,' said Hasan. 'Probably saved us. This made us brothers. I won't harm you or your family. You are good Turks, good Muslims. For my part, I bloody well need to be celebrated for being me.' He punched the air with his fist. Loosening his hand, he continued, 'When I saw my mother dead in her bed, I asked myself, *What was the purpose of her life?* To give birth to me, is the only thing I could come up with. My father belittled it. I'm going to grab this life and go for it. Louise had better weaken and then work out, because I want to be rich and known, and own things.'

'Such wantings go against my life principles,' said Ali quietly. 'You know me well enough to know that. Therefore, we have to go our separate ways.'

Yonka saw Ali drop his head into his hands as if overcome by what his friend was saying. They were so busy talking, they forgot to order stew, only drank. It was now time for them to pay and leave.

Hasan got up and threw money onto the tablecloth. A lamp bulb near them flickered and went out. Ali remained seated, draining the last drop of his raki, while Hasan walked out of the pergola restaurant.

★

Back in Club Vivendus, it was Hasan's last job each evening to close the hammam building. In the changing room, to his surprise, two hooks were occupied. Guests left things behind. Once, it had been a big-cup skin-coloured bra. Another time, one trainer. How did they not notice when they got dressed again?

This night, a pair of sandals had been left behind, and a woman's flowery summer dress, with underwear in its pocket, hung abandoned. Hasan lifted a gift bag from the hook next to it. Hilfiger. He whistled shortly; it was the most expensive shop in Bodrum. He pulled out a man's shirt. First class, expensive and in his size. Tonight, he might have lost Ali's friendship, but had been compensated with the gift of a perfect shirt. He pulled it out of the bag, folded it twice and stuffed it under his polo shirt.

Turning to his duties, he went to the main water tap and shut off the flow. He had opened the control box on the wall, when he felt the shirt slip down, but caught it in time. He had to hurry and get this stolen shirt into his room as fast as possible. The voice he thought he heard shouting from far away was in his head. Perhaps it was the effect of the raki on an empty stomach? *Haram*. Ali had mentioned this most important word twice. His mother had taught him; his father ignored it. Hasan felt the spasm of that familiar pain. It was a mixture of shame and

122

an insisting voice shrilly ordering him to take advantage of opportunities when they presented themselves. He had found and deserved the shirt. He had a right to want more in life and, if it cost his friendship with Ali, so be it. Undermining strong women by harming them was, after all, the only thing his father ever taught him.

Hasan closed the control box, hurried to the padded door and locked it with a padlock. No one had seen him take the shirt. Holding onto the bulge under his polo shirt, he left the hammam building and ran across the lawn from one patch of shadow to the next, until he reached the staff quarters behind the kitchens. He trampled up the stairs to his room on the second floor. Safe inside, he stuffed the shirt into the leg of one of his tracksuit trousers in the chest of drawers. Crashing out on his bed, he felt so good about himself, he pressed the button on the CD player next to him on the bedside table: *Buddha Bar Ocean*.

*

Louise, on the tiled heptagon, wiggled her toes. Her two big toes with wrinkled skin could easily be mushrooms that mycologists found in swamp areas. A noise came from behind the padded door: footsteps, a clacking. Noises people made doing things with things. She shouted and ran at the door, only to slip and fall back on her bottom. She laughed.

'Luckily, I am well padded,' she said to the empty room. Nobody came in.

A new blast of hissing steam burnt her scalp, too

vulnerable under a thin layer of wet hair. She gasped as she heard a door being slammed. She skated to the padded door, but could not open it, no matter how hard she threw herself at it.

'I'm still in here!' Silence. Her tender ear against the door produced ringing in her cochlea, nothing more. If someone had been in the changing room, that someone was now gone, had left the building, slamming the door.

She tried pushing the padded door again. It was locked or obstructed. That someone had done this. How? There was no handle or keyhole.

'Help!' she shouted.

The door did not give. She was closed in. Sweat diluted with condensation streamed down her body. Nothing made sense. Were hallucinations part of the hammam experience?

She had to get a grip of herself. By now, dinner was over, even the evening show was finished. A closing-down round was surely imminent. Electricity to get this steam heater working cost money, as did the light of the lamps.

Resigned, she returned to sit on the platform. It wouldn't be long and she would be let out. A hiss producing burning heat jolted her. She dragged herself to the nearest tap. No water came out. She tried the next and the next. The cold water had been shut off. She assimilated this for several minutes, bad minutes, of her life. It hissed. She was wrapped in scalding steam again.

'Mum,' she wept, crawling around on the platform like a poison-darted animal. And then she stopped, because she had heard a new noise, a ticking. That was a change from before. It meant something. Of course. The heating system must have been switched off as well as the water. The steam generator cooling down could produce ticking. As long as she did not panic, all would cool down and be well. After all, she still had light in the room. Perhaps it wasn't as late as all that.

It hissed. She shielded her face with her pareo, not minding to be naked from the waist down. It ticked again. 'Four,' she said out loud and moistened her dry lips with her tongue.

It hissed. The emerging steam had not cooled in any way, but it still ticked. 'Nine,' she said. She curled into a foetal position to protect herself from the heat. Water boiled at one hundred degrees. Therefore, there would be one hundred ticks before the boiler stopped producing steam. 'Ten,' she counted and felt better for having worked that out.

It hissed. She felt as if she had jumped into a furnace. She slid down from the tiles and crouched in the runnel, as low down as possible. Heat rises. 'Eleven,' she counted. The metal slots burnt into her cheek. Through the ceiling above her came steam with its hissing.

'For God's sake.' She climbed back onto her tiled area. 'Twenty-three,' she counted. Her swollen tongue licked over stinging, cracked, parched lips. Why, with all that moisture, was she so desperately thirsty? Dehydration caused strain on the heart. And yes, she felt angina pain.

'Forty-seven,' she counted and nestled her head in the crook of her moist arm. After sixty-six, she unrolled and got up again to lick condensation beads off the wall tiles. The ceiling hissed out steam right above her, as hot as ever. 'Eighty two. Why do you tick?' she shouted into the room, swaying in blankets of steam.

She drew on memories of happy times in St Gingolph to take her mind elsewhere for a while. However, with a drawn-out hiss, steam was pushed into the room to bring her back to now. She gasped for breath. The hundred-degree countdown had not worked. Some evil creature had cut off the cooling water, but not the steam machine. No blue glass eye could do anything about that.

It ticked. She felt nauseous. She let it get the better of her and retched. Her convulsing stomach only produced acid liquid, which burnt in the back of her throat. It ticked and again hissed hot steam. Her heart laboured in her chest. She felt dizzy. Perhaps by now it was one hundred and forty-seven, or fifty-seven. She had lost count. Who cared, anyway?

It hissed. She screamed. 'One hundred and... Two hundred... Ten thousand... Please, someone help me!'

It hissed. Louise slid off the tiles and slumped into the draining runnel, unconscious.

*

Shortly before six in the morning, Ali had worked himself through the garden, pumping insecticide. Several puffs into bushes, and insects of many sorts would not pester holidaymakers that day. He came to the hammam building as he did every morning. At the back was an overflow tube, and the little water which came out of it soaked away into the earth. Strangely, this morning a large puddle had formed. Something was malfunctioning in the hammam.

He slipped the tank off his back and went into the changing area. A flowery dress had been left behind, and some sandals. The door to the steam room was closed with the padlock. He heard the hissing of steam and checked his watch. Why was the hammam boiler on at this time? It made no sense. Ali knew that Hasan had the key. The young Turk galloped through the gardens to the building behind the kitchens.

Hasan, in pyjama bottoms only, hair tousled around his puffed face, opened the door. 'You,' he said, seeing Ali in the corridor. 'You came to tell me we are still to be friends?'

'No. There is something wrong with the hammam. You need to unlock it so we can investigate.'

'The hammam opens at ten only.'

'Then give me the key and I'll check.'

Ali ran back with the key and unlocked the padded door. The heat inside took him by surprise. He squinted around in the steam, disconcerted for a while, before checking along the draining runnel. Then he saw the pink feet.

★

At ten o'clock sharp, the Boss called an emergency meeting of four in the yoga room. A green stucco Buddha in the lotus position on a narrow bamboo table smiled benevolently as the four took seats around a table brought in from the terrace. They were the Club Boss, the Club's appointed lawyer, Ms Kiraz, Dr Salim, who had been called in from the Izmir Hospital as he was the back-up for the Club for cases the nurse could not handle on her own, and Duncan, a retired English ex-pat employed by the Club's insurance company as loss adjuster.

First, Dr Salim was asked to describe Miss Picard's medical condition. He had been driven to the Club in a private ambulance to help the unconscious woman laid out in the Club's first aid station. He spoke softly, but managed to get across the severity of damage done, not just to the lungs and heart of Miss Picard, but also to her liver and kidneys, exposed to extreme heat and dehydration for at least eleven hours. She was now on oxygen and an intravenous fluid drip and doing better, but he stressed that her injuries were potentially life-changing. There was even a real possibility of fatal complications, should there be a heart or lung history in her family.

Ms Kiraz, the lawyer, clicked her tongue. The Boss invited her to speak next. She brushed her voluminous, curly dark hair back over her forehead. Her black eyes shone onyx.

'Miss Picard will sue Club Vivendus. She has no other option. She will be advised by Swiss lawyers. Experience tells me that they will demand two and a half million, minimum. American dollars, not Turkish lira. I advise you, in order to minimise damages, to be able to show that you have done everything in your power to assist the victim.'

The Boss, clearly stressed, got halfway out of his seat. 'We, the Club, have taken immediate action in calling the Izmir Hospital. Dr Salim is a senior consultant. All emergency equipment is available in the ambulance he came in. I have personally not only contacted Miss Picard's next of kin, her mother, but also called for a Christian priest, who should be here shortly to give Miss Picard spiritual guidance. A helicopter is booked to fly her to the American Hospital in Istanbul, where they are getting ready for her.'

He was interrupted by Leyla, the club's receptionist, coming into the room to give him some papers. He dismissed Leyla and sat down again to read. There was much tension in the room.

'It's a fax. A reply from Mona Picard in St Gingolph.'

'Louise's mother,' said the lawyer, beckoning with her hand to be given the papers.

Kiraz read. Outside the window, a shrill bird made a lot of noise. 'Hmm,' started Kiraz. 'As I said, the Club is being sued for three million Swiss francs. There are no flies on Mona Picard. She has already contacted the best lawyer in Geneva, and is on her way here.'

'How does Louise react to this?' asked the Boss.

'She is too weak to do too much reacting,' said Dr Salim.

'People have accidents,' said the Boss. 'They also have accidents during their holidays. That's why this Club is insured, certainly up to three million.'

'Hold it,' said Duncan, who had until now kept quiet. 'Could someone shut up that bloody bird outside?'

Kiraz went to the open window and shouted something into the bush. Satisfied with the ensuing silence, she returned to her seat.

'As if it were that easy,' commented Duncan. 'The Club may not be the guilty party here.'

Kiraz argued that the Club's running of the steam room, for tourists not used to the nature of the installation, was *prima facie* negligent. Hard evidence would be needed to overturn that.

'Let me tell you about one of my cases.' Duncan looked at the others briefly before continuing. 'A hotel insured by us was sued for several millions by the family of a woman, for failing to control all of their cutlery at all times. I put that right,' he said with pride. 'They didn't get a penny.'

The others waited for the rest of the story.

'A man, paying back his wife for infidelity, used a hotel steak knife to cut her throat in their room.'

'Extreme,' commented Dr Salim.

'Foul play. My favourite phrase,' Duncan went on. 'You dig a little and you find foul play.'

'Surely, in Louise's case, it is human error by the man in charge of the hammam?' suggested Kiraz.

'I,' said the Boss, 'hired Hasan in the name of the Club to be responsible for sports equipment, including the switching on and off of the hammam. Unfortunately, I cannot see any way out of this.'

'Because you aren't considering foul play,' said Duncan. 'There was bound to be something going on between Hasan and Louise; there always is.'

'Do you have proof of that?'

'Not yet. Let's get some people in here and ask questions.'

'Miss Picard is too ill for that,' Dr Salim said quickly.

'And Hasan will tell us packets of lies,' said Duncan.

130

'But there is the woman who went on the shopping trip with Louise. And there is Ali, the handyman, who found the victim, and most of us know he is Hasan's closest friend.'

The Boss called Leyla back in and told her to bring the Belgian woman and Ali to the yoga room.

'Brigit was upset about the hammam disaster,' said Leyla. 'Everyone in the club is talking about it.'

'Thank you, Leyla, blabbermouth,' said the Boss, after Leyla had left. 'You put them on reception, and it becomes a gossip bar.'

Brigit soon arrived and told them that Louise had much enjoyed the trip to Bodrum. She had bought a beautiful shirt for a man she loved. Hilfiger, the most expensive. Louise had seemed interested in trying out the hammam.

Duncan hoped to hear the identity of the man Louise loved, but Brigit did not know.

Ali advanced into the room with much reluctance. He had to be asked three times to sit on the chair facing the table. He squirmed. Eventually, he admitted that Hasan was not his brother any longer. When asked why, he said Hasan was planning to do bad things which Ali did not want to have anything to do with.

'Ha!' said Duncan loudly.

After more questions, it became clear that Hasan had this theory about women, that strong women were useless for men, and weak women were ready to be exploited by men. If women were strong, they could be reduced to becoming weak and manageable. Hasan's father, before he went to prison, had taught his son that.

'On the evening of Miss Picard's arrival, I saw Hasan talking to her near the bar,' said the Boss. 'And he made her get him drinks, which is forbidden.'

Duncan noted the Boss's words and would not let Ali leave. He kept asking about practices for weakening women and, in the end, Ali admitted that Hasan had claimed to have found a way to make the rich Swiss woman weak enough for him. That is when Ali had given up on his friend.

Once Ali was out of the room, Duncan said, 'Hasan tried to fry her alive. Criminal harm. I told you.'

'It does look as if what we thought was an accident may, in fact, be a deliberate crime,' admitted Kiraz. 'In which case…'

'The Club is off the hook, and my insurance company does not pay,' Duncan finished for her.

'I have to write a report for the police,' the lawyer said, as the door was opened. Leyla appeared.

'Sorry to interrupt again,' said Leyla. 'The Red Cross helicopter has landed on the football pitch, and Mrs Picard has arrived in a taxi from the airport. She wants to talk to Dr Salim urgently, and refuses to let her daughter be flown to the American Hospital. She wants her to be flown back to Switzerland.'

Leyla stopped talking, because she was shoved to the side by a man in khaki with a Red Cross armband.

'You're blocking the door,' he said. Once inside the room, he asked belligerently, 'What's going on here?'

Behind him, Leyla disappeared.

'First,' the helicopter pilot looked at the four sitting around the table, 'I am told to land on a beach where tourists are sunbathing. A sandy beach with my T129, which is equipped with a tail rotor and has small-wheeled landing gear. Once I set down on the playing field, a hysterical woman orders me to fly her daughter to Switzerland. That's one thousand two hundred and nine air miles from Bodrum. My old military helicopter only has endurance of three hours max. Flying through Greek, Albanian, Italian, and French airspace, one of them will recognise me as a tactical reconnaissance helicopter and shoot me down. Even if not, it would cause massive political aggravation. For Turkey, with its present domestic problems, it is not the moment. That aside, I've only half a tank of fuel left.'

Behind the pilot's back, the receptionist materialised again. 'Sorry to butt in, but the priest you sent for has married Louise and Hasan. And the bride couldn't even get out of bed, so dizzy she was.'

'The clever bugger!' Duncan exclaimed.

At that moment, Mona Picard made her entrance.

'You may congratulate me,' she trumpeted. 'My daughter has just got married. When Louise is well again, there will be a real wedding, a big wedding in St Gingolph. You're all invited.' Before allowing herself to take a breath, she went on, 'I was so right to send Louise to Club Vivendus. She found her happiness, a man, a husband. And so quickly.'

'Madam, your lawyer is suing Club Vivendus for three million Swiss francs for the accident in the hammam, and now you invite us to Switzerland?' The Boss deflated Mona's bubble.

No pin dropped on the floor. Mona rearranged her thoughts in her head. 'Louise's health is damaged because of you, big boss of Vivendus. My daughter will never run or jump again. She will be out of breath and vulnerable to chest infections. As for the strain on her heart walls, only a consultant can tell me how bad it is. That is all your doing.'

Mona, looking at Kiraz, noticed a smile. 'What are you grinning about? Who are you?'

'I am the appointed lawyer for Club Vivendus. Your daughter has just given her heart to a man and, I might say, she will have to pay for it dearly. We have reason to believe he deliberately harmed your daughter in the hammam.'

'Is this woman trying to be funny?'

'The matter is serious,' Duncan took up. 'The accident, if such it was, was caused by Hasan not following the rules when shutting down the hammam last night. A technical investigation is being made by one of my colleagues.'

Mona's reaction was not what they expected. She stayed calm, and looked straight at Duncan. 'You are English,' she said with a dose of charm. 'One of those English bulldog-type men.'

'Hasan will be proven guilty and will have to foot your claim of three million Swiss francs,' said Kiraz. 'Three million have to come from somewhere, unless you drop the charges.'

'You are getting on my nerves,' Mona said to Kiraz. 'Hasan loves my daughter. A mother's heart can tell. He would never hurt her, and if you insist on being unfair to him, I will have to bring in my own Swiss lawyers on this case.'

134

Kiraz got out of her seat and walked up to Mona, handing her a piece of paper. 'A preliminary in-house report of what happened the night the hammam was left on.'

Mona stuck the paper between her lips and dug in the handbag dangling from her shoulder. She set the reading glasses on her nose and read briefly. 'It's in Turkish.'

'Turn the page,' Kiraz suggested.

'I have read it.' Mona wiped her glasses off. 'And it is nonsense.'

'You find yourself in a no-win situation,' Duncan pointed out. 'Drop the charges.'

Mona, without looking at him, fidgeted for a while. 'I would never sue Hasan. I may still sue Club Vivendus for negligence. At the end of the day, you are responsible for your employees.'

'Speaking for the Club,' said Duncan, 'I am confident that I have enough evidence to prove malicious harm, which absolves Club Vivendus of responsibility.'

'All right then, I will also drop the case against Club Vivendus,' replied Mona. 'The one I *will* charge with negligence is the doctor. Has he wrapped her in ice? No. Has he performed an ECG? No.'

'Madam, please,' Salim begged. 'I have three children and live in a two-bedroom flat above a kebab restaurant. It smells. I hear the goats squeal when they are being slaughtered in the backyard. I am vegetarian. The hospital has not enough money to pay me more. I had to drive my eldest son to his first Koran lesson in the ambulance with a dead woman in it. The morgue closed early that day because of the extremely high temperature. I can't afford my own car. How am I to pay three million liras?'

Mona looked down on him as if he were a lice-infested dog. 'It is not three million liras you have to pay me.'

'Oh, thank you for taking pity on a poor, hardworking doctor, who did everything to save your daughter's life,' replied Salim.

'It is three million Swiss francs, and it was ultimately you who failed to treat her adequately and promptly. Don't try to push this onto my beautiful new son-in-law. His parents own the Grand Hotel in Andorra, you know. And his uncle is chief consultant at the General Hospital in Bulgaria.'

THE ROMAN EMPIRE

'Is there really such a thing as the Military Uniform Society?'

'You bet there is. That is why I have invited two of their officers to fly here from London.'

'Mayor,' said the treasurer. 'You never cease to surprise us, but today you might be going a bit astray. Ransvoort is a small, peaceful town with no military history of its own.'

The meeting was called. They took their seats. The first points on the agenda were the budget, revenue and expenditure, and then re-election of council members.

When it came to the list of items to vote on, they were all cancelled and replaced by one single important issue – the Ransvoort municipal library.

There was unrest in the room. What was wrong with the library?

The mayor addressed the meeting. 'Our library, as you know, is underused. It is housed in a large, brick building with two thousand square metres of space. The library only needs about five hundred. Yet, we pay to heat the whole property, maintain it, clean it…'

'Volunteers help out in the library,' the treasurer remarked.

'Thankfully. They do a wonderful job, but they can't buy the latest books, balance the budget, replace the gutters. That is why…' The mayor paused and asked for silence. 'That is why I have invited two members of the Military Uniform Society in London to join us today. Please…' The mayor made a sweep with his arm toward the two guests. 'Mr Calder and Miss Bixley.'

The man rose. 'I am James Calder. We thank you for the invitation to join in your town meeting, so that you can hear what the plan is and vote on it. The society is offering to buy the municipal library building and turn it into a museum of military uniforms and military paraphernalia.'

The Ransvoort councillors silently processed this information.

The mayor spoke again. 'About two million tourists visit Amsterdam every year. They will be offered a little side tour to Ransvoort's museum. The local hospitality facilities can benefit enormously from this. There will be other benefits for all of us. We will become a town with money in the kitty, besides gaining an international name.'

'If we want a museum, why not exhibit something else? Art, perhaps,' suggested a female councillor.

'How many art museums have you visited in small foreign towns?' Calder asked. 'The best art is in the Louvre, the Prado, New York. I understand that men are interested in military history, battles, and so on. Men identify with soldiers, and men will come and visit the museum. But that is not all. We plan to make this museum so special that it will appeal to women

138

and children as well. Miss Bixley is better at explaining this.'

Miss Bixley was a woman in her thirties, whose long bangs tickled her eyelashes as she looked around. 'Our society is generously endowed and has small premises in Pimlico, but no museum. We already have a collection of military paraphernalia given to us as gifts. Our cupboards are full of the most unusual talismans soldiers were given by their wives and lovers to protect them in battle. To give you an example, there is a gold amulet with a round clasp which holds a lock of blond hair – beautifully crafted by Asprey in 1805, presumed to have belonged to an officer in the Peninsula War. There are other things, like small diaries, some with detailed drawings, going as far back as the First Anglo-Dutch War in the seventeenth century.'

'Where do you get the uniforms you plan to exhibit?' the mayor interrupted.

'There are war memorabilia in many homes, small auction houses and antiquarians all over Europe,' replied Miss Bixley.

'My grandfather found a pickelhaube helmet,' contributed a councillor.

Miss Bixley gave him a pleased little nod. 'The society buys precisely such things. Across Europe, the soldiers and commanders wore intricate uniforms, embroidered, with epaulettes, gold thread, ornamental buttons. The success of such a museum lies in the details: men at war – it is human and moving, and should be shown, so as not to be forgotten. The small sacrifices, the little ribbon the wife sewed inside his jacket. Everyone knows what

Napoleon wore, or Nelson. The museum exhibits will be about local units, proud fighters, flags, medals, letters to wives, drawings made to amuse their children back home.

'It will take our specialist researchers three years to gather enough exhibits, and it is expensive. An authentic Swiss lance from the Battle of Marignano is worth over ten thousand pounds. And so is a gold epaulette from the uniform of a French dragoon in the Napoleonic Wars. It is not the glass cabinets which cost the most, nor the mannequins we will have hand-made from jute material rather than plastic. We will exhibit soldiers' handkerchiefs, their socks, as well as their swords and halberds. Three years for this gleaning. The project is exciting. We need a modestly priced building in an accessible part of continental Europe. I ask you to imagine the film and music we will show on entry. A cafeteria with a selection of the rations eaten by soldiers from all parts of the world, some on bamboo plates, some in metal bowls. This has great potential.'

'Your enthusiasm is catching, Miss Bixley,' said the mayor. 'I believe that such a museum would be a positive thing for our town.'

'I am not sure that a museum dedicated to military things suits the spirit of the times, and I suspect other colleagues may agree with me.' The lady councillor spoke again.

'We are not pro-war,' replied Miss Bixley. 'Quite the opposite. But we don't believe that forgetting is the answer. We do have an alternative building in Sweden in mind, but Ransvoort is the ideal location, and we hope you will support us with your votes.'

'I thought you might be here again.' Victoria approached Thomas, who sat on a limestone rock which the Ice Age had dropped in the meadow. He did not look at the view, even though the fields were interwoven with heightened colours. His legs in shabby jeans were crossed, and on his nose were glasses which were tinted orange by the light of the approaching sunset.

'Still writing your historical novel, even in fading light?' asked Victoria.

'Well, yeah, it takes years.'

'I wouldn't have the patience,' Victoria said, 'not for something like that.'

He flinched. Victoria had the knack of making him feel small and unworthy. He realised that she did not set out deliberately to upset him; it was just the spoilt way she lived which made her oblivious to the feelings of people less fortunate. His brother Aaron was mostly to blame. He had expected her to live up to his standards and ideals from the start.

Of course, their life was better than Thomas's. Aaron was the elder son and now ran the family cardboard packaging factory, since the death of their father, and he and Victoria lived in the manor house with the widowed mother. Thomas, meanwhile, was teaching history in the local secondary school, and paying off a mortgage on a former miner's cottage. The only thing he had over his elder brother was having made a child; he and Ellie had a toddler called Tilly, the joy of the brothers' mother. Having offspring, however, effectively put him at a disadvantage again, because the cottage was too small for a comfortable life with a child.

Thomas closed his notebook and pushed the knife-sharpened pencil behind his ear.

'How precious.' Victoria pursed her lips. 'Writing a novel in this day and age with a pencil.'

'Tell me.' He looked at her standing in front of him, blocking the sunset and putting him into her shadow. 'How is the baby-making coming along?' He felt guilty for deliberately touching on a sore subject.

'That also seems to take time,' she said. 'I now have a good gyno who is trying to find the reason for the difficulty.'

'It can't be that my brother doesn't know how to do it,' said Thomas. 'Eager beaver at eighteen, he seduced girls on the back seat of his car. In fact, I believe Aaron invented the practice.' His little nasal laugh caused Victoria's large blue eyes to narrow. She moved her head rapidly from one side to the other. She would now walk away, quickly. He knew her. He admired her. He let himself down every time with her. It had to be because he felt inadequate in her strong presence, and suffered from this weakness.

She was already a hundred yards away, and he regretted their conversation so much that he jumped down from the rock and ran after her.

'What?' Unwillingly, she turned round and stopped.

He took a deep breath. 'Victoria, I am sorry about what I said. My mind was with Roman gladiators and you suddenly appeared in front of me. The two worlds did not gel. I like you; I think I am lucky to have such a beautiful sister-in-law. There. I can finally bring myself to say it. I definitely have no right to let my frustration out on you. Just remember: I don't have as easy a life as my brother.'

Victoria stayed put and listened, her head down.

'It's not that I want your sympathy, or pity,' Thomas went on. 'The planning committee has given me permission to add a playroom next to the kitchen of the cottage, only because ours is the end one with the bit of extra land. That is really good news, but I have to build it myself to afford it. Ellie and I don't get to live in Doreen's big house.'

'The Atkinson packaging factory, with all its problems of modernising, is not a great money-earner at the moment,' replied Victoria. 'And sharing the manor with your mother, who still runs it as if she were a ship's captain, is not as great as you seem to think.'

'Everything has a price.'

'Do you teach that to your class to prepare them for adult life?'

'In Yorkshire, most of them know that only too well. I spend my time clawing forbidden smartphones out of sweaty hands.'

'Perhaps they learn more from Google than from you.'

'Thanks, Victoria. Somebody has to do the school teaching.'

'Thomas…' she said with a slump of her shoulders, '…your brother has demons of his own. He was told by his GP to take a daily brisk walk for his health. Of course, he took this as a personal affront, went out and bought a colt, which he plans to ride once a day. Aaron

143

being Aaron, it had to be a black pure-breed Arabian, for which the barn has to be adapted, a groom hired and God knows what else. At least your mother is chuffed about it in a twisted sort of way, muttering about how important it was to the Queen Mother to have horses around.'

'Perhaps Sardine can play the groom,' suggested Thomas.

Victoria laughed. 'Sardine is being kept busy by your mother all day long. And didn't you get the memo? He's not to be called Sardine any longer. His name is Owen. She insists. Apparently, he's given up eating sardine sandwiches. Doreen goes to great lengths to gentrify him. You see, my dear, life in the manor is not all smooth sailing. There might even be scandal lurking.'

'Heaven forbid,' Thomas exclaimed, in pantomime fashion.

'There is something going on between your mother and Owen – ever since your father died,' said Victoria. 'Didn't Ellie tell you she saw them together in town? I have certainly caught Owen creeping up the stairs in the manor at late hours.'

'Very royal family again,' said Thomas.

Victoria did not understand.

'John Brown, the Queen's ghillie and forbidden lover,' explained Thomas. 'Never mind if you don't know. I don't teach this to my history students, either.'

'Aaron said he will be spending a lot of time in London to secure the factory's future. Why don't you come to the manor for tea? Surely you need to pick up some books for teaching? Please bring Tilly. It would make your mother so happy.'

'That is generous of you, Victoria.'

'Not at all. You are an Atkinson like the rest. You have a right to know what goes on in the factory and to visit the family home. You could write the manor into your novel.'

'Except that the Romans were here nearly two thousand years ago.'

'I see. The whole book is about the Romans, like the statue in York?'

'The very one, in front of York Minster – Emperor Constantine. His father, also an emperor, died in York in 306.'

'Any women in the story?'

'Little is known about Mrs Constantine. She is of absolutely no interest to anyone. If that is not discrimination…' he joked.

'They hadn't gone through the suffragette rage by then.'

'Voilà, an explanation, the mere thought…' Thomas said, his mind back in Roman times.

'You know so much about the past, Thomas.' Victoria smiled her blue-eyed smile, as if to call him back to her with it. 'Talking to you, sometimes I feel you are so at ease with past civilisations that you must be an escapee.'

'We are all survivors of them. Thank you for the compliment, though.'

'Did Romans really live in Barnsley?'

'If their Emperors died in York, a town which they called Eboracum, the army or entourage certainly spent time in Barnsley.'

'What did those guys do over here? Or, more to

the point, what could be done in the second and third century?'

'Conquering, tourism, drinking, womanising. Barnsley might have had the coolest tavern in the realm.'

'Thomas, your schoolkids are lucky. You make history come alive.' She advanced carefully on him. 'May I kiss you?'

'Please don't. It would be too devastating. I wouldn't make it through chapter seven.'

'Sorry,' she said and, to his disappointment, stepped back. 'But you will come round with Tilly?'

'With Aaron there, the dynamics are always charged.'

'Aaron can't help but dominate,' said Victoria. As she spoke, Thomas noticed folds under the corners of her beautiful mouth, small skin pockets collecting sadness.

'My brother has always been that way,' he said. 'The teacher sat him at the front desk, not because he was the brightest, but so that he could not traumatise the student sitting in front of him.'

Suddenly, she reached out and grabbed his arm. 'Talk of the devil.'

Thomas twisted round to see a man on a black horse. The rider was below them, cantering along a lane between two fields, their green having turned grey with the fading light. He gave two quick knee-jerks and the horse threw back its head, picked up speed and galloped off into the vaporous ribbons of evening mist. Aaron's jacket flapped.

'He looks good,' admired Thomas.

'He knows it.'

★

Aaron galloped right up into the cobbled forecourt of the manor in Woodley Park. At the barn, he dismounted and pulled at the reins to force the horse into the dark space. It objected by snorting angrily and tossing its head, the white of the cornea showing next to the black iris. The horse's pulled-back lips revealed regular ivory teeth clamped over the metal bit, white spittle in the corners. Overpowered by Aaron's determination rather than physical strength, the colt ended up in his wooden stall. In retaliation, he kicked with one of his hind legs, the hoof iron embossing additional half-moons into the already damaged wood.

'Calm down, will you?' yelled Aaron at the animal.

'Is there always going to be such a hullabaloo when you return from your ride?' At the barn door, Doreen's silhouette stood out against the security floodlight which had come on in the forecourt.

'Beastly horse,' panted Aaron and bolted shut the stall. His mother watched him walk towards her in a peculiar bow-legged manner.

'Sitting on that horse is not improving your figure.'

Aaron lifted a bucket from a hook and filled it with water, much of it splattering onto his knee-high boots. 'Is it really too much to ask for Sardine to give the animal fresh water twice a day?' He glanced up at his mother.

'I need to talk to you about that.' Doreen ran her finger down the dark-veined wood of the barn doorframe. 'Let's have a cup of tea in the kitchen.' That bravely said, the finger stopped over a dark nodule.

'As you wish, Mum.' Aaron went back to the horse

with the water. Shortly afterwards, Doreen and her son crossed the cobbles to the kitchen garden, where the scent of lavender, sage and lemon balm hovered.

The kitchen was the only cosy place in the whole house because of its spontaneous mess. Different makes and sizes of plates stood in the plate rack; similarly mismatched mugs hung from hooks underneath. Pots and pans dangled from a round, metal rack. Cooking basics were stored in jars marked *flour*, *sugar*, *rice*, *pasta*. On the window sills, either side of the bevelled glass door to the garden, was a collection of small plant pots in long, narrow zinc trays, containing cuttings stuck into sifted earth. Only a few showed promise.

Through an arch at the back was the utility room with a sofa, a coffee table and a television on a low table – Owen's day room, which he now claimed as his with a dry, short bang of a well-fitted door from the outside. Trumpeting nose-blowing ensued, so repeatedly that it became intolerable to those in the kitchen. Just when Aaron was going to interfere, Owen appeared under the arch, padding in thick socks.

Owen had been stock-keeper in the family factory. His redundancy due to computerisation had coincided with the death of old Mr Atkinson and the consequent need for a handyman in the manor. He was a stocky man in his early sixties, his dark hair greying, his skin tanned and his features strong, but untidy. His pond-green eyes were too close together. Under a substantial nose was a mouth too small for the face. He greeted Doreen and Aaron with a lopsided grin showing teeth, some of them discoloured. Doreen had already put the kettle on the gas

148

ring. It started to whistle. She unhooked mugs – three of them, without a hesitation – and poured.

'Darjeeling,' she smiled.

Aaron thought his mother's profile this evening looked less familiar, harder and coarser. *Is she spending too much time with this Welshman?* he wondered.

Owen appropriated the largest mug, the one with the four-leaf clover pattern under glaze. With it, he left the kitchen to go back to his cave.

Aaron leant back in the chair until his back felt the hard support of the wood spindles. He was aching all over after the ride. He was not in good physical shape. He turned down the offer of one of the biscuits his mother had piled onto a plate, like shingles onto a round roof.

'Owen is a practical man.' Doreen obviously felt she had to explain. 'He is doing a great job in the house.' Her old eyes were shining, as if they were new. Girlishly, she slipped sideways onto a chair at the round table where she smiled at her son, chin in her hand, her elbow on the waxed tablecloth. A gratified mother contemplating her pleasing firstborn. With something like pride, he had noticed the still-small waistband of his mother's skirt.

'It's a handsome colt, I give you that.' Doreen opened their conversation with a compliment. 'But it should not be living here. It needs more straw, other horses, proper grooming. You didn't think of that. It's like the Rolls Royce which did not fit through the door of the garage.'

'I thought you asked me in here to talk about...' Aaron pointed his thumb towards the arch and whispered, 'Sardine.'

149

'It really is a very long time since his sardine and raw onion on rye,' said Doreen. 'Owen now enjoys cucumber sandwiches and drinks tea.'

'He has become quite a project for you, Mum.'

As she said nothing, just lifted her chin off the heel of her propped-up hand, Aaron continued. 'Does he have to be gentrified to be a match for you? Victoria said that Ellie saw you two in town, rubbing shoulders, laughing and flirting, and not even noticing her when you passed her in front of Boots. Victoria said Ellie was embarrassed by it.'

'Ellie is such a bad catch for Thomas that she has no right to be embarrassed,' said his mother. 'Bored in her poor man's cottage with only Tilly to burble to, Ellie has taken to inventing Mills and Boon stories.'

'I don't know,' Aaron said slowly. 'I've noticed Sardine has the run of the whole house, which he wouldn't have if Dad were here.'

'I need his help all over the place precisely because Dad is not here any longer.'

'Your bedroom at ten at night?'

'Don't be ridiculous. I am redecorating.'

'Ever since Dad passed away, you have become unravelled.'

'How about your wife, glorious Victoria, who tells me she has invited Thomas for tea, even with you away? According to Victoria, he needs to pick up books for his teaching. If you ask me, she is playing with your brother as a lynx would with a mouse.'

'Where did you get lynx from?'

'I didn't have time to think of a better comparison than just cat and mouse.'

150

'It's not a secret that Thomas, the family nerd, left some of his many books behind when he moved out,' said Aaron. 'Every wrapped present he ever received was book-shaped. Also, if you think Thomas is making a play for Victoria, I'm not worried. Thomas is a bore. He doesn't know how to live. He settled for a pauper cottage on Collier Way. It fits his passion for history. Maybe he dreams of living in the Middle Ages or, even better, Roman times. Victoria is not going to flirt with that sort of man. He has no money. He has no taste. He has no dick.'

'He managed to father a child with Ellie.'

'Thanks, Mum. A girl, born prematurely. We're working on producing a boy. Victoria is taking hormones in order to increase the potency of sperm counts.'

'If that is what your physician tells you, I suggest you go somewhere else for fertility advice.'

★

Two weeks after this conversation, Doreen was in Market Street buying Christmas wrapping paper and ribbons. Owen had helped her order Christmas presents online. She felt a bit lost in this fast-moving IT world. Expressing her gratitude to Owen for his help, she had made him order his own Christmas present – an Italian hand-made wool suit, and a shirt and tie.

Walking out of the town centre, she passed the Church of St Clement and reached Collier Way. To her dismay, she noticed not just a broken wicker fence on the ground by Thomas's end-cottage, but her younger son in a T-shirt hacking a shovel into the ground, digging the trench for the foundations of the new room.

She stopped at a discreet distance. Thomas, unaware of her presence, forced the shovel head into the soil, groaning every time he did so, and then deposited behind him the result, creating a row of little piles of earth. The effort was enormous; the result pitiful. He was not even a foot deep into the ground, and that only along one side of the walls, pegged out with red string.

Doreen turned on her heels and walked briskly all the way back to the manor.

★

When Victoria and Aaron were called downstairs by Owen and entered the salon as requested, Doreen described the pathetic scene of Thomas digging.

'This is an embarrassment.' Doreen's cheeks were still blotched red from the forced exercise in the cold air.

'He needs a digger,' said Aaron. 'There are several companies who hire them out. Don't upset yourself, Mum.'

'It's not so much Thomas I'm upset with,' Doreen took up. 'It's what people around here think of the Atkinsons. How come they don't give their son some money to live a decent life? Twenty thousand pounds for this extension, and the dedicated educator, son of the rich Atkinsons, can't afford that. It is shameful for me – and, of course, you.'

'Thomas chose to be just a teacher. He married a girl from parents with no money. He has no ambitions. Let him dig.'

'You can be so cruel sometimes,' reprimanded Doreen. 'If I had twenty thousand pounds doing nothing, I would give it to him.'

'But you don't, and you shouldn't,' said Aaron. 'I'll go and talk to him about hiring a digger tomorrow. Even Thomas can afford that.'

★

The next day was the first day of December. Overnight, the temperature had plummeted and Barnsley was frost-trimmed.

After a short and rough-handled gallop around the frozen country park, Aaron made the steaming horse walk sedately up the street to the Church of St Clement, where a woman with a pram objected to his riding. He dismounted, but got the seam of his coat caught in the saddle cantle, which tore away the sleeve, revealing the seam stitches like bones in a herring. He swore so loudly – not at the woman, but his life in general – that dense white condensation clouded his head.

Continuing to walk alongside his horse, holding it by the lead strap, Aaron reached Collier Way and his brother's cottage. Horse and man stepped over the fallen fence and into the garden, where Thomas stood contemplating the digging efforts at his feet, the earth now scummed with ice.

'I don't think I can dig today,' Thomas said.

'If you use a hired digger, you'll have the foundation dug in two hours without pain,' said Aaron.

'I have just come to that conclusion myself,' said

Thomas, to Aaron's annoyance. 'But first, I want to show you something rather unusual I found whilst digging.'

The colt, which Aaron was holding, became bored. Pawing, his front hooves caused parts of the trench side to collapse.

'Thanks for bringing your stupid animal to make my work go backward,' said Thomas.

'Sorry,' said Aaron and spat at the horse's face.

Thomas tapped his temple with his finger.

'An Arab trick to tame their horses,' said Aaron.

'That, being most unlikely, do you want to see what I found in the ground?'

'Is there really nothing to which I can tie the horse? Why don't you have any trees in your garden?'

Thomas looked around him and then pointed. 'There. Him.'

Him was a man approaching, dressed in a dark coat over a dark suit, a white collar band showing around his neck. When the vicar reached the broken-down fence, he stopped to greet the brothers.

'Thomas has found something in the ground,' Aaron announced randomly.

'What?' asked the vicar.

'He hasn't shown it to me yet. Come in.'

The vicar balanced over the seesawing fence panel and clumsily hopped onto the grass.

Looking back down onto the broken wood, the vicar was just about to say something, but Thomas was faster.

'Please, don't preach that good fences make good neighbours.'

'I wasn't going to.'

154

'We're good then,' took up Aaron. 'Hold this.' He passed the horse's lead strap into the hand of the priest.

'Oh no,' he objected. 'I have no experience with beasts of burden. None at all.'

'It's not a beast of burden. He is a thoroughbred.'

'He has to carry you on his back, though.'

'Whatever you say, Reverend. The horse is tame. If you hold onto it for just a few minutes, Thomas can show us his findings.'

'It might be a treasure.' Thomas, eager to oblige, sounded excited.

'Show us the treasure, then.'

The vicar eyed the horse suspiciously, but held onto it, both thumbs squashed onto the strip of tan leather.

At the end of the trench, Thomas got down on his knees. Aaron merely crouched. 'Look, right here,' said Thomas. 'My shovel became stuck between these tangles of roots.'

Aaron reached out and touched them. 'Black and gnarly.'

'I've searched on Google.' Thomas was enthralled by his find. 'We're talking old, old roots from white vines. Conclusion, right here used to be a vineyard. The Barnsley people drank their own wine.'

'And that concludes your precious find? Old vine roots?' Aaron straightened, dusted down his breeches and shouted back to the vicar, who was close to the horse's head, talking to the animal, whose pricked ears twisted ominously.

'We're making friends,' the vicar shouted back.

'That's not all I found.' Thomas sulked when the

three of them stood together. Fishing around in his trouser pocket, he produced what resembled a fat, greenish coin in the crux of his calloused hand.

Aaron closed in on it. 'What am I looking at?'

'A Roman coin. I strongly believe it has the embossed head of Aurelius, and the typical garland and writing around it. The words and portrait are worn down.'

'Not surprising in this lime soil,' the vicar contributed.

'Aurelius was a historian in the reign of Constantine, at the end of the second century,' said Thomas. 'I found more coins. Some were entangled with rotten shreds of cloth material, which I guess they had wrapped around the vine roots to protect them from frost. I'll go and get the other coins to show you.'

'Better hurry,' said Aaron. 'The vicar is about to be dragged out of the garden.'

With purpose in his gait, Thomas hastened to his cottage back door.

Aaron took over the horse's lead strap.

'Your horse did not react to the name of Jesus,' the vicar, having regained his composure, complained.

'He's not Christian. Few of his kind are.'

Not sure how to react to this, the vicar took up the subject of the vine roots. 'They must date back to the time of the black monks in Bretton Priory. Imagine. They owned the land we are standing on now. Come to think of it, they were from the Cluniac order, which began in Burgundy. No wonder they had a vineyard. The monks did not grow wheat to bake bread for the poor. They got drunk.' For a man who seldom laughed, the vicar was in stitches. 'What a marvellous find,' he enthused. 'Drunk as skunks.'

The colt nodded his head repeatedly, causing spittle to fly from his mouth. The two men stepped back.

Thomas reappeared, carrying a small wooden tray, on which was a collection of earth-encrusted coins.

The vicar picked out a large one and held it up to the cloud-covered sky. 'I'm not wearing my glasses, but I believe it's made of gold.'

'Most of the ones they minted had up to forty per cent silver,' said Thomas. 'The rest is bronze and, yes, there is gold. A find can be called a treasure if it contains gold or silver, and is older than three hundred years.'

The vicar breathed in. 'Well, Thomas, you might have found a treasure, and that in the grounds of the old priory and near my church. I can almost feel the spirits of the bygone gambol around us.'

'How much do you think this find is worth?' interrupted Aaron.

'To the right person, a lot I would imagine.' The vicar was eager to continue this conversation. 'I confess to being a bit of a numismatist myself. It started with my puzzlement at some of the coins I found in the church collection box. It's very important you don't try to clean the coins. A lot of damage has been done that way. It's a job for an expert.'

'Put that tray on the ground,' Aaron ordered his brother. 'I'll take pictures and contact some people.' Using his mobile, Aaron photographed the coins, the larger pieces in close-up. He took pictures of the trench, the roots with the rotten cloth.

'That'll do for starters.' Aaron put his phone away. 'Hopefully, we can crowdsource some info on Twitter.' He picked up the coins and placed them on his spread handkerchief, before knotting its corners and pushing the bundle inside his breast pocket.

'What are you doing, brother?' said Thomas. 'I found them. I dug them up. They are mine.'

'Somebody might want to check them more closely. I'll keep you posted on the outcome of my research, both of you.' Aaron walked out of the garden, pulling the horse behind him. The animal crunched more of the fence as it went, not without glancing back at the vicar who was dusting down the shoulder pad of his black coat.

'It is laudable that you trust your brother to take care of your find,' he said to Thomas.

'Aaron has connections, and he comes across more forcefully than I ever could. I need twenty thousand pounds to build the extension. He knows that. He will not let me down. Surely.'

'He is your brother. I don't know his character. He never attended any of my services.'

★

It was the middle of December. The weather had turned unusually mild. Thomas was practising mixing concrete. He also went to the Sunday service at the Church of St Clement, where the vicar had constructed his sermon entirely on the theory that the people living there before them had tended to vines, linking it to the role wine played in the Bible.

158

Thomas let his mind wander along the stained-glass windows and the candle-burdened flower displays on the altar. Inside him flickered resentment that he had not heard a word from Aaron about the coins. Infuriatingly, every sample of concrete had turned out too sloshy, or unmanageably dry and sticky. Thomas needed expert help, and for that he needed money. Ellie complained about the lack of space. Since the decision to build out, the existing cottage seemed to have shrunk.

The Friday after that, Aaron had still not contacted his brother. Thomas decided to pay the manor an unannounced visit. It was ten days before Christmas, and minute snowflakes whizzed around in the freezing air. Thomas's hands on the bicycle handlebars smarted from the cold. Applying the brakes hurt. In the window at the top of the staircase, the curtain twitched; Victoria watched him get off the bicycle and lean it against the entrance gate pillar. Thomas warmed his hands by clapping them together. She used one of hers to give him a demure little wave.

Entering the hall, he heard a soft tapping noise – unidentified and yet familiar. The tapping stopped. Guiltily, Thomas glanced around him. In the silence, he tiptoed to the open door at the back of the sombre hall. In the kitchen, his mother stood at the table, the mixing bowl clamped under one arm. Presently, she took up beating batter again, the fast-moving wooden spoon hitting the side of the earthenware bowl with regularity. That was the noise he had heard.

At the other side of the round kitchen table sat

Sardine, relaxed, watching her energetic activity. She stopped beating and tapped the spoon handle against the rim of the bowl. Blobs of batter fell back into the bowl, the consistency of which, Thomas noticed, would have been perfect for his concrete. Doreen looked at Owen and held out the wooden spoon, one hand under the batter-coated implement. The Welshman got up from the chair, leant over the table and opened his mouth.

'Mmm.' He licked his lips. 'Better than ever.'

It was a simple, but intimate, little scene.

Behind Thomas, up on the landing, Victoria appeared. She wore a black dress, as if she were in mourning, and beckoned him to come up to join her. When he was close enough to her to be overwhelmed by the scent of her body warmth, he stopped.

'This is a surprise visit, isn't it?' she said. 'I haven't invited you for tea today, have I? Sometimes, I worry about going gaga.'

'At thirty-six, there is no danger of that. I came to speak to Aaron.'

'About those coins you found?'

'Tell me, did he say anything to you about what he is doing to sell them for me?'

'He is contacting people; that much I know.' Then, after a brief pause, during which he looked at the purple of her eyelid shadow, she added, 'I'm not sure it is my place to tell you.'

'You can tell me anything. I am your devoted friend.'

'Dear Thomas…' she paused again '… I am so sorry, but nobody seems to be interested in the coins. They are rubbish, probably not Roman at all – Aaron's words. Perhaps some play money, like Monopoly.'

'Roman Monopoly?' Thomas exclaimed.

'Hush. Aaron would not like me to talk to you about the coins.'

'I'll trade you the Parthenon for Hadrian's Wall,' Thomas joked, but his heart was not in it. 'Look, the mere fact that I found them after almost eighteen centuries means they aren't rubbish.'

'Perhaps I misunderstood,' she said, looking suddenly smaller and vulnerable. 'I just want to prepare you for a possible disappointment. Your brother did mention faulty minting, as well. There seem to be metal blobs stuck to one side of the coins. Perhaps not all of them, I don't know.' She paused again. 'Aaron found it funny that, even in the third century, master money-makers obviously had trouble with their suppliers. Aaron was, of course, comparing this to the family factory, which has run into quality-control problems.'

'I am glad my brother finds my Roman coins amusing.'

'Perhaps it is you, Thomas, with your passion. You should take them to a museum and show them what you found.'

'With my bicycle?'

'Sorry.' Victoria put her hand on the stair rail, the very one he had never dared to slide down. 'You've got so many things going for you. Don't be jealous of Aaron. You two are just very different brothers.'

'Faulty Roman coins,' he picked up from what she had said earlier. 'There has to be a historical explanation.'

The telephone rang downstairs; nobody answered it. 'Aaron must have gone out.' Victoria checked her watch. 'I have so many things to do.'

'Tilly is yours in many ways,' he tried to hold her back. 'You are godmother and aunt. When older, she will run to you to complain about her parents.'

'Anyway,' she brushed over what he had just said, 'we'll be seeing you at Christmas. Doreen is inviting you, Ellie and Tilly.'

'A charity invitation?'

The telephone was still ringing – and she did it to him again: she ran down the stairs, eager to get away from him. He probably bored her.

'Thank you for visiting,' she shouted back up, while clattering across the chessboard-tiled hall.

In the courtyard, his bicycle was no longer leaning against the pillar. Sardine crossed the cobbles, and the two men acknowledged each other with a nod.

'Mr Atkinson took the cycle into the barn,' said Sardine. 'He said it might freeze out here. Sorry, I couldn't do anything about it.'

'Well,' said Thomas, embarrassed that Sardine knew he had been in the house without asking to see Aaron.

'Right now, you can't get it back, because Mr Atkinson locked the barn with his key. Between you, me and the goalposts, I believe he went out to buy his horse some tranquilisers. Things will have to calm down round here with a baby.'

'Victoria, pregnant? Really? She didn't tell me.'

'I overheard them say the foetus is hanging on by the skin of its teeth – for the moment, at least.'

'Unborn babies don't have teeth.' Thomas turned to leave.

'Perhaps he went to the bank,' Owen said.

*

Thomas stomped through Barnsley; his cotton socks were soaked through the shoes. The bank. His brother had sold the coins and was depositing the hundreds of thousand pounds in interest-bearing accounts in his own name.

When Thomas eventually tumbled into the warmth of the cottage, Ellie was in the small kitchen, seventeen-month-old Tilly dozing, slumped in her arms.

'Do you mind telling us…?' Ellie started.

'Stop right there,' Thomas barked forcefully. 'I had to walk back all the way because my brother confiscated my bike. It is freezing out there; I might have lost toes to frostbite. I felt like a soldier in Napoleon's army retreating from Russia.' Thomas brushed snowflakes off his dark blond hair. 'Why are you and Tilly back already? How did it go at the clinic?'

'They tested her lung capacity,' replied Ellie. 'A very unpleasant procedure. She cried a lot, but is asleep now. Her lungs did not get enough time in the womb to develop fully. I am so sorry she came so early. I should not have done all that washing by hand and reaching up to hang it on the line. Nor should I have cleaned the cottage the way I did.' She started to cry. 'I wanted things to be neat and tidy before the baby came.'

'Poor little mite.' Thomas stroked over his child's

fine, blond hair before kissing the top of her head. 'Victoria might be pregnant.'

'Really?' Ellie stopped crying. Instead, she looked befuddled. 'Might? What does that mean – *might*?'

'Apparently, a weak sperm has caught on for the moment. I don't understand.'

'I can see that. Men should not talk to woman about pregnancies.'

'I didn't ask to be told. By the way we, all three, are invited for Christmas to the manor.'

'I have nothing to wear.'

'Women should not be told about invitations,' replied Thomas. 'They never have anything to wear. I'll be in the dining room, writing my book. Keep away from me.'

'With pleasure.'

Before she closed the kitchen door on him, she asked, 'Why are you wearing your pullover inside out? The label shows and it is not one to be proud of.'

He checked down his front. 'That,' he said, his chin pleated, 'is one of those things. I dressed in a hurry this morning. Do you know that Aaron hasn't done a thing about the Roman coins?'

'You trusted him. I wouldn't have.'

★

Thanks to Owen, the portal of the manor was twinkling in lights like in years before. *The hall was decked*, and they sat around the festive table.

'Sardine is sitting in Dad's chair,' Thomas whispered to Victoria.

'He will probably carve the turkey as well.' She made it worse.

'I just can't get used to it.'

'He plays man of the house. Your mother needs it.'

'Happy Cringles!' Aaron, in a spontaneous move, held out his cracker to Ellie. 'You have to pinch where it is gathered. Harder. Like this – excellent, and pull.'

A dry crackle bang, and something small rolled out. 'You won, Ellie. Well done. Here is your prize.' It was a miniature compass, which Tilly claimed.

'It must be a bummer for a historian that those he is interested in died so long ago,' continued Aaron.

'Thomas still manages to give them successful CPR,' replied Ellie. 'The Romans practically live with us.'

She clawed the paper with the joke from the wall of the cracker. Aaron pinged the glass. Ellie read out loud, 'Why did the scarecrow get the Nobel prize? Come on you,' she coaxed, but then read the answer. 'Because it was outstanding in its field!'

'That's clever,' said Victoria. 'I mean, for a cracker joke.'

Ellie turned to Victoria. 'Are you feeling well? Not nauseous? I have to admit,' Ellie, went on, 'you look glowing.'

Aaron added exuberantly, 'It looks like we've done it this time, and we are sure it's a boy. Everybody,' he raised his champagne glass, 'to *Alexander*!'

Owen grinned generously. 'Miss Victoria. Finally a bun in the oven. That'll be another mouth to feed.'

Victoria bashed the table with her balled fist. 'Honestly... That man...'

'Owen comes from a family of eight children,' Doreen defended him. 'He was kind enough to prepare and cook the turkey with all the trimmings.'

The turkey, when Owen brought it in, was too pale, the stuffing too dark and soaked in rum.

'Remarkable,' said Victoria sarcastically. 'All that, without a single sauce stain on his designer shirt, which complements his expensive new suit.'

There was a brooding silence, before Doreen sniped, 'A mother of boys better be prepared to make allowances for the wives her sons bring home.'

There was another dull silence.

'As for you, Owen…' Doreen got out of her chair to pick up the carving set from the sideboard, 'you cooked it. You get the honour of carving it.' She presented him with the knife and meat fork which had nestled in red lining.

'It is a pleasure to please you, Madam.'

'See,' Victoria whispered to Thomas, 'there is something going on between them.'

'Pass the cranberry sauce,' Doreen commanded.

'Granberry, granberry', repeated Tilly.

'I've just re-read D.H. Lawrence,' announced Ellie in her thin voice. 'The story of Lady Chatterley.' The wine had heightened her cheeks. Under her full-length flowery Laura Ashley dress, her nipples were easily located despite the brassiere's outlines. 'It makes more sense to me now than when I read it the first time, before I was married.'

Aaron, his head down, was rudely checking his phone on his lap for messages.

Doreen cleared her throat. 'Why don't we talk about Thomas's Roman coins? How is the selling of those going?'

Owen pointed to Aaron. 'He's not wearing his paper hat,' as if this were mandatary in order to take part in the conversation.

'There.' Over the dish of *devils in blankets*, Aaron offered his Christmas cracker to Owen. They pulled. Tilly held both hands over her shell-pink ears. Owen unfolded the yellow paper hat from his side of the torn cracker.

'There you go.' He held out a wobbly yellow paper crown. 'For the lord of the manor.'

Aaron scrunched it up and tossed the paper ball back over his shoulder.

'Why are families always at odds with each other at Christmas? I want to know,' Doreen asked around the table.

'In Roman times,' Thomas glowed with eagerness to enlighten, 'they celebrated winter solstice with a pagan festival. They called it Saturnalia. In other words, the Romans invented Christmas. It is recorded that one of the traditions was rowdiness. There was loud singing, dancing in the street, and nudity. On the first of Saturnalia, bad behaviour by servants was tolerated, rewarded even.' He smiled.

'As you have taken on promoting the ancient Romans,' said Ellie, 'you really deserve to be paid by them. Are you sure your brother has not sold the coins?'

'Nice one, Ellie.' Aaron leant back in the chair. 'I have a sister-in-law who doesn't trust me.'

'You have a brother who fancies your wife.'

'If that were so,' Aaron responded, 'you have a husband who fancies my wife.'

'And a partridge in a pear tree,' Owen concluded the conversation with a thundering baritone voice. 'Who wants dessert?' he sobered them. 'We're having chocolate-filled meringue.'

Tilly looked up expectantly.

'One taker, any others?'

'Mother, did you let him make that as well?' said Aaron. 'Have you given up completely?'

'Your mother, the amazing Doreen Atkinson, has made the traditional Christmas cake as usual,' announced Owen. 'All I did was accessorise it.'

'Ellie was right about your mother and the handyman,' hissed Victoria when Owen was out of earshot. She stared right into Aaron's pupils. 'Careful, or even you, first born, will lose out on your inheritance.'

The entrance bell rang in the hall. Shoulders shrugged round the table, until Ellie led the vicar into the dining room.

'Sorry to intrude,' he said. 'I came to wish you a happy Christmas.'

'You're late for turkey, but in time for pudding,' said Victoria.

'I can't stay, I am afraid, but thank you.'

'Course you can. Why else would you have come?'

'Outspoken, isn't she?' The vicar tapped at his lower lip.

'Don't mind Victoria.' Doreen put her napkin next to her plate. 'Why don't you join us, Vicar?'

168

Thomas jumped up and fetched an extra chair from the adjoining living room. He wedged it in at the bend of the table, saying, 'That should do for a latecomer.'

'What has the vicar done to you, dear?' said his mother.

'What has the vicar done?' Thomas repeated petulantly. 'He gives shelter to down-and-outs. One of them, a brickie on parole, said my foundations weren't straight enough to build on, and I wouldn't get past building regs. What I'm doing is bloody hard. You try.'

'He might know what he is talking about,' Ellie said timidly. 'I don't want to risk a wall collapsing on Tilly. Thomas should get a professional in.'

Thomas rubbed his thumb against his index finger. 'Where is that coming from, huh?'

'On that front, I am the bearer of good news,' the vicar announced. 'Unless, of course, Aaron has managed to sell the coins to a museum to your satisfaction.'

'Dream on,' Ellie said unpleasantly.

The vicar tisked. 'It's Christmas. Peace on earth and goodwill to all men.'

'That's a recent invention,' said Thomas. 'As I have already told the family, winter solstice in the third century was the very opposite of holy and goodwill, more like debauchery and bad behaviour.'

'What can you expect of a primitive society?' The vicar needled Thomas. 'During the subsequent seventeen hundred years, we have become more civilised as Christianity spread.'

'And yet,' Thomas could not leave it, 'it is a fact that, at Christmas, the divorce rate spikes, family feuds flare up. It goes right back to winter solstice and the Romans.'

'Poor Ellie,' said Doreen, 'she has that every day.'

'I'm with the Romans,' declared Owen. 'You have to have at least one day in the year to talk the way your mouth is made.'

'It is one day in the year when we all should remember to be kind to others and be grateful that Jesus was born,' the vicar tried to make a repair job. 'Let's not forget, those Romans were heathens.'

'Wrong!' Thomas glowed with purpose. 'The Romans were the first to bring Christianity to Britain.'

'Before or after they fed Christians to lions in the Colosseum?' asked the vicar, and immediately apologised to Doreen for his forthrightness.

Doreen twisted the gold wedding band she had never taken off. 'We are getting sidetracked here. The vicar has not finished saying what he came here to say.'

'Thank you, Doreen,' replied the vicar. 'As I tried to say earlier, the director of the college, to whom I spoke of Thomas's coins, has spoken with someone he knows in a heritage society. Apparently, they are interested, excited even. They believe, as does your son, that Constantine and his entourage stayed in Barnsley at the end of the second, beginning of the third century. They have given the go-ahead to make Thomas's cottage an official excavation site, and in a few weeks a crew of archaeologists will come and start digging. The drawback is that your garden will be topsy turvy and, as they anticipate digging down through the floor of your cottage, you will have to be relocated into temporary accommodation, only for about four to six months. They promise to make good, and are willing to contribute financially up to what their small budget allows, perhaps half the cost of a double room in the Finkle Green B&B. What do you say to that? For a short time, the world will focus on Barnsley and on St Clement.' The vicar waited for applause.

'*Sol lucet omnibus*. The sun shines for everyone,' Thomas translated himself.

Ellie heaved with anger. 'So now those guys in their togas and sandals are pushing me and my baby out of my home, and we have to pay to go into a ghastly hotel room. It's really spiffing news, Vicar.'

'It would, of course, work out cheaper and more comfortable for you if Mrs Atkinson invited you to stay in one of her guest rooms for the duration.'

'The manor's only guest room is for our guests,' said Doreen.

'I'd better be off.' The vicar squeezed out of his chair and made moves towards the door.

Ellie sat slumped in her chair.

'I was only trying to help.' The vicar, after a glance back at the table, saw himself out.

Ellie came back to life. 'It's the fault of that Constantine. Nobody else is interested in such old rot except my husband.'

'You are so wrong, darling,' replied Thomas. 'The Romans are the founders of our civilisation. Modern languages are based on Latin. Nobody intelligent can ignore this.'

'Bla bla bla,' Doreen imitated her grandchild. 'If nobody wants any more dessert, Owen can clear away. Let's read

171

out cards from friends who cannot be here to celebrate with us. Here's one.' Doreen put her reading glasses on her nose and opened the card. 'Wishing you a festive time, and for your wish to come finally true in the new year, dearest. Hope to visit in spring. Signed, Aunt Julia.'

'Who the hell is Aunt Julia?' asked Aaron.

'We don't have an Aunt Julia,' said Thomas.

'I do,' said Owen curtly, and put the dish with the pudding remains down on the sideboard. 'The card was addressed to me.'

'How awkward.' Doreen handed the Christmas card to Owen, who wiped his hands along his Italian wool trousers before taking it. Doreen closed her eyes for a moment, as if her eyelids were overwhelmingly heavy.

'Have I told you that, in my novel, I have come to the time the Romans stayed in Barnsley? Soon my book will be written.' Thomas tried to lift the mood the only way he knew.

'With a Masters in history, Thomas will be a great success. Royalties will be pouring in,' said Aaron.

'How generous of you, Aaron, to praise your brother,' said Doreen.

'I told you, Mother. And I am telling you all again, nobody wants to buy the coins Thomas has undug. Nobody, absolutely nobody. They are rubbish, and I am out of it. Here, you can have them back.' Aaron put a tied-together cloth pouch on the table. 'I'm done with trying to sell them.'

'Would someone please claw the compass out of Tilly's mouth and tell her what a compass can do?' said Doreen.

Owen started to carry plates back to the kitchen, while Ellie forced Tilly to spit out the Christmas cracker compass.

The silver cake knife fell off the cake plate, smearing chocolate onto the tablecloth. Thomas moaned as if he had been stabbed.

'What's the matter with you?' asked Doreen in an annoyed tone.

'I can't help thinking of Constantine having the sword kicked out of his hand by a drunk. Luckily, they found it and fixed it back on.'

'What century was that?' Doreen tried to placate her son by pretending to be interested.

'Four weeks ago. Don't you read the *Chronicle*? The homeless drunk was no doubt one of the vicar's protégées. The emperor would have been devastated by such a lowly deed. He took pride in his warrior attire and his sword. An unworthy Barnsley man did that to him, after all the emperor has given us.'

'Dearest,' said Ellie. 'It's a modern statue, made of bronze.'

'Wifey is right, bro,' said Aaron. 'Those Roman blokes are dead; they are so dead. Get used to it.'

'*In libero enim mentibus omnium servierunt diis eorum,*' said Thomas. 'Constantine Chlorus said that, and it is still a basic truth in philosophy and frequently quoted. With free minds, all are to worship their gods. The coins I held in my palm he probably held in his. Just imagine.'

'Don't have an orgasm over it.'

Tilly went into a meltdown because Ellie had not given her back the compass.

Aaron shook his head. 'Is that the best behaviour you can expect from your daughter? My Alexander will be made of solid wood: handsome, dark and brave. At three, he will handle the stallion.'

Owen, who had joined them at the table again, said, 'You'll need Gorilla tape to keep your lad on that horse. Rolls of it.'

'Not funny, Sardine. He will be bright, a charmer. Women will swoon in his arms. Before that, of course, he will be going to Eton.'

'Everyone,' Doreen raised her hands, 'let's just get Victoria's baby into the world first.'

'I'll be able to straighten out young Alexander,' said Owen, oblivious to sensitivities. 'I sorted out three of my younger brothers. One of them became a cop, another a prison warden. The third, well, he became a hairdresser. He was made of a bendier wood.'

'Thank you, Owen, for this enlightening contribution. You mean well. Better not say more, please.' Doreen clasped his elbow. On the floor next to the sideboard stood eight empty bottles of champagne in a cluster.

'Too hot, this suit.' Owen shrugged the jacket off, rolled it and gave it to Doreen to look after. Under his armpit, dark patches showed on the cyclamen shirt.

'You can force him to stop talking,' said Victoria, 'but you can't change his nature. Remember the dog Grandma Atkinson used to have…?'

'Enough, Victoria, enough everyone,' said Doreen. 'We are not Romans. I need fresh air. Let's go outside.'

'It is snowing hard,' said Owen.

'Doreen is right. Let's go into the garden,' suggested Victoria.

'Wouldn't it be fun to play with snow, sweetie?' Ellie coaxed her child, who poked around her open mouth with saliva-glistening fingers. 'She can't get enough air into her lungs without breathing through her mouth.'

Tilly retched and threw up. Everything she had eaten was back on the high chair table and down her pretty dress.

'Poor sick child.' Doreen remained in her chair, defeated.

Owen, wrapping a wool shawl over Doreen's shoulders, said to her, 'When you don't expect a change for the better, it happens.'

'Your Aunt Julia meant you and me getting together in her Christmas card, didn't she?' said Doreen.

'I told her about you.'

'Did you see that?' hissed Ellie to Thomas.

'Let it go,' he replied. 'They grew close. My father is gone. It happens to people. It is not a sin.'

'As long as it stays at a friendship level.'

Thomas understood that his wife meant him and Victoria. 'It will not go further. I promise.'

She checked his face as if she did not know it.

'You, too, Ellie, might be attracted to someone one day, and I would understand.'

'Who on earth could that be, the way I live?'

'The vicar?'

'Get away with you.' She shoved him from her side.

★

In April, it rained into the trenches dug into the garden of the end-cottage on Collier's Way. A panel was strung across the road reading: *Danger. No access.* A canvas tent was erected in the middle of the closed road, a table in it and a few objects on that table. The archaeologists had started digging two weeks ago, the day after Thomas Atkinson, wife and daughter had moved into the B&B, and still not found anything Roman. There was a small beer bottle half-filled with earth, a pen still in working order, and the leg of a plastic doll. The school was doing mock GCSEs and Thomas worked hard to prepare students for it. Many had chosen history and the Romans, and the principal put it down to the teacher's infectious enthusiasm. Thomas had brought them to the excavation and given them soup spoons, encouraging in them the excitement of digging for priceless indicators of the past. He had buried several of his coins, which they dutifully returned after the excitement.

Shortly after that, their neighbour paid them a visit in the B&B. The excavators had damaged the waste pipe their houses shared.

Thomas glanced away. 'Well, they have to repair the damage at their cost.'

'Did you sign a contract?' the neighbour pressured.

'No,' said Thomas.

'I didn't think you would have. You are the dreamy type.'

'You can't insure dreams, so what is your problem?'

'Not my problem. Your problem. The shit is all over the place. The council will come and repair for close to

176

three thousand pounds. I'll send – no, I'll *bring* – you the bill.'

After the neighbour left, Thomas was sitting on the two-seater sofa in the living room, drinking from the bottle they had received at Christmas from Aaron.

'What can we do?' Ellie sat on the floor in front of him.

'It's probably not as drastic as this idiot of a neighbour makes it out to be.' Thomas passed the bottle to her.

'Three thousand pounds is definitely drastic and the council always wins. We have to go to Doreen and Aaron, and ask them for money.'

'Begging? Never.'

'Then go and sell that.' Ellie forced the wedding ring off her finger. Her lower lip wobbled. 'The way you look at Victoria, it should not be on my finger, anyway.' She crawled on the carpet towards him with the ring between her teeth. 'You went on your knees giving it to me. You brought me down to my knees. I now spit it out…'

A swishing noise came from the entrance door directly into the living room. An envelope was pushed under the door. 'The bill,' Ellie fretted.

It turned out to be an invitation to celebrate Tilly's second birthday at the manor. *Weather permitting* was added in brackets.

'I could do with something a bit fancy,' said Ellie.

'I thought you'd say you had nothing to wear for the occasion.'

'I have my flowery Laura Ashley. I'll shorten it to calf-length for an April do.'

'Good. A dress for all occasions,' he said with relief, but unwisely.

'You are the worst husband any woman could be punished with,' she erupted. 'You haven't the slightest clue how to treat a woman, do you?'

'What should I have said?'

'That I deserved a new dress. That you would buy me a new dress.'

'We haven't got the money.'

'That's no excuse.'

'Why not?'

'Because.'

'I don't understand.'

'Precisely.'

That night, Thomas slept on a camp bed in the tent in the middle of Colliers Way, because his wife had closed him out of the room in the B&B. It was a moonless night, and the outlines of the few objects the excavators had found mocked him from the tabletop, which was higher than his rudimentary canvas camp bed.

He tried to empty his mind enough to fall asleep, but the figure of five pounds forty would not go away. He only had five pounds forty left in his bank account, enough to keep the account open. Despite some measly help from the heritage society accounts department, they would have to move into a single room under the eaves at the B&B. Tilly would have even less room to play. What would sleeping with an angry wife be like on a single mattress? Everything was raw and painful, and the metal bedframe dug into his back. His head hurt. His mind ached with the dizzying smell of wet asphalt.

Aaron. That was a solid word he could hook his thoughts on. Double A added to Atkinson, his triple-A brother, taker of oxygen. Tilly had been the only triumph in Thomas's painful life. Now Victoria was pregnant, and no doubt an Alexander Augustus Atkinson would take over the family, the factory, the money, the memory of their father, as soon as he was potty-trained. He would have to protect sweet Tilly from the boy.

Goddess Victoria on her plinth would not oppose her husband – who, after all, was a wealthy provider. Nor would Victoria ruffle her mother-in-law, who offered her the manor house to stay in and would subsequently naturally leave it to her in the will. He, Thomas, had nothing. He had dug day and night to enlarge his humble abode and unearthed coins of no value. The pipe was broken. A three thousand pound bill swung over his head like Damocles' sword. The floor of the cottage had to be redone, which apparently was in the two thousand pound region. There was a specialist helping premature children with weak lungs in Edinburgh Hospital, but she only took private patients.

The sudden noise Thomas heard was heavy rain drumming onto the tent's canvas. Right above his head was the joint which did not join. Thomas started to cry like a little boy. Never had he managed to go to Rome for a holiday; the tokens the Romans had let him find in the ground were just a cruel teasing of what could have saved him from penury and hardship. Ellie was right; he was a useless husband and a useless father. He could not even afford to help his darling daughter breathe.

The rain increased; the drops became a continuous

179

dribble. His father had treated him with kindness. Thomas could go as far as believing that his father had favoured him over arrogant Aaron. But, of course, with Thomas's lack of luck, the kind parent had died early. Thomas moved the canvas bed a bit further to the left. Now only his feet were getting wet. If the archaeologists found valuable Roman gold coins, he would find this so unbearably unjust that he would take out the five pounds forty and hitchhike to Rome. Standing in the Colosseum the way they used to, he would, he would... What would he be able to do?

★

Three days later, Thomas had such a bad cold that Ellie let him come back to the room in the B&B. Unfortunately, Tilly caught the virus and struggled to breathe. They sat her up, rubbed her back; they tried to teach her to use an inhaler. The two-year-old needed urgent help, and they could not afford to give it to her.

Ellie pawned her wedding band and bought two kilos of potatoes and carrots for the money she got for it.

'Only gold-plated,' the man said in the pawn shop. He would, wouldn't he?

Ellen was wearing her flowery Laura Ashley in bed as a nightdress. Making the point that it was a garment for all occasions.

He hated her words and the dress so much that he slept on the carpet by himself.

The neighbour was suing over the burst waste pipe; a letter confirming this came with the post.

'We're doomed,' said Ellie.

Before he responded to that, there was a knock on the door. Neither Thomas nor Ellie wanted to open it.

'Hello?' came the muffled voice of a woman.

Unwillingly, slowly, Thomas opened the door.

'Ouff, you live high up.' A young woman they had never seen before staggered into the small room. 'I am,' she gathered air, 'I am Miss Bixley from the Military Uniform Society in London.'

Ellie looked at Thomas, who said, 'You must be in the wrong place.'

'You found buttons digging in your garden,' said Miss Bixley. 'I was told by the vicar of the church over there.' She pointed into the corner of the room. 'This is marvellous.'

'Buttons?' Thomas was mystified.

'The battle of Adwalton Moor in 1643. Lord Fairfax's army against the Earl of Newcastle. We found one of his uniform jackets, but not the buttons – until now. Aaron is your brother, isn't he?'

'And how!'

'I saw pictures he circulated on the internet. He believed them to be Roman coins, but they are buttons. The blobs on one side are the soldered-on loops for the thread to go through. The uniform buttons for an earl were minted in silver and gold, and they had the heads of emperors on them. I can just see the earl staggering out of the inn befuddled. The first British wine-growing experiments were in this area. He flung his uniform jacket away to hug a wench. That jacket rotted in the ground, but the buttons did not. The gold braid needed

181

twelve buttons either side, and two larger ones at the top to start the weaving. You found all of them. It is very exciting. I am authorised to offer you twenty-five thousand pounds for them.'

'Aaron put you up to this,' said Thomas. 'It is a cruel joke.'

'All right, twenty-six and a half. I do not have permission to go higher than twenty-seven. Can we shake hands on twenty-seven?' Confused, Thomas held out his arm. 'The buttons?'

Thomas gave her the cloth-wrapped pouch. She opened it and studied them. 'Goody!' she exclaimed. 'Show me your cheque book and watch me do it.' She showed him, on her smart tablet, the transfer of twenty-seven thousand pounds into his bank account. And she left.

Tilly looked up at her mummy and daddy. 'You did not say goodbye to the lady with the funny hair.'

'It was a dream,' Thomas said.

'I saw the money transfer,' said Ellie. 'It was real. Call the bank.'

'We're going to Rome!' Thomas beamed. 'Tilly, I'll show you where the great lived. Veni vidi vici.'

VIENNA

Maxine was at her desk on Monday morning in the Austrian Federal Police headquarters on Kopernikus Gasse in Vienna. She was concentrating on her historical report on the Fritzel family, eleven years after the case broke, when an urgent message from her boss pinged on her screen.

With a double degree in social politics and forensic psychology, she had been hired in a special police support role. That job had been created as a result of the Fritzel case, in which the father had imprisoned his daughter in the basement, and made children with her. An initial analysis had been conducted by the Austrian Psychiatric Institute, where Maxine had her first job after her MA. The work had found validation with the criminal section of the Austrian Federal Police. Few countries had such abhorrent sex abuse problems, and that is why Maxine held this unique position without any serious police training to back it up.

Maxine's boss, Senior Chief Inspector Zuckermayer, in his corner office from which some green of the public park was visible through the window, twisted his chair right round to face her. She felt apprehensive.

'Another case for us has just come up.'

She brushed imaginary fluff from the taut skirt stretched over her bony knees as she sat in an uncomfortable chair, his desk between them. Maxine made police eyebrows rise with her tight skirts. Her long legs were good. She was twenty-seven.

Zuckermayer explained. 'Last Saturday, the thirtieth of April, early afternoon, a guest in the Hotel Ziegelhof was found astride a boy of eight, molesting him. The child's cries for help brought the hotel owner to the room. There are more details, and a mobile phone picture was made. I told the owner that you were on your way to investigate.'

Maxine tried to imagine the scene in a bedroom of the charmingly preserved seventeenth-century hotel, which offered the homely Ziegel Bar, and a garden with a large pond on which a famous pair of black swans glided, birds which never flew away. Hotel Ziegelhof was a jewel in the crown of Vienna's tourism industry. It was expensive to stay overnight, of course, but judged a worthwhile experience in gourmet dining. No adults abused innocent boys in such a hotel as the Ziegelhof.

'What are you waiting for?'

Maxine was jolted from her contemplation.

'You're supposed to be on your way.'

'Sorry, Chief Inspector,' Maxine said, glancing at the pile in her pigeonhole against the wall.

'I'll attend to the important cases shortly,' he offered, while she wriggled herself up, pulled down the skirt which had ridden up, and went to the door. She felt her boss's shy eyes on her backside. It gave her self-assurance. There had been suggestions that she might consider reserving this style of attire for out-of-office hours, but Maxine liked herself in tight skirts, and they could lump it.

Once, she had been forced to defend herself. 'With my legs pushed together so tight, I am an unlikely victim of rape.'

It had been the wrong thing to say. She caught herself saying wrong things regularly. She was one of the youngest in the police force, a female among a large pack of men.

'Just to be clear,' she said at the door. 'I am to go there alone to make a detailed report. There is no plan for an arrest?'

'No immediate action in that direction,' said Zuckermayer. 'The offender identified by the hotel owners is a regular in the hotel.'

'I see. An Austrian with a sudden attack of feverish *paedophilitis*!'

'By the way...' Zuckermayer now prevented her from leaving the room by adding a personal remark to finalise the short meeting. 'Your mother is doing rather well, according to poll predictions.'

'Yes,' Maxine said. 'She is.'

'It looks as if Barbara Hummel will become our mayor. A good thing, a good thing.'

'I am proud of my mother, of course. See you later.' She left the office, accidentally slamming the door. It was a mishap that would be forgotten in less than three minutes by a healthy mind, but which could arouse catastrophic anxiety in a troubled psyche. Maxine had graduated *summa cum laude*.

Zuckermayer remained alone in his corner office.

★

Mincing across the Rathaus Platz, Maxine met her mother striding into City Hall, chin up, hair swishing over her shoulders. Barbara Hummel was a woman one noticed: tall, slim, elegant, with summer-blue eyes and dark cherry lipstick.

'Where are you going, daughter of mine?'

'To investigate a child abuse case in Hotel Ziegelhof.'

'Be careful what you put in your report,' replied Barbara. 'Hotel Ziegelhof is one of Vienna's best. Remember, I am going to be a traditionalist, but green, mayor. Tourists come to Vienna because of the horse-drawn carriages, the opera house, and gourmet meals served with *Gastfreundlichkeit*. Ziegelhof has five stars in that department. Besides, the Wengers are friends of mine.'

'They vote for you.'

'That too, of course.'

'Mother, I have to run.'

'Not in that skirt, you won't.'

'What is it with everyone and my skirt?'

'No damning report for Hotel Ziegelhof, promise me,' Barbara insisted again.

'Promises in politics are like burps from trout,' replied Maxine. 'Bubbles that rise and go poof at the surface.'

The mother laughed shortly, while clasping her daughter's shoulder with a manicured hand. 'You say the drollest things.'

Mother and daughter went their opposite ways. The sun came out and gave the Rathaus Platz an instant lick of gloss. In the distance, the harness bells of the horses, trotting along, jingled in the clear air. It was the beginning of May, Vienna at its best.

★

Frau Wenger was waiting for Maxine in the Ziegel Bar with its old fireplace, smoke-darkened ceiling beams, and wooden chairs with carved hearts in their backs. It was just gone ten in the morning and the bar was unmanned.

'I'll take you upstairs to show you where it happened.'

One behind the other, the women went up the carpeted stairs and walked along a corridor on the first floor. Some floor planks gave an atmospheric creak. Halfway down, where fresh marguerites in a pewter flagon on an antique sideboard added a touch of innocence, Frau Wenger opened the door to a double room. Besides the wide bed, there was a solid oak armoire, an easy chair upholstered in dark-green striped fabric, plus a narrow chest of drawers with a lamp on top. There was also the expected dressing table with mirror, and a pink Dralon drum-pouffe in front. It was furniture found in every hotel bedroom, although it was rarely used by anyone for its intended purpose. People needed laptop surfaces and plugs for chargers, not hairdryers.

Maxine pulled a tablet computer from her bag and

installed it on the dressing table. She tried to sit on the pouffe, but that did not work with her skirt; instead, she pushed it out of her way and bent over the computer.

'If you don't mind,' she started. 'I'll ask the questions and you answer them as truthfully as you can.' She turned round to check the effect of these words on Frau Wenger.

'Sure, absolutely,' Frau Wenger nodded eagerly. 'You see, the guest who was doing things to the boy is a regular. He signs in as Castle Key Housing Development. They pay for the room. I presume he is the director of that company, or owner, or someone important. He has been coming for the last five or six months, twice a month, usually staying for three days in a row: Friday, Saturday, Sunday. During the day, he goes out to work, he once explained to my husband. In the evening, he often meets with business people downstairs in the Ziegel Bar, which is good for our business. But then something unpleasant happened.'

Maxine, alert, concentrated on Frau Wenger's facial expression.

'Herr Castle Key, as we call him, asked for a large kettle for his room to make soup meals for himself. This is not good for our business.'

'Can you give me a name?'

'Knorr instant soups, mushroom cream mostly.'

'The man's name.'

'Ah, the man's name. Franz Kupfer.'

'Age?'

'Fifty-seven years old and should know better.'

'Name of the boy?'

'We don't register child guests.'

'Why was the boy in the Ziegelhof last Saturday?'

'He is the son of a woman who booked a single room with a child's sofa bed. It was her first visit with us. She and the child had only arrived shortly before the foul deed happened. She signed in as Ingrid West-Kupfer.'

'The same name as Franz Kupfer, the alleged offender.'

'I suppose so. There are many Kupfers in Austria. He lives in Salzburg, and she lives in Bern, Switzerland. You know, the place where they have bears in pits in the middle of town? Sometimes, people fall into them and are eaten. Although I suspect some of them are pushed.'

'Frau Wenger, you like stories with dark endings, books about crimes, murders, stories about men behaving unacceptably, don't you?'

'I guess it is interesting to learn about what people, bad people, are up to. I am like everyone else in that way.'

'Perhaps, but right now it might be influencing my investigation.'

'If you take it that way, I will get my husband to talk to you. He thinks he is cleverer, anyway, and he took the picture of the man with the boy.'

'You do that.'

'It is a mystery to me,' Frau Wenger added, before leaving, 'that the criminal police bureau let their women officers wear street-corner skirts.'

Herr Wenger arrived with Ginty, the chambermaid, a young woman about Maxine's age, who had a straight hair parting with long tresses over it, wrapped around her head: the picture of old-style Austria. Both gave clear and concise answers. Maxine typed much of it onto her tablet.

Nobody had used the room since the event, two days ago. The bedding had not been changed, either. Ginty pointed out that there were urine stains on the duvet, urine from the child peeing from fright, and spots of blood near the pillow.

When asked to tell what exactly happened, Herr Wenger spoke. Changing a bulb in the lamp on the stairs, he had heard a child calling for help. He dashed to the room from which came the disturbing noise.

'I had heard the boy shouting before that,' contributed Ginty. 'Castle Key was chasing him down the corridor, trying to grab him.' Eagerly, she went on, 'Once he caught the boy, he dragged him, kicking and screaming, into his room and shut the door. I got to it just in time to give Herr Wenger my master key.'

'With which I opened the door,' he took up.

It was clear to Maxine that the hotel owner and chambermaid had a much smoother relationship than the owner couple between them. Maxine had a habit of noting down seemingly unrelated details in her work. It had paid off in the past. She asked Herr Wenger to describe what he saw after unlocking the door.

'The boy, the son of the woman guest in number twelve, lay flat on his stomach as if thrown onto the bedcover.'

'A duvet,' said Ginty.

'His head was turned towards me at the door. His mouth was open and loudly protesting, while our guest, Herr Castle Key, in trousers but no shirt was astride him, pinning his legs down under his weight. Both his hands were in the boy's trousers, feeling around in them and shouting angrily, "Give it to me. I need it. Give it to me".'

'Disgusting,' reacted Ginty. 'He is only eight.'

'At this point, I took out my phone and took a picture.' He produced his phone, and furious scrolling revealed to Maxine that he was not a patient man. Eventually, he pushed the phone close to Maxine's face. A balding man with an angry face, a nude torso, was sitting on a panic-stricken young boy, Harry Potter T-shirt rucked up as high as his shoulder-blades. The man's hands were pushed into the child's jeans.

'Can you text this picture to me, please?' asked Maxine.

'Will do.'

'Right now, in front of me,' she insisted. 'People mean to do it, but often don't, or can't.'

She gave him her mobile number and he typed, swearing twice.

Once she was satisfied with the picture on her device, Maxine continued with her questions. 'During Herr Kupfer's stays, did anyone visit him in his room? Man, woman or teenager? I will want to see the register later.'

'I never saw anyone visiting the man,' said Herr Wenger.

Maxine noticed that Herr Wenger scratched his eyebrow with his ring finger, on which was no ring.

'That is not quite true,' he amended. 'I remember now. His mother came several Saturday mornings.'

'Once, I had to let her into the room because Castle Key was out,' added Ginty, who nodded with earnestness.

'His mother? What made you so sure?'

'A woman in a long black raincoat with a hood over her head,' said Ginty. 'She wore granny glasses and walked slowly, and bent, but quickly disappeared into the room when I came into the corridor.'

'Did she have *Mother* written all over her?' asked Maxine.

'I heard her say "Darling, how are you?" with motherly concern, before he literally yanked her into his room, perhaps because he was ashamed that he was still a mummy's boy.'

'You are making assumptions, Ginty,' criticised Maxine. 'Don't.'

'Cleaning his room the next day, I found a tissue with a trendy lipstick colour in the bathroom pedal bin,' Ginty went on. 'And another time, a small diamond earring lay under the bed. It was only glass in the end. I had the jeweller in town check it for me.'

Frau Wenger, at the bed, stretched the duvet to assess the urine damage done to it.

'There is a lot more going on in my hotel than I am aware of. You have to report these things to me.' Frau Wenger looked at Ginty.

'Tell you there is lipstick on a Kleenex? Child's pee on the duvet cover? You are always busy with important things.'

Maxine clapped her hands together several times. 'Back to the man you identify as Castle Key, kneeling on the boy. What happened when he saw you at the door, witnessing what was going on, even photographing it?'

'He climbed off the bed right away and adjusted his trousers,' said Herr Wenger.

'Be more specific. For instance, was his fly undone?'

'I didn't look that closely.'

'How about you, Ginty?'

'I remained outside in the corridor. That was a more correct way for me to behave.'

'What did the boy do?'

'He clambered off the bed,' replied Herr Wenger. 'The man gave him a helping hand. He even pulled the T-shirt back down over the boy's trousers.'

'Was the boy bleeding from anywhere?' They shrugged. 'Do you remember if anything was said?'

Wenger tried to remember, a furrow between his eyes. 'Castle Key tried to talk his way out of it. "It is not what you think. I was only trying to teach the boy a lesson. Grown-ups need things, and boys have no right to hide them" he said.'

'What a pervert!' Ginty exclaimed. 'Apart from balding badly, he looked so normal to me. He even gave me a five euro note as soon as he got here. I guess he can afford it, rich as he is, building whole new towns in Austria.'

'What happened after the boy was up and straightened out?' asked Maxine.

'Not much,' replied Wenger. 'I sent Ginty back to her duties. The boy took off down the corridor towards his mother's room.'

'And Castle Key?'

'He said young boys were a pain in the ass and closed the door in my face. I thought about it over the weekend and called your department this morning.'

Maxine was typing on her keyboard. When she came to a stop, she straightened up. 'I need to talk to the mother of the boy and the boy himself.'

'You'll have to go to Bern for that,' said Herr Wenger. 'This woman is unlikely to book again with us in a hurry after what happened to her son.'

Maxine went back downstairs with Herr Wenger and Ginty. At reception, she checked the current and previous guest registers, noted down addresses, and set off on foot back to police headquarters.

During her absence, Zuckermayer had made no inroad in her pigeon hole. She reported to him that the suspect, Franz Kupfer, was a big shot in Castle Key Housing Development, but that the information she had been able to collect was inconclusive, because the witnesses were not the brightest and produced contradictory accounts.

'In what way?' her boss wanted to know.

'A bent old mother visiting her son on weekends in his hotel room during a business stay-over, and leaving trendy-coloured lipstick stains on Kleenexes behind.'

When Zuckermayer asked what Maxine planned to do next, she said she needed office clearance to pay Castle Key a visit.

'The child molester is, according to the Wengers, a big cheese in that company.'

'I'll get the ball rolling,' promised Zuckermayer.

★

Two days later, Maxine took a taxi to an ultra-modern, characterless office block on the outskirts of town. The young black receptionist, at a desk which resembled an island in a sea of glass walls and marble flooring, looked her up and down, and even lifted out of her chair to fully appreciate the limited extent of the tight skirt.

After a wait in a minimalist seat, leafing through magazines called *The Modern Architect* and *Property Week*, she was called to see the director of Castle Key.

'What do you want from me?' he asked rudely, stabbing pins into the map fixed to the wall. He was a middle-aged man who clearly worked out. A lot. Under his expensive shirt, his biceps rippled. The muscles on his neck were like ropes. His skin was pleasantly tanned, his profile strong, and the mouth well-shaped. This was not a man who got sexual pleasures from prepubescent boys.

He stuck in the last yellow-headed pin and turned round to concentrate on the visitor. 'A policewoman,' he said, the tone mocking.

'Seconded to the police force.' She felt she had to tone things down and, in vain, expected him to invite her to take a seat. He was unnerving for women.

'I have a few questions, and then I'll leave you to your pin-pricking.' The moment she said this, she regretted her impulsiveness.

'Pricking?' His raised eyebrow showed he was not letting her get away with it.

She remembered her yoga exercises and let her shoulders sink. 'Three simple questions, that's all I came with.'

'The pinned area on the map is up for grabs, south west in Mödling,' he said. 'It looks unpromising at first sight, but I know that it has great value, because a Chinese company wants to buy it. More than five hundred homes can be built on it, with woodland area preserved, a brook running through it. It offers children future tadpole memories. How much greener can CK get?'

'Apart from trying to sidetrack me, what do you know about children?' asked Maxine. 'Young boys in particular. A young boy staying with his mother in Hotel Ziegelhof.'

'Nothing. I am not fond of that rustic establishment.'

'Do you not stay at the Hotel Ziegelhof every other week? And is your name not Franz Kupfer?'

'That's your three questions, but I'll be generous with you today. Did you not force yourself into a tight skirt to distract me?'

'Answer my question.' After a second she added 's'.

'I've never stayed at Hotel Ziegelhof, but have had a beer with colleagues in their Ziegel Bar. And my name is Konrad Marsch, owner and managing director of Castle Key.'

'Do you know a man called Franz Kupfer?'

'Your questions are piling in and my generosity is running thin.'

'I'll leave soon, I promise.'

'From the daughter of a political candidate like Barbara Hummel, promises have to be taken with a pinch of salt.'

'Do you intend to obstruct a police investigation, sir?'

'Oh dear. I am generally known to be constructing things and not obstructing them.'

'There are other ways to get my questions answered.' Maxine secured her bag over her shoulder.

He relented. 'Franz Kupfer is employed by me to figure out the lie of the land. He is a geometrist. You know: the guy who looks through a thingy fixed to a tripod standing in a field, which tells you that all the cows will be gone soon and houses will be standing shoulder to shoulder.' He paused to check for a reaction.

'This is how our planet is getting ruined.'

'Do you want to live a cow's life?' Marsch glowered at her. 'You've got the tits for it.'

'Indicatively, everything in your mind is sexually oriented,' said Maxine. 'Besides, you have just stepped over the line by sexually embarrassing me. It has been a crime since the latest discrimination act.'

'Arrest me then.' He held out both arms, wrists touching. 'Handcuffs didn't fit into the lining of your sexy skirt?'

'Now I add sexual harassment to the collection of accusations against you.'

'Come off it. A policewoman looking like you and dressing as you do cannot be expected to be treated as a postulant nun. What has Kupfer done to arouse your interest? To me, he seems a rather dull man.'

'Is he married?'

'Do you fancy him, by any chance?'

'Stop playing games. Is he…'

'He and his wife have been separated for years, by now surely divorced. He remained in their family home in Salzburg, while she lives with her parents in Bern.'

197

'Is he gay?'

'He is a dour person, never tells jokes, always intensive.'

'He is a contractor whom you employ periodically? And he lives miles away from Vienna. Therefore, he stays in a hotel when he works for you. In this case, Hotel Ziegelhof. I assume he is well paid.'

'The services of a geometrist cost a fortune, a totally overpaid profession,' said Marsch. 'But to satisfy building control, I can't do without it. Besides, he has worked for me since I started up.'

'I think I have found my man,' she grinned, copying what a police colleague said during her short training course.

'Please, don't do anything to him,' said Marsch. 'I still need Franz. And I have influence in Vienna. Remember your mother. Her political interests must be on the forefront of all your actions. Barbara Hummel will be just the mayor Vienna needs in these troubled times.'

'Times are mostly troubled because you threaten to construct acres of modern housing all round us, destroying the natural habitats of animals and overloading the centre of Vienna with traffic.'

'Finally, you got over my *obstruct* and turned it into *construct*. I thank you. How did the police force ever get to employ such a tight bunny-assed kitten?'

★

In her villa near the Tiergarten, Barbara Hummel stripped down to bra and panties and tilted the cheval mirror to show the whole of her. She had laid out the dress she was going to wear on the double bed behind her, a marital bed in which she had slept alone since her husband Bernhard had died of cancer.

'I'm going to be Mayor of Vienna,' she said to herself. 'How am I going to lose weight fast?' She poked her face closer to her own in the reflection. 'How? Ta da, the fat lady, mayor of Vienna,' she mocked herself, making an effort to pull in her stomach, and imagined the journalists smiling smugly. 'No wonder,' they would conclude. 'They eat Wiener Schnitzel with noodles, Zacher Torte and endless pastries.' Barbara heaved a sigh. 'I will be going down in local history as a Viennese pastry bag.' She began to jump up and down. Calories could be burnt that way. *Hop hop.*

'Mum,' shouted Maxine from downstairs. 'What are you doing? The house is shaking.'

'I am getting ready to go out,' Barbara shouted back.

'I came to talk to you about the incident in Ziegelhof. I've been investigating it all week, but it can wait. Bye, Mum.'

'Wait.' Barbara ran out onto the landing and leant over the banister. 'Don't go. I want to hear this. I need to hear this.'

No answer came back. The house felt empty to Barbara. Her daughter was gone. Downstairs, the longcase clock dinged. Against the roof window above her, she heard the tock tock of heavy raindrops, precursors of more rain to come. She waited a while longer before returning to the bedroom, where she sat on the side of the double bed in which her daughter had been conceived, twenty-eight years ago, when her young husband could not get enough of her.

Would he have admired her for being put forward as candidate for Mayor of Vienna? Coming into the house, would he now take off his shoes before stepping onto the white living room carpet? Probably not. It did not matter any longer. He had left her, gone his own way, hiding in himself a terrible malfunction of the human body, called cancer.

For her, life was not over. She had a chance to be elected mayor. She was fifty-nine. She was a woman with needs still. She got off the bed and, throwing her arms out, she started to sing.

'*My dearest, my dearest,*
I'm on the way to you.
No wind or rain can hold me back.
My dearest, my dearest, on the way to you.'

Wearing a grey, raglan-sleeved dress, she went downstairs and grabbed her black raincoat, and set off down the street towards Hotel Ziegelhof. It was midday on a rain-grey Saturday, and she would not be back before Sunday.

★

'Darling, you look wonderful,' Franz admired, his back to the rain-dotted window of the hotel room, once she had pulled the door closed behind her and hung the wet coat on the door hook. She went to join him at the window. On the pond in the hotel garden, the swans fed from the bottom, their black tail triangles in the air.

200

'They do that when it rains,' he explained.

'What do men do when it rains?'

'They cuddle future mayors. Come closer.' Franz Kupfer tightened his arm around her and shook her. 'I missed you like crazy. Could barely do my job all week.'

'Measuring hills and meadows?'

'Missing you and sex.'

'Franz.' She pushed the fringe to the side of her wet forehead. 'I was already on my way last week, when you texted me to cancel our meeting. *An unforeseen complication*. What happened?'

'There was a problem at Castle Key,' said Franz. 'My boss wanted to discuss it in the Ziegel Bar. Something to do with a Chinese company competing over territory we're interested in. I could not risk anyone discovering that you were with me. I cancelled for your sake.'

'And a little bit for your sake, surely? Having sex in a hotel with me does not make you look like a nice guy. Although, in theory, you can do pretty much what you like. Your ex-wife lives in Switzerland.'

'Your husband has passed on. You, too, are free to have a relationship with me.'

'Bernhard is very much still at my side during this election,' said Barbara. 'I mean, the image of our love is helpful to me. Who he was, they still like. Even the cancer card pushed me into pole position. I am ashamed to have to admit this.'

'Did we come here to talk or make love?'

'I'm just rattled by what Maxine revealed to me and can't get it out of my mind. Imagine child-abuse in one of these Ziegelhof rooms.'

'Surely not?' replied Franz. 'There are only thirty rooms in this hotel, and I have never seen a child during my many stays.'

'Maxine will not leave a stone unturned, combing through every room that was occupied last Saturday. In this room, she'll find you, alone.'

He laughed out loud, even tapped his chest with his fist twice. 'Your daughter sounds like a real nitpicker. You can tell her from me that I don't like children, never wanted any, never had any.'

'Actually,' Barbara said, stepping out of her dress and leaving it crumpled on the floor, 'she is a very accomplished young woman, and must never find out about us.'

'That's precisely why I cancelled last Saturday and spent the afternoon working in the Ziegel Bar with my boss. We now have a new Saturday in front of us, and much catching up to do.' He went to the freshly made double bed.

She joined him, stretching herself out next to him, making kitten noises. He bent over and kissed her mouth, deep and long, while she looked up at him with her calm, blue, lucid gaze.

After he had let go of her, she still could not leave it alone. 'There won't have been many single men registered in the hotel last weekend. Maxine is bound to regard you as a suspect. Her next move might even be to Bern and talk to your ex.'

'Bern is outside Austrian jurisdiction,' said Franz. 'Leave Ingrid alone. She is safe with her parents on their farm, living ankle-deep in cow dung.'

'Do you not care any longer?'

'My wife told me ten years ago that I was a hateful, destructive man. I tried, but she found someone more lovable whom she brandished in front of me. That did not work out, either. Seven years ago, Ingrid went back to live with her parents in Switzerland. I don't want to talk about it any more.'

'You are right, darling,' said Barbara. 'For our precious few hours alone, let's try to be happy and make ourselves comfortable.' She hopped off the bed like a teenager. From her bag, she pulled a small metal vase and a bunch of flowers. She filled the vase with water in the en suite, returned to the room and put the flowers on the small dressing table.

Pushing his back into the pile of pillows, Franz watched her, his hands crossed behind his head.

After fluffing the flowers with a satisfied little sigh, she took out a box of Kleenex and put it into a drawer. Then she unpacked a few clothes and distributed them into drawers, before pulling both curtains to hide the dark, rainy day outside and switching on the lamp on the chest of drawers. The soft light turned her naked body satin gold.

'Every time you come here, you take possession of this room, trying to turn it into a home, a home for us, with flowers and knickknacks, distributing things into every drawer, taking out my clothes and folding them more neatly. This is a hotel room, Barbara, just a hotel room.'

'Nesting instinct,' she said, laughing at herself. 'I can't help it.'

203

'And leave my toiletries in the bathroom alone. They don't have to stand in formation.'

'Sorry,' she said. 'I've probably lived alone for too long and have turned into a spinster.'

'Come to bed and contribute to a non-spinster experience.'

'I'm so glad you didn't cancel today.' She climbed up on the bed and pushed her upper body close to his manly chest. After an awkward silence, both in an uncomfortable position, she reached out and tried to unlock the hands behind his head.

He reacted instantly by grabbing her wrists. 'Don't mess with my hair.'

'Your hair seems different today.' She concentrated on the thick, chestnut brown strands falling across the dome of his head. 'Lighter.'

'I've changed shampoo.'

She buried her face in his hair.

'What are you doing?'

'Smelling your new shampoo.'

'Don't do that. You're acting weird.'

'I've never known a man who is so fussy with his hair,' she said. 'Can't get near it, can't touch it, can't smell it.'

'What?' He glowered at her in jest. 'All the men you've so intimately known loved to have their hair messed up by you? It's high time for you to be with one who doesn't like it. Look how much *you* will appreciate it.' He went with both hands at her hair, roughing it until she looked like Struwwelpeter.

Seeing his contrite expression, she kissed him on his

mouth, her breasts cool against his heaving hot torso. The hair was forgotten.

*

In the corner office, with Zuckermayer at his desk, Maxine started, 'My mother said...'

'Never start a sentence with *my mother said*, or I won't vote for her.'

'Actually, she only said she wanted to know about the Ziegelhof child abuse case.'

'You know the answer to that,' he responded. 'Our investigations are secret until solved.'

'Surely a mayor has to know what is going on?'

'Barbara Hummel is not mayor yet.'

'Forget what I said,' was the best Maxine could come up with. And then, in a more professional tone, continued, 'I don't want to alert Kupfer to our interest until I have interviewed the abused boy and his mother. I need to get clearance to go to Bern.'

'OK,' said Zuckermayer. 'But I can already tell you that we will not get permission to interview an eight-year-old without a child psychiatrist being present.'

'I have a degree in psychology,' she reminded him.

From below, the hooting of car horns indicated some traffic problem, but it seemed to come from a dimension adjacent to the one in which she found herself with her boss. Human life was as compartmentalised as an open-sided skyscraper doll's house, she thought to herself. Knitted puppets in separate chipwood squares to go about their lives, making decisions, lying, dreaming.

Using cut-out doors between squares, she had to bring it all together. That was the desired goal.

'We are aware that you are qualified,' Zuckermayer said. 'I'll talk to the Swiss and will let you know.'

★

Maxine flew from Vienna to Zurich and took the train from there, as Bern did not have an airport. The farm she was heading to in a rented Renault was quite a way up a winding road. When her satnav told her she had arrived at her destination, Maxine wondered whether she would be welcome.

A plump woman of medium height, with pale legs in large green wellies, had heard the Renault. She was in the process of watering geraniums on the windowsills of a chalet. The spout of the watering can dribbled on the floor after the woman stopped her activity to stare suspiciously at Maxine emerging from the car.

Maxine advanced on her. 'Ingrid West-Kupfer?'

The woman nodded reluctantly. 'Are you the new district nurse?'

While Maxine struggled to respond appropriately, Ingrid went on, 'Eugen is much better. He's eating again. His grandfather bought him a dog. You needn't come up here.'

'There is a misunderstanding,' began Maxine, talking slowly and with clear diction. Suddenly, though, in a raised voice she added, 'You're pouring water on my shoes.'

Ingrid looked down and decided to set the watering can on the ground.

'I am Maxine Hummel from Austria. You were visiting Vienna on Saturday, the thirtieth of April, with your son.' Maxine used the *useful empty moment* technique.

'And you are, no doubt, one of my ex-husband's girlfriend bitches,' the woman responded to the psychological subterfuge.

'Again, a misunderstanding. I am from the federal police and came here to ask you questions about your stay in Hotel Ziegelhof.'

'I haven't done anything wrong.'

'I'm sure you haven't, but let's just find out about it first.'

At that moment, a boy appeared around the corner of the dwelling. He was linked with a furry dog by a stick from his hand to the dog's jaw.

'Is that...?'

'Eugen,' called Ingrid. 'Come here.'

On close inspection, the eight-year-old Eugen looked like Hansel in the Grimms' story: thin legs, dangly long arms, an untamed tuft of hair across his forehead. His knees bore marks of old cuts and bruises, and the fingers, with which he had managed to wrangle the stick from between the gleaming white canine teeth, had cuts and grazes on them.

'Nice dog,' said Maxine, who did not like dogs. The Bernese Mountain Dog must have sensed it, for he bounded towards her and jumped up. She felt his paw claws on her tender thigh flesh through the flimsy cotton of her cloche-cut skirt. Had she worn one of her usual tight skirts, this would not have hurt. For the occasion of an officially paid trip, she had for once conformed to normal attire – although, when she had set out that morning without the comfort of being swaddled, she had felt vulnerable. Walking along, air came up from under the wide skirt to chill her legs.

'Can we go inside and talk?' suggested Maxine.

'Inside are Grandpa and Oma,' objected the boy.

'Of course. Perhaps we could take a short walk up that path, just you and me.'

'And Siggy.'

'And Siggy,' she mollified.

As the two with the dog set off up the dirt track, Ingrid stopped them. 'Not so fast. I received a letter from the Bernese city council. Eugen is under ten. You are not permitted to use him as a witness without an appointed legal person to protect him.'

'I am hardly going to hurt him after travelling here specially,' said Maxine.

'I don't understand you,' Ingrid insisted. 'Rules are rules in Switzerland.'

Maxine was losing her patience. 'You, Ingrid, are over ten years old. I can ask you any questions I want, so why don't you and I take a walk together?'

Maxine had not noticed an ancient man approaching, listening to their conversation. He was leaning heavily on a stick which he planted at an odd angle.

'Life is life,' he said in the Swiss dialect, which resembles the Austrian language. 'I am old and I know.' Coming up closer, he tipped the rim of his Tyrolean hat with the knob of his walking stick in polite greeting. 'Ingrid, my daughter, went to Vienna to face Franz about his shabby behaviour. At their wedding, he promised me he would look after her, but then forgot all about it, putting his work and money first. After a marital fight, she ran out on him, which allowed him to keep their home in Salzburg. Nowhere to go, an Austrian helped her out for a while. Ingrid was not thinking straight in what she did then. She had a baby with that Austrian, but did not marry him. Now she is safely back with us. But there are no good schools up here in the Bernese Oberland. My grandson, Eugen, should go to a good school. He is a good boy. Now I have answered all your questions and you can go back home.'

'How does Eugen feel about his father?' Maxine countered.

'What can the lad feel? His father has left.'

'Dad,' Ingrid interrupted. 'Don't give away more to this woman. She may well just be Franz's latest. She is exactly the type he likes: undernourished, nervy, a career woman.'

'In the interest of Eugen,' Maxine asserted herself, 'I am here representing the juvenile law, which seems to have been broken.' She looked from the old man to his daughter. 'Can either of you tell me what happened in Hotel Ziegelhof on the Saturday Ingrid went to confront her ex-husband?'

The old man started to talk. 'Franz is an impatient bugger. When Eugen came back from Vienna, the boy was shaken. "It's not my fault," he kept repeating and crying. His fingers were bleeding.'

Maxine looked at Ingrid. 'Did you get a chance to talk to Franz?'

'We arrived in the hotel about lunchtime,' replied Ingrid. 'The receptionist said Franz was in his room,

209

room number seven, on the same floor as ours. We went upstairs and unpacked our overnight bags. It is difficult to keep an eight-year-old patient in a room, while I made a list of what I was going to raise with Franz. As it was, Eugen left to go for a wander.'

'And?' Maxine waited for her to go on.

'Eugen obviously ran into Franz. Franz is jealous because I had a son with a man who picked me up after we broke up,' Ingrid acknowledged in an effort to be helpful. 'But I do not know what happened after that, or what upset my Eugen. Can you tell me?' Ingrid looked at Maxine, who was trying to push the busy cold nose of the dog away from her legs.

'The chambermaid described to me what happened after Franz recognised Eugen in the corridor,' started Maxine. 'Despite the boy's protestations, Franz dragged him into his room and physically imposed himself on him.'

The old man spoke up. 'Is that how you speak in Vienna? Here, we call it giving the boy a good spanking.'

'Oh God, that is so bad,' Maxine winced. 'I need backup.'

'What you need, young lady,' said the old man, 'is going back to Vienna where you've come from and take a warm bath.'

'I will do that,' replied Maxine. 'But first, you have to tell me truthfully, will Ingrid file charges against her ex-husband Franz Kupfer, for what he has done to Eugen in the Hotel Ziegelhof in Vienna? For, if she does, we are facing a court case.'

The old man rubbed the sole of his walking boot

210

over a loose pebble. 'Why would she want to do that? I have done that to Eugen many times.'

'Oh, God.'

★

On the last day in April, Ingrid had arrived at the hotel in a taxi from the station. Eugen was with her. After they had registered, they went up the carpeted stairs to the first floor, along which they walked to the very end, Eugen trailing his hand along the antique sideboard. The single room Ingrid had booked over the phone had a made-up sofa bed pushed into a corner, and a window giving out onto the road in front. Once Ingrid had unpacked the bag containing a change of clothes for herself and her son, she went down to reception to find out whether Franz Kupfer had checked in.

Ingrid returned and announced, 'He's here.'

Eugen was pulling at the ribbon around the upholstery on the chair.

'I brought your Harry Potter T-shirt,' she tried to distract him. 'Do you want to wear it?'

'Yes,' he said.

She got the grey sweatshirt off him and then attempted to pull the Harry Potter top over his head. He ducked. He could dress himself. He was eight and not a baby any longer.

'My chances of getting financial support will only improve if I catch him with yet another woman,' said Ingrid half to herself, 'proving he is a philanderer and never took our marriage seriously.'

211

For her son's sake, Ingrid made an effort to control her anger. She noticed the trimming of the chair cover dangling. 'Stop destroying the upholstery, will you?'

'The black bits jump off like beetles when I pull.'

'They're called tacks, and you have to pick them up and push them back into the trim the way it was.'

Eugen tried to do as his mother said. It was fiddly work. 'Ouch,' he shouted. 'I keep pricking myself. It hurts.'

'You'd better let me do it. You're smearing blood on everything.'

'It's boring here,' he complained. 'Why did we have to come?'

'It's grown-up stuff.'

'I am eight.'

'I want to smoke out my first husband.'

'Franz,' said Eugen. 'He doesn't like me.'

'It is high time I made him face the responsibilities of his past actions,' replied Ingrid. 'I want you and me to live in Salzburg in the house Franz and I bought and decorated when we were newly married. I even sewed the curtains. It is wrong to be forced to burden my old parents because he left me with no money.'

'How can you get Franz to give you money when he doesn't want to?'

'Guilt,' she said, and Eugen sucked blood off his fingers.

'Franz meets up with a girlfriend in this hotel at weekends. She gets all his money. I was an innocent young bride. He promised me fairy castles, and then spent all day helping build houses for others, getting rich in the process.'

212

'Why didn't my dad give you money?'

'That is different. Your dad was a roofer and he fell.'

'Did he like me?'

She sighed under her breath. 'He had a big heart, but no money. He died before you were one year old.'

Uncomfortable with the emotions coming from his mother, Eugen stood up tall and informed her that he would go for an adventure.

'Don't get caught by a creature from Harry Potter's school.'

'It's called Hogwarts, Mum.'

She let him leave the room.

Out in the hotel corridor, Eugen was disappointed by the blandness of a place which ideally would have been decorated with dangling bats and overrun by red-eyed snakes, while, along the growling grey walls, the echo of curses should entice him to magic them open with the right spell. Instead, there was the smell of polish and a sideboard on legs. He approached it with caution. Perhaps, the many drawers held some magic.

Eugen opened the top one. Empty drawers had more to reveal than full ones. In the next, he found a short, stubby pencil. There was nothing more to it than that. Perhaps that was the clue. He opened another. From the very back of it he pulled a thick scalp of straight, dark, animal hair.

'Awesome,' he breathed. This had to have come off Aragog, the giant spider who lived in the forbidden forest. Eugen kept opening drawers to find more of the man-eating animal, when Franz appeared behind him and caught him by the scruff of his neck.

This was not a nice man. He did not deserve to have a piece of the magical spider.

Franz breathed down Eugen's neck, and the boy twisted in his grip and kicked his shin as hard as he could. When Franz let go, the boy pushed the piece of pelt into his trousers.

★

After a few months, the Ziegelhof child abuse case was shelved. No charges were pressed, no clear evidence of sexual misconduct was proven, and nor did a repeat occur.

Barbara thanked her daughter for not having dragged the Ziegelhof name through the mud and hugged her tight. Maxine untangled herself from the embrace. A horse-drawn carriage clattered by and stopped.

'You want a city tour?' the coachman touted.

'We are Viennese. We live here.'

In police headquarters, Maxine was treated with condescending pity for having mucked up a good opportunity for the department to shine. The Fritzel case from little Amstetten had made world news. The Austrian police force had been in the spotlight for days. The case would never be forgotten.

Maxine was put in charge of the problem of travellers setting up camp in Mödling, where Castle Key was preparing to build affordable new houses. It was definitely a career demotion.

★

Ginty, on her free afternoon, set off from Hotel Ziegelhof at a rapid pace and, by the time she reached the Rossauer Bridge that led over the canal, she was almost running. Finally, she came to a halt, looking up and down Zwerg Gasse, and located the hairdresser's shop. Standing in front of it, she caught her breath. This was an important day in Ginty's life.

In the hairdressers were three women being worked on. The manageress looked up at her. 'How can we help?'

Ginty could still bolt, but that was not in her conscientious character. Instead, she exhaled heavily before saying, 'I want my long hair cut off, like this.' She unfolded a torn page from a magazine. 'The other day, a policewoman about my age came to the hotel, and her haircut was trendy and not like mine.' Ginty tossed a tress back over her shoulder. 'Sometimes, I even wear them wound around my head. Now, that is naff.'

'You're the girl from Ziegelhof,' the manageress recognised her and wrapped her hand around one of Ginty's long, thick tresses. 'Good hair,' she admired. 'For this important job, I'd better get you Rolf.'

Once Ginty was seated and her shoulders covered by a cape, and Rolf's narrow scissors were poised in the air, he asked, 'Are you sure you want such a short cut? If I do it and you regret it, it will take years to grow back.'

'It took all my life. I've never been to a hairdresser.'

'You have quality hair. I will try to cut it so that the long strands can be used for wig-making.'

'Really? Someone walking around with my hair!'

'You can even sell your hair to Talbergs, Vienna's hairpiece makers,' said Rolf. 'I know them. I can help you with it. There are more people walking around with wigs than you would believe. Most hair for them comes from Asian women. One can see it immediately. That hair is difficult for hairdressers to look after, and the hair is too unyielding for men's toupees. One of our regular male customers stays in your hotel.'

'The Ziegelhof?' she confirmed. 'What is his name?'

'I can't tell you that. Hairpiece wearers like to keep it to themselves.'

'I think I know who he is,' Ginty said. 'He definitely does not want his mother to know he wears a hairpiece. That's why he hides it in a drawer of the sideboard in the corridor, in case she goes through his stuff in his room.'

Rolf brought the scissors to her head. Ginty closed her eyes. 'I want to look trendy,' she muttered. 'I want to look trendy.' She started to cry. Her mother and grandmother used to brush *that* hair. On special Sundays, she had worn two big red bows.

Rolf kept snipping.

When Ginty came out of the hairdressers feeling alien to herself, two things happened simultaneously. She saw two large, black birds flying through a blue summer sky; they had long necks and trailed their legs behind them – the Ziegelhof swans.

Ginty went to the newspaper-dispensing stand. On the front page was a banner headline: *KONRAD MARSCH DECLARES LATE CANDIDACY IN RACE FOR MAYOR.* The photograph showed Marsch at his felt board, pricking pins into a map.

MAKE IT GO AWAY

On the Isle of Wight, Prior Cyril quickened his pace towards a monk in the rose garden, shoes briskly kicking back the material of his frock.

'Sorry to interrupt your garden contemplations,' he called out, wiping perspiration off his balding forehead, then ducked out of the way of a bee. 'I need to consult you on a general matter.'

It was a sunny mid-June day in 1967. From the extensive lawn beyond the rose garden came the unmistakable puttering of a petrol lawnmower. Behind the remarkable Byzantine monastery with Moorish architectural elements, the sky was an uninterrupted honest blue. The row of windows on the upper floors of the building glinted, giving the illusion that the glass in them was not flat. Through gaps in the rose bushes, the monks could see visitors refreshing themselves, on benches attached to wooden tables. Children's shrill voices pierced the air; a dog was barking excitedly.

'Aren't you venturing a little too close to our open-to-the-public coffee shop?' asked Prior Cyril.

Brother Leonard lowered his eyes. 'When they see me, they come running with their box cameras. A

217

souvenir of a monk in front of the splendid abbey. They clearly appreciate that.'

'Or is it a splendid monk in front of an abbey?'

'The income from the restaurant helps us. Besides, the gift shop sells our home-produced honey. What did you come to talk to me about?'

'It is like this…'

Leonard smiled. Even if it was far from being like this, Prior Cyril often started a conversation that way.

'…our abbot's sixtieth birthday is coming up.'

'End of August.'

'Some of us have talked about a joint gift. Knowing his interest in the design of historic buildings, something along those lines for his office.'

Brother Leonard listened and clearly visualised the office. He knew it well from frequent visits relating to what was considered to be his 'rebellious streak'. He did have too vivid an imagination, besides a constant urge to be outside, to walk in nature whatever the elements and bring back wildflowers and budding tree branches. These he kept in empty milk bottles, which could then not be returned.

'I came up with the idea of trying to find the original architect's drawings from when they built the abbey in 1907,' said Cyril. 'I think that would be a splendid present for him, especially as it was one of the monks, Paul Bellot, who drew up the plans.'

'A monk architect. I didn't know.'

'The old, abandoned abbey lay in ruins. At the start of the twentieth century, some French Benedictine monks decided to move to the Isle of Wight. A new abbey had to be built. And one of the French monks had studied architectural design in the Ecole des Beaux-Arts in Paris.'

'Interesting,' admitted Leonard, 'but are the original plans still around?'

'That is, of course, our problem,' admitted Cyril. 'Two monks ventured to the archdeaconry record office in Newport, but did not find what we are looking for.'

'The French would have wanted to keep Paul Bellot's drawings, surely.'

'Perhaps, but what would be the interest of something built somewhere in Great Britain?'

Leonard thought about this before contributing, 'The plans might have ended up with other old papers somewhere.'

'That is what I think as well. There is the Buxton Manor antiques barn,' Cyril said. 'They advertise paintings, vintage maps and other dated local paraphernalia. Perhaps the drawings ended up there. Or perhaps some descendant of someone involved in the building of the abbey can help. It is worth looking into.'

'Maybe we should consider giving our abbot a brass, fan-shaped fireplace guard for his office on his birthday.'

'That would not be personal enough. Would you go up to Buxton Manor and talk to the owner of the barn, explaining what we are after? You are the most worldly amongst us and, liking gardens and flowers, you can probably find the right words.'

'How could I go on such a quest and approach the owner, who is a woman, without the abbot finding out about it?'

'We will cover for you.'

'All right,' said Leonard. 'I'll go up to the manor and talk to her, though she sounds a real fright.'

'Oh, what do you know about her?'

'Both her parents died. It was in the local newspaper. She is unmarried and runs the large house and the barn on her own. That is not normal for a spinster.'

'She is not going to harm you,' replied Cyril. 'Her parents were respected people. The abbot had some dealings with them in the past, as he does with the major houses in the area. It is not a blame on the daughter if her parents died. You are a forty-year-old, fully trained monk. Use your people skills and keep your distance.'

'All right, Prior Cyril. I obey and will go.'

*

What had been omitted from the obituary of Sir Rupert and Lady Daphne Harris of Buxton Manor was that both of them had serious character flaws. They had treated their only daughter, Seraphina, with harsh cruelty, taking out on her their own frustrations, built up during their tender years when they themselves were pushed around without respect by their disciplinarian parents. Difficulties in the Harris marriage, and too much whisky, produced aggressive feelings towards the child. Seraphina was helpless, and they abused her verbally and physically. At the age of eight, she received an indent in the skull from her mother's pastry roller. It was clearly visible and talked about in the village, thanks to Ben Beccles, the Buxton Manor caretaker.

The Harrises only sent their daughter to school when she reached nine. Driven there and picked up by Beccles, Seraphina rarely spoke to other children or played. She had a defiant glint in her dark, almond-shaped eyes which other children feared. As a teenager, she was taken out of school and confined in the manor. Only the doctor saw her away from it, on the occasion he gave her advice on starting menstruation. He was outraged that Sir Rupert had told the girl she was unclean and how, on days she had thoughts about boys or other forbidden things, the angels punished her by poking her inside the dirty, shameful place.

Now at thirty-three, with her parents dead, she was still living alone in the vast Jacobean house with mullioned windows and six chimneys, each serving a large fireplace. Old Beccles still did the garden and looked after the house, as best he could. He was upset to hear her ladyship frequently weeping in the drawing room. Probably not in mourning for her unkind parents. He, too, had suffered from them; his servitude had only been made tolerable by the appreciation of the locals for the stories about Buxton Manor's inhabitants which he provided.

*

Brother Leonard, ignorant of psychotic cruelty, a man who dedicated his life to the glory of God, sniffed the air and felt jaunty about being outside. He was walking up a wooded hill to one of the most noteworthy houses on the Isle of Wight, to perform a task he had been entrusted with – the abbot's birthday present.

221

At his feet, the road leading up the gentle hill was dappled by the myriad of trees surrounding him. He stepped into a sun patch and saw his cut-out shadow on the ground in front of him. He lifted his hand and waved to himself. As he passed an old oak, his shadow dissolved. He pressed on, from silhouette to dark, until he saw the entrance to the property. With a last effort up a steep incline, he arrived. The gates stood open, and he passed between the gate posts and along the barn onto the pebbled forecourt. Liver-coloured stones immediately worked themselves over the rim of his sandals to bother his naked toes.

Laboriously lifting his feet with every step, he came to the Tudor-arched oak door. There was a small, inset window protected by a cast-iron grill, as he imagined a prison door to look like in a Dickens novel. A pale, bluish face materialised in the aperture.

'Hello,' he thought he had just said. However, being honest with himself, it had been a mere croaky whisper. If this was the woman he had been sent to deal with, he would have to turn back right now. Daring to check again, he realised that his imagination had tricked him. He reached out and pulled the bell rope energetically several times. The little bell on its metal spiral nearly came off. He wanted to get this mission over with.

The door did not open. With luck, she was not home. Or perhaps the ghostly face he had seen behind the bars was an intruder, who had murdered Seraphina Harris in her sleep last night. It was that sort of house – one with a long history, crackling up its quarry stones like the tendrils of dark ivy. He bent down and clawed a pebble from between his toes without unstrapping the sandal. Of course, she chose this moment to appear and be faced by his black-clad backside rather than his rehearsed words of greeting.

He straightened up. She gave a little sneer. His head felt hot from the blood which had flowed into it while bending down.

'You look flushed,' she said. 'Do you have a fever? I can't tolerate infections. State your case and then go back to your abbey. That's where you're from, black monk, isn't it?'

He licked his teeth; this mission had already gone wrong.

'Are you deaf and dumb, or here to collect money? I don't give to charity.'

He shook his head and clasped the flat, silver cross dangling on a chain over his chest. His frock felt itchy and hot, despite the bell-shaped sleeves, especially at the nape where the lowered hood gathered, restricting his neck movement.

They eyed each other with mutual distaste.

'I came here for help,' he said, wishing he could rub it out and say something better.

'You are injured. There is blood on your foot. An angel pricked you, because you did something bad.'

He looked down. A pebble wedged between two toes had cut into his flesh. There was indeed fresh blood on his sandal.

'It doesn't hurt,' he reassured her. 'Not at all.'

'Self-flagellation. Is that what you do in the abbey?'

She made him feel rigidly self-conscious. It was alarming.

223

'Come inside,' she gracelessly invited. 'Since the death of my parents, tyranny has gone from the manor. You do not risk anything.'

'It is chill in this house,' he uttered in the stone cave of the entrance hall.

'With walls five feet thick, it is to be expected.'

'It is a splendid manor, pure Jacobean style,' said Leonard. 'One of the oldest and best on the island.'

'Well, well, well. You are clearly able to do small talk. I can't abide small talk. Why did you come here?'

'I'm going to get right to the point,' he started. 'I understand that in the barn you sell old maps and drawings of noteworthy buildings on the island.'

'I have some. One is of the old coastguard station built out into the sea. Never seen one of the abbey, apart from a large oil painting I sold years ago to an American.' Seeing how Leonard reacted to that, she added, 'Don't regret it. It was done in the Cubist style, and badly at that.'

They found themselves in the sombre drawing room, where everything seemed to be imbibed by wood smoke, and drab from wear and tear. He noticed the indent on her forehead above a large, pale face without make-up. Tiredness or sadness showed in the small, slack folds at the corners of her eyes. The flesh of her arms, emerging from short sleeves, appeared soft and unpleasantly carnal. She stood, feet apart, hands clasped in front of her, staring at him, a monk clad in black from neck to ankle.

'You are after historic documents concerning your abbey, aren't you? I can already tell you that you will find none in the barn. What sells are seascapes, cows and landscapes.'

'Have you come across someone who was involved in the building of the abbey? That would have been sixty years ago.'

'We owned land then, a lot of land.'

He noticed half-charred logs in the large fireplace, but no iron set to clean things up. He guessed they would have been weapons for parents to hack into unloved children.

Above the mantelpiece, where one normally expects a mirror, or a valued picture, hung a straw hat.

'My father's hat.' She had followed his eyes. 'He died wearing it. I put it there to reassure myself that his head is not in it any longer.'

He squirmed. She made it sound as if her father's head had become severed from his body. That was, of course, what had happened to King Charles the First, who hid from Cromwell's soldiers in Carisbrook Castle on the island, before being smuggled out by the royalists to Buxton Manor, where he remained until they came for him, sedan-chaired him to London and, on a winter's day in 1649, chopped his head off in public. All those years ago, Buxton Manor was already standing on this hill, on this island, the house with its secrets the same.

'You can have the Panama hat,' she offered. 'It was expensive. Like the one Picasso wore in photographs of Cannes.'

She unhooked the hat and advanced on him with it.

'Please, no.'

'You are fair-haired. You could burn in the sun.' She pushed it onto his head.

'Please don't do that,' he said too late. This dark house and obnoxious woman seemed to impose discomfort on him.

'Bit by bit, the Harris estate grew smaller. Grandfather sold the land on which the new abbey was to be built. At the time it caused a big hoo-ha, selling to the French.' She smiled so timidly that it did not penetrate the sad mask of her face.

Leonard felt pity for her.

'I have a friend called Donna. She is an artist-painter, like her grandmother Dotty before her. Despite the acrimony about the French building on the island, Dotty chronicled the progress of the building with charcoal drawings.'

'Oh dear,' replied Leonard. 'I am not up to squabbling with a mad female painter.'

'Aha. We don't like women,' she said. 'But then, your job gives that away all by itself.'

'My job?'

'Celibacy, or the flames of hell.'

'You don't seem to be a man-lover yourself.'

She clapped her hands. He hiccoughed.

'We have a lot in common,' she concluded, got up and went to stand close to him. The scent of her perfume went up his sensitive nose. His eyes started to water.

'Don't cry, virgin monk.'

What an invasive bitch, he said to himself.

Her head moved forward, and he felt her lips on his. The kiss was short, but the thrill was major. As a boy, he had

226

once kissed the black part of a young horse's muzzle and never forgotten the sensation of silk bliss on his lips. What had just happened challenged this cherished memory.

'My parents had a folder with a collection of Dotty's drawings,' Seraphina went on, cold-voiced. She clearly had felt nothing. 'Your toes are still bleeding.'

He looked down. 'The pebbles in your forecourt.'

'Let me put this right.'

He was helpless, standing in the Panama hat, uncomfortable and weak, and now she was on her knees in front of him, unstrapping his sandal, a gesture so personal his stomach lurched. He was forced to keep himself upright by placing a hand on one of her rounded shoulders. To further discomfort him, she started to rub up and down his calf muscle.

'Fit as any middle-aged monk I can think of.' She laughed in a way which was unpleasant to his sense of decency.

'What woman gets to know a monk?'

Why the hell have I let myself be manipulated by a dangerous woman? What accursed hallucination has been sent by the devil to derail me?

'Lie on the sofa,' she ordered. 'We don't want the cut to become infected. My mother died of an infection which spread from a cut in her leg. Twice its size, the leg got. Dad managed to get her into his car to bring her to the infirmary, but he forgot to put the handbrake on when closing the gates behind him. He ran after the car. It crashed into a tree. Mum died on impact. Dad had a heart attack from the stress and the running. I saw it all from up in Charles's room. Stay put. I'll be back.'

She left the room. He hoped this would give him a break in which to rally. His breathing was short and fast, giving a whiny sound every time he exhaled. He lifted his head from the stuffed armrest of the aubergine-coloured sofa. The straw hat fell off his head. He felt a little better.

She was back too soon with a packet of concertinaed cotton wool and a bottle of TCP disinfectant, and sat down at the other end of the sofa.

'Put your bad leg up on my lap.'

As he didn't obey, she peeled back the hem of his frock, grabbed his ankle, lifted and pivoted it to end up on her thighs. Gently, she started to dab his toes with a piece of disinfectant-soaked cotton wool. It did not sting, not like the mercury his mother had applied to grazes on his knee. He held himself up with his bent elbows to retain some control of what she was doing. The uncomfortable position tightened the material of his collar at his Adam's apple. He had no way out. He closed his eyes and let her do her job as first aider; there was an innocent explanation for that.

To his horror, she started to clamber over his body, inch by inch and, most awkwardly, her left foot hopping on the worn carpet, the right knee bent and pushing along the gap between the seat and vertical cushions. Her soft breasts and belly slowly brushed against him. Finally, his elbows caved in under her weight, and she collapsed on him. Her body became one with his. He felt overwhelmed by flesh, invaded, crushed. He forced his brain to come up with his favourite prayer:

God of wind and water, stillness and storm,
Give us faith to seek you in times of trouble.

'Ouch,' she exclaimed, and grabbed his cross which had poked her, and pulled the chain roughly over his head. He soothed his scratched ear by pressing his hand against it.

Nobody else but he had touched that cross since the abbot had put it around his neck on the day he had taken his vows. He started to panic, and his ears were filled with a loud rushing noise. If he fainted now, someone would have to be called and he would be taken in shame from this hell house.

'Don't pass out on me,' she said, close to his face. To his relief, she clambered backwards and off him, off the sofa, to stand in the hateful room.

He pulled himself up and swung his legs to end in a sitting position, his frock back down over his legs.

A rustling sound came down the chimney, followed by the dribbling of debris.

'Rooks,' she said. 'The last storm took the chimney cap away with it. These vile birds nest in my trees. They sit on the chimneys, probably have done since the manor was built.'

The time had come to leave. He hobbled out into the stone hall and to the oak door, while she behind him carried his sandal, the back strap hooked over her extended finger.

'Look, it's possible my parents' folder of Dotty's charcoal sketches includes some of the abbey,' she said, her shoulders up like a gull's wings in the chill. 'They left me with hundreds of books and papers, all in a mess. Give me a week, and I will see what I can find for you.'

'It is not for me, but our abbot,' said Leonard. 'He has an important birthday coming up.'

'I see,' she said. 'You were sent on a quest by your brother monks.'

He was pleased for no reason except to note that, for a bitch, she still had some logic in her.

When she waved goodbye at the door, he concluded that, in the end, they had parted in some kind of equanimity. Walking down the hill, he stopped, as if someone had tapped him on the shoulder, and turned to look back. The façade of the house, built in 1605, was uniformly perfect and untampered with during all these years. Except for... he narrowed his eyes...

'A pulley,' he said out loud. Above the upstairs window in the side apex was fixed what looked like a wooden pulley. At that moment the window was opened, and he could see Seraphina at the sill looking out, having run up the stairs to the room she had called Charles's room, to have a last glimpse of him, the departing black monk. Part of him felt flattered, while another part still wondered why someone had fixed a pulley to the quarry stones of that fine house.

*

Back in the abbey, reporting the outing, Brother Leonard was not entirely honest with Prior Cyril, who listened, chin in the bony heel of his hand.

Cyril was known for his clever brain and astute thinking, while he, Leonard, as many had pointed out, showed an undesired tendency to fabulate.

'When I got to Buxton Manor,' Leonard started, 'I found the property to be a major architectural example of the Stuart era.' *How unfabled was that for a start?*

Cyril was not impressed, Leonard could tell. The prior contemplated the growth of the nails on the hand which did not support his head.

'The pebbles in the forecourt were so sharp they hurt my feet. It was almost like a fire walk test for me. Seraphina Harris at first was totally unhelpful, but relented enough to look for a folder of original charcoal drawings from the time the abbey was being built.'

'Did she offer you refreshments?' enquired Cyril.

'I refused any personal interaction,' replied Brother Leonard, 'apart from talking at a distance, remaining in the hall – except for quickly nipping out to check the paintings in the barn, which were all of seascapes and cows in meadows.'

'Could you be learning?'

'But now I have to go back to pick up the promised sketches.'

'Will she charge us for them?'

'From how I interpret what she said, she was going to give them to us. Her family was proud of the abbey.'

'It sounds as if this would be a suitable gift for the abbot,' said Prior Cyril. 'We can always have the best of them framed.'

'Maybe you could go up to the manor to pick up the folder?' Leonard suggested, and then secretly held his breath in dread of what would be said next.

'She would expect you to return, and that would be

right,' said Prior Cyril. 'We will give you a price level up to which you can negotiate, if you find the drawings worthy of our abbot, and if she does ask for money.'

'All right, Prior Cyril. I will study the art of charcoal sketching of that time to learn what to look out for. Then,' he gave a sigh, 'I will go up there again.'

'It is like this.' Cyril wasn't letting him off the hook yet. 'You've enjoyed going there, the woodland walk, the adventure. God will put you through another test next time. You failed this one.'

Leonard looked at the prior in surprise.

'You are not telling me the truth.'

'But... But I have. I have.'

Cyril nodded, his mouth pinched shut, which accentuated the carved, deep folds from his nose to the corners of the thin mouth.

'Mrs Harris is a lonely, badly treated woman,' he said. 'You, a man in his best years, unavailable, having taken the vow of chastity, must surely have been an irresistible challenge for her.'

Blustering, Leonard tried to repair the disaster. 'All right, I didn't tell you enough about the pebbles. They are sharp and mean, all the way from the gateposts to the house. The lady protects herself well.'

'Is she a handsome woman?'

'Is she a handsome woman?' Leonard repeated, giving himself time to come up with an answer. 'She is pale and looks beaten. The memories of her parents hover around, especially in the drawing room, where everything is worn or torn, and the chimney lost its cap. Dead rooks are falling into the hearth.'

232

'I thought you said you were only standing in the hall?'

'It was clearly visible from the hall.'

'The abbot has asked to see you. You'd better brush the horse chestnut blooms out of your hair, which is in any case too long.'

★

Ten days later, loaded up with copious advice and reminders of his status handed out by Prior Cyril, Leonard was walking up the hill through the forested area. The sky was black, and the fir, beech, ash and larches around him had lost all lustre. He had spent hours every night on his narrow bed, half-thrilled by and half-dreading his next meeting with Seraphina, but now he wondered whether the lack of sunlight was a deliberate doing of God to keep him on the straight and narrow.

Before leaving on his mission, Leonard had picked up two small plastic bags from the abbey's kitchen and wrapped his feet as a precaution, before slipping into his sandals. Spiritual advice was sensible, but the physical aspect, he thought, ought not to be neglected.

When the manor appeared, with more confidence this time he padded across the fire walk to the door.

Seraphina had written to the abbey, *For the attention of Brother Leonard*, to say she had found the drawings. And now Leonard pulled the bell rope for a second time. The bell tingled so timidly, he had to encourage it with another pull.

233

'You again.' She opened the door.

'You wrote…'

'Don't be so jumpy. Come in.'

He did as he was told. She went close up to him. He stepped back. This was to be a test for him to redeem himself from the bending of truth after his first visit here. He could do it. He wanted to do it. It had been his grandmother on his mother's side from whom he had inherited the fabulating trait. The old Irish lady had been noted for telling compelling tales. Sadly, he never met her. She died the day he was born, and the priest at the time was supposed to have said, 'One life lost creates a new one.'

'Glad you came.' Seraphina fell to her knees in front of him. He looked at the white scalp in the parting of her dark hair. Was she bowing to him? Some villagers, not familiar with the religious code, did that.

'Your toes have healed.' She straightened up. 'They look like fishfingers before being battered, the way you've wrapped them in plastic. Socks,' she said, so directly into his face he could feel the spray of her saliva. 'Do monks not own socks?'

'Feet are tell-tales of many things in a man and should be shown,' he replied. 'Like nuns have to brush hair away from their forehead to show the canvas of honesty.'

She reached up and pressed the heel of her hand against the damage done to her skull. 'The folder I found for you is upstairs in my parents' bedroom.'

'I can't go upstairs.'

'Then I'll have to throw it down for you.'

'Yes, please.'

'This is sick.' She showed annoyance; he noticed her earlobes becoming raspberry-coloured. 'I've gone through all this trouble for you.'

In the chill, dark hall he felt a prisoner of her moods. As he wondered how to cope with her, a very loud and unusual sound was heard. It was as if, higher up in the house, a large crate or tray of ironmongery had been hurled down a flight of stone steps.

He stood rigidly. The door to the drawing room in which she had crawled over him was closed. A timid, heart-shaped light was visible through the keyhole. Perhaps a mysterious person was in there. Certainly electricity was being wasted.

'Are you coming up?' Her upper body showed over the stone balustrade.

He started to climb the stairs, one stone tread after another. On the landing was a vast oak chest. The lid was ajar, as too many blankets had been pushed into it. In the corner stood a man-high brass candelabra with just one candle in it, albeit a fat one. The girth of a candle, however, did not affect the efficiency of one wick. In this case, it wasn't a sufficient way to cast light, should the day grow even darker. In the abbey's chapel, they had dozens of candles in sticks. They flickered beautifully, like the fluttering of the devoted-to-God heart which was his since he had joined the order eighteen years before.

'I'm in here.'

He heard her voice and pushed the door from where the sound came, to find her sitting on a soft bed under

235

a carved canopy. On the rug at her feet lay books, like carelessly scattered tiles. The bedcover tulips were covered with books in a similar way.

'You made it,' she said, looking up. All frustration had gone out of her. The earlobes were a normal pale. 'There is a dedication inside the lid of the folder, which I hadn't noticed before. The collection was a gift to my grandparents from Dotty.'

'Are we alone in the house?'

She eyed him more intensively.

'Your caretaker,' continued Leonard. 'Does he sit in the downstairs drawing room sometimes? The one with the fireplace chimney which lost its cap?'

She seemed to curl inside herself. 'Ben Beccles is not allowed in there.'

'The light is on in that room. Did you know?'

'It happens,' she said a bit too casually.

'It is a waste of electricity. Also, while talking light, one candlestick on the stair landing is not enough, especially as there are no lamps installed.'

'Enough for what?'

'Enlightenment.'

'They invented electricity. I tend to use it. Perhaps not so on-turning for you, as you are no doubt inundated with candles in your spiritual abbey. Add incense, and you could be called a junkie.'

'Candles for me are…' That had to remain private, untouched and secret. He had to get off the subject of light and ghostly people in empty rooms. 'What was that noise of things crashing down the stairs?'

'Mummy's silver. I used to be forced to clean it.

Served me right. I had no life, no friends. Nothing else to do. Don't worry. The silver is not aerodynamic. I put a tray of it on a narrow ledge. Probably the honey spoon was the last straw on the camel's back.'

'I have to go back to the abbey. What do you want for the sketches? I was given a budget.'

'You are a useless businessman. You have not even examined the merchandise you are offering to pay for.'

She picked the folder closest to her buttocks on the soft bed and pulled open the ribbon bow which held it together.

'Come and see.'

He edged forward nervously. Close to her, he remembered her scent.

'If you don't start to look through the artwork, the booklice will beat you to it.'

He advanced into battle, the reassuring feel of the cross against his chest like an armour. She showed him the drawings in a way which made him sit next to her like a little boy. The charcoal lines depicted the building during different stages of construction. It was done with talent.

'The abbot would cherish this,' he said spontaneously.

Her arms locked around him tighter than the frock ever did. She pulled him onto the bed with her. The hard covers of some books dug into his side, but what she did next to his black frock, and him in the frock, made him lose control of all consciousness, or perhaps his whole being was catapulted into another galaxy where sensations reigned, unknown to earth dwellers. This was the catastrophe he had been excitedly afraid of for a long time. He was lost. He was reborn. He was guttering like a candle.

When she covered his body again with his habit, it felt like a curtain lowered over an obscene play. She was clumsy in her moves; the seam became entangled in the back of a ring folder. He excused her, because she was not a monk who had pulled the habit over his body thousands of times.

The image of Prior Cyril appeared in his mind, the hand supporting the chin of a leading monk who could only condemn him if he knew what Leonard had just let happen.

'I have to go and deal with this.' Leonard got off the bed and tapped to the door, the sandal straps open still.

'Don't forget your cross.' She held it out to him. 'It came off your neck when we…'

'Goodbye.'

He almost skidded down the stairs on his flat, leather soles. From the room of wasted electricity came the cackling of laughter. The small keyhole heart of light was now dark. He crossed the enormous flagstones in the hall and tried his best not to step on a crack. His Irish grandmother was said to believe that walking on a crack would bring bad luck. He pushed the oak door and, for no reason, turned to see whether Seraphina had followed him to prevent him from leaving. A slim, fast, dark shape grew and sped across the ceiling above the staircase. He blinked, taken aback, but dared look again. The one candle that he had pointed out was not enough to light the stairs was probably drowning in its own candle wax and, fighting extinction, was throwing shadows against

238

the whitewashed walls and the ceiling. This was a cursed house. He felt the chill of being observed from several corners, and a bit mushy in the genital area.

Engaging on the pebbles, he wished the flames of shame would lick up his body and burn his penis to a frazzle, before consuming him entirely.

'Love you,' he thought she shouted from the window of Charles's room.

He took the sandals off and started to run down the steep road, enjoying the burning sensation of concrete friction. He went on running through the woods, over roots which had pushed through the tarmac, and stones which had rolled onto it. The more it hurt, the more absolved of guilt be believed he became. But, at the same time, he realised that his guilt was so enormous that an ocean of embers could not singe away the shame, especially not as he had enjoyed it more than anything else ever. Maybe he should just curl up at the foot of a bush in a ditch and hand his soul over to the devil.

When the abbey came into sight, he lacked the oxygen to go on. Before making a next step, he had to vow to himself never, ever, to let anyone know what had happened in Buxton Manor. What Seraphina would make of it was her choice.

'Was this your first time?' The timbre of her voice had been intrusive.

'What do you think? You who are so experienced in whoring.'

'It was far from whoring. It was a first time for me, too.'

239

'You must know how utterly untrue that sounds,' he had said.

'Sorry for being me,' she had responded and disarmed him again.

The abbey. The abbot. Prior Cyril. God, no. In his confused haste to leave, he had forgotten to pick up the folder with the drawings.

'Doomed!' he shouted up at the canopy of trees, and no rooks croaked or birds flew in fright; no-one answered. God had turned away from him. This time he had blown it.

Walking into the grounds of the abbey, he vowed to pray one thousand hours as a self-inflicted punishment. More urgently, though, he had to wash out his cotton underpants into which his guilty penis had wept milky tears of shame.

Seraphina Harris, a greedy woman, wanted too much money for the artwork, was the lie Leonard had decided to use. And, subsequently, vehemently make it clear that he would never agree to be sent on any errand beyond the walls of the abbey as long as he lived.

*

Cyril realised that Leonard's commitment to the abbey was genuine, and that he had stayed well clear of the fairer sex, which he so manifestly feared and detested. Cyril even tried to soften the outrage in his fellow monk.

'Miss Harris is not evil,' Cyril offered, as they walked through the rose garden, Cyril eying apprehensively the bees which were eagerly sucking nectar from flowers with their tongues. 'She is just a lonely woman with money and nothing much to do all day long. I feel I sent you into the fangs of a lioness, and you took it badly. I am sorry. You will never have to be alone with a woman anywhere ever again.'

'Thank you,' Leonard mumbled, chin almost touching his collarbone.

That night, after two hours of prayer, he returned to his cell with the apple he had helped himself to from the fruit display. He lay on the hard, narrow bed in his small cell and relived the sensation Seraphina's body had produced on his. He put the green apple on his nude belly where the navel was, and contemplated the fruit: Adam, the apple and Eve. But what the story was about was the snake, the devil in disguise.

At three in the morning, Brother Robert from the cell next to his knocked on his door. 'Are you all right, brother? I hear you yelling.'

'Not to worry,' shouted Leonard, biting into the apple and appearing at the door. 'Nightmares,' he explained, and took another bite from the juicy flesh of the fruit.

'We all have them.' Robert suggested the two of them went to the chapel to pray for an hour or two. Leonard was grateful for the love Robert showed him and extended the prayers until the sun came up.

At breakfast, he made a point of passing the abbot at his table on the dais at the head of the room.

'I love being a monk,' he enthused.

'Glad to hear it. Brother Robert told me about your nightmares. Eating apples does not make them go away.'

'You are right.' Leonard bowed his head not just to God, or to his superior, but also to the thwarting of any carnal twinge that could ignite his body ever again. He was a clean monk, from now on until his death.

At the abbot's sixtieth birthday lunch, swan pie was served, and the Queen had sent a telegram. The abbot received a Victorian fan-shaped fireguard for his office. He seemed pleased with it.

★

Up in Buxton Manor, Seraphina found herself pregnant.

'Sod's law,' she said to her father's hat, back up on the hook. 'Your fault. I will have to find a way to make it go away. I never gave you or Mum away, did I? There will be no baby, no shame, as there is no father for the child, and nobody who would want to help me or a bastard infant.'

If she deprived herself of air for long enough, the being inside her would suffocate, surely. Seraphina practised holding her breath, but found this an inefficient way to make the pregnancy go away. She would not have the courage to poke herself through the vagina with a crochet hook. Jumping from the staircase landing might kill the baby, but leave her with two broken legs if she was lucky. No, it was not a solution.

Beccles must not find out about her condition; that was important. He, no doubt, had seen the monk visiting. She came up with the line that the abbey had sent a monk to the island's historic houses to find pictures of the monastery.

'I sent that religious nut packing,' she said.

The caretaker nodded. She did not trust him. He loved to spread gossip about Buxton Manor in the village pub. Her coupling with the monk would probably give him free beer from the landlord for life. He must not know.

As time passed and Seraphina's bump grew larger, she became more desperate. The more advanced the pregnancy, the harder it would become to make it go away.

'Drowning,' she whispered, waking from a nightmare, before she realised it was three in the morning and the autumn rain was knocking against her window.

Pour fertiliser into her vagina and lie on the bed, feet up against the headboard. Perhaps simply stop eating and starve the foetus.

When she was seven months pregnant, she wore loose clothes and avoided Beccles. Cot death was discussed on the radio breakfast broadcast. No medical explanation for that. She concluded that it would be easier to make the problem go away once the baby was outside her body. A pillow over the head could produce cot death.

Eventually, it dawned on her that she would have to have someone help her with the birth. The mere thought that the growing being inside her had to come out of her somehow made her dizzy. The belly button opening was clearly an old wives' tale. Seraphina panicked. In January, on impulse she walked all the way to the abbey without having worked out what she could gain from this move. Behind those walls, somewhere in the vast building, was the father of her growing child. What did she know of him or his life? Could he be persuaded to change lifestyle, and come and live with her as a husband and father? *Dream on*, her mind told her. The most frivolous thing about him was that he liked an abundance of flickering candles. She was on her own.

She turned away from the monastery and walked all the way back. Abandoned, she would give birth to a monk, a small monk. A monkey. But how? How would the baby get out of her body? Why had she never been told? She examined herself in the shameful place. There was no opening there for a baby to come through. It could not be vomited out, either. Perhaps a mother's bump burst, and then she had to be sewn together again? That is why babies were born in hospitals. But her mother had given birth to her in the manor. It had been said often enough how much it had hurt without gas.

Seraphina had left a shopping list for the caretaker, and he appeared at the door.

'It says here,' his dirty thumb holding the list, his cataract-dulled eyes scanning it, 'two dozen wax candles.'

'We need more candles.'

He switched on the light in the hall.

'The manor was built in 1605,' she added. 'They did not have electricity then. So…'

'As madam wishes.' He walked off with the list, and she saw him deliberately drop it on his way out. He had no respect for her. He had seen her being beaten by her mother, cursed and shoved around.

She yearned for the flickering light of candles. Enlightenment, believing in a higher cause: wasn't that more or less what the black monk had said?

'Beccles, you dropped your list.'

Hearing her voice, he turned slowly. 'So I have.'

'Candles. I want candles, the way I wrote on the paper. Make it four dozen.'

'Very well,' he said, gave her a dirty look and departed again, faster this time.

That day, she felt an animal kick her from inside her own body. Panic shot through her. The baby in her was growing, healthily kicking. That was not in the wishful dream of making it go away. She came to the conclusion that the only way out was to kill herself. Charles the First had been lucky; his death was 'assisted'. What had he been thinking, up in the room above her, before they came for him?

That room was also the location of her worst memory. It was the *game* room, to where the hunted carcasses were raised with the pulley and hung, for the fowl meat to become gamey, and the mammal meat high. In her childhood, curiosity had once driven her up there, on an afternoon when her parents had invited important guests to dinner. There had been great tension in the air. Lady Daphne was in the kitchen, overseeing the preparations for a game pie.

The door to the forbidden room had been left open; over the beam were ropes and meat hooks on chains. Beccles had shot pheasants and they were hanging, their legs bundled together, their heads dangling on elongated necks. Bits of venison on hooks and chains were dripping blood onto the planked floor. She had climbed on the chair, probably trying to save a pheasant's life, when her mother entered, apron dusted with flour and the pastry roller in her hand. A bad memory, a bad room.

Seraphina had no way out of the horrors. One consolation was that, if one did not poke ghosts, they pretty much left one alone; they were not interested in interaction.

Beccles returned and tilted the basket until the candles rolled out of it. 'Forty-eight, as madam requested.'

He turned his back and left. With difficulty, she bent down and picked them up, collecting them in the dell of her ample skirt. The door opened again; Beccles threw a large box of matches her way. She missed catching it. The door closed.

'Father,' she said up to the hat over the fireplace. 'I am going to your game room, and there is nothing you can do to prevent me.' She worked herself up the stairs, hampered by the load of candles in her skirt over the bump of the baby in her body. Her breathing rasped. 'You,' she talked to the unborn, 'will make most things impossible for me. There is nothing here for you. I care enough for you to spare you a miserable life.'

She entered the cursed room, this time to have a good look around rather than just dash to the window to wave at the monk. The exposed ceiling beam was still the same. Chains and ropes, some with hooks, were thrown over it. The smell of blood and meat turned high was gone. The floor planks did not glisten with the dripping of blood. Here and there lay the black feathers of rooks stuck to the planks.

She let the candles roll into the large salt tray on the floor. Nothing was left in it but dust fallen from the ceiling and, in a corner, the dried-up body of a tiny fieldmouse which had not been able to climb out over the rim. The grabbing clamps to hoist the salt blocks up into the room with the pulley lay either side of the tray.

Seraphina dared to look around her, more focused. From a nail hung netting bags, into which smaller pieces of meat would be stuffed, to be hooked up to dry and age. A last burst of afternoon sun came through the window, making the dead-animal-meat room almost friendly. There was one net bag hanging still, but no meat was in it. Insects and maggots, not to forget rook beaks, over time had done away with it completely.

Seraphina lit the first candle. She dripped wax from it into the tray, and fixed the candle upright in the wax. She used its flame to do the same with the next, and the next. Often she had to stop and arch her back; this was not an easy task with a baby in one's body, which felt as if it were ready to be born. Finally, all four dozen candles were lit. They did flicker like a golden expanse.

She dragged a stepping stool under the beam, stepped on it and reached up to catch a rope. She pulled at one end of the rope to shorten it, and did her best to tie a noose and slipknot. With her eyes, she measured the height of the stool. When she was satisfied that, without the stool under her, she would dangle, she got back on the stool and focused on the burning candles. She drew the noose over her head and concentrated on the candles. She did not move. The noise she heard was that of a rook's strong wing flapping in the confined space of the chimney flue.

'Little monkey,' she moaned. 'I can't do this to you. Somehow we'll manage, just the two of us. I will be a kinder mother than my mother was to me. I will protect you from prejudice and harm.' Overcome with emotion, she nevertheless managed to utter, 'I will love you all my life.'

And then, with determination, she lifted the rope off her neck and stepped down from the stool.

'We don't need candles. They have no magic. They do not bring enlightenment. They are a waste of money.'

She waddled to the salt tray and managed to squat. She pulled in a deep breath and blew out the wicks closest to her. She inhaled again, stronger, and blew out some more. She kept blowing harder and harder. A pain shot through the lower part of her body. She felt a tearing inside her, as if her innards were being ripped out. She had started to give birth. She lowered her knickers and clamped her fingers onto the rim of the tray. The pain flared up; she needed to push. She panted and wept. It seemed to go on and on. She was assaulted by spurts of unimaginable pain. At the next onslaught, a boulder tore her body in two; the head was born. With another push, the baby's body slithered out of her.

Seraphina trembled, exhausted. She went on her knees. And there it was – a miracle on the floor beneath her, a baby girl still attached with a tube. Babies did not have such tubes. It was something which grew inside mothers. She bent forward, picked up the tube with her teeth and bit through it several times. The baby was so small and so beautiful, Seraphina started to weep, her tears falling onto the miracle human, which did not object, did not move. *Had she killed it by severing the tube?*

'Smile, little monkey,' she said and kissed the baby on its wet forehead. She still did not move. Seraphina picked her up and put her ear to the little chest. There was no heartbeat, no breathing. She shook the infant. She sat back on her haunches and rocked the infant in her arm. She begged the baby to live, promised her daughter many things. The baby she had wanted to make go away had been born dead.

Beccles appeared. 'Madam,' he said to the woman sitting in a mess on the floor, 'there is a customer for you at the barn.'

REMEMBRANCE DAY

Lewis chose to stay in the car, which he had parked on the kerb. *Not to crowd the small house* was his excuse. Melissa helped the children out of their seats in the back. As she went with them through the front garden of the end-terrace house, the children in front, bunting their new trainers against the shingles on the path, Lewis took out his smartphone, diverted his eyes from his wife and children and engaged with messages from his office.

Inside the narrow corridor of the house in East London, Melissa picked up the post from the vinyl carpet protector. An ivory-coloured, size A5 letter was loosely sealed. It bore the ER stamp of Buckingham Palace. She peeled the flap back and pulled out the letter. She flicked the switch, but the flush ceiling lamp did not work so, in the sparse light coming over her shoulder from the window above the door, she started to read.

'Dad!' she shouted with excitement.

'I'm not dead yet,' came back from the room to the right.

'Mummy,' said Florence, 'it smells funny in Granddad's house.' Isabelle, her elder sister, pinched her nose and grimaced.

251

'Listen to this.' Melissa stood at the door to the room facing south, known as the parlour in bygone days. The comfy armchair near the glass-warmed window let the old man observe who was coming and going in the road. Ducking under their mother's arm, the seven- and five-year-old girls ventured into the room. Without greeting their grandfather, they headed to the fish tank on the navy-style chest of drawers.

Melissa's father, Major Horace, now eighty-one and retired from the Royal Marines many years ago, wore a striped pullover, crumpled trousers and, as usual, no socks over his feet in tartan slippers. Melissa had bought the slippers last Christmas, because she did not want her girls to see the curved purple toenails, in case it put them off their grandfather and old people in general.

'Why is there always such a racket when you visit?' Horace challenged his daughter.

'Listen to this, Dad.' Melissa started reading the letter in her hand. '*Addressed to Major Clarkson bla bla bla. Copy to ER Protocol, signed Buckingham Palace private office.*' Melissa waved the letter in the air like a stiff flag, adding, 'The Queen.'

'Did the Queen send Granddad a letter?' asked Isabelle. Both girls looked at her, wide-eyed.

Horace sat back, lifted his right arm and let the hand flop on his bald head like a rubber starfish. 'Your mother is shouting about it, but the Queen ran out of envelopes.'

Melissa, watching her father behave the way she was used to, continued. 'I opened it because the flap was unglued and because you never read your mail. Here it goes.' She continued reading the letter.

'Dear Major Clarkson,

The committee of war heroes has decided to add a special event to the forthcoming Remembrance Day ceremony at the London Cenotaph. Having gone through our records, it emerged that you are the only remaining paratrooper of the Royal Marine unit whose efforts helped us in the Falklands War. We are aware that, since then, forty years have elapsed and that you are in your early eighties. Just before the laying of the Royal Marine wreath, you will be honoured with a medal presented by Her Majesty. There will be a special chair brought for you, after a short walk down Whitehall. Our Protocol Department will be in touch with you about details of this occasion. It would be helpful for us if you had a younger family member or friend with whom we could liaise.'

'They plan to put the doddery hat on me on Remembrance Day for all to see.'

'Dad, this is an honour. I wish Mum were still here for this. She spent so much time alone while you were warring abroad.'

'It was preferable to warring at home,' he replied. 'Absence makes the heart grow fonder. Isn't that how the saying goes?'

Melissa, ignoring him, continued. 'You do realise it will be on the telly throughout the Commonwealth, the world. You were a major, the most experienced, the leader in your unit. Parachuting onto a moving warship is the bravest thing people can imagine. The Queen in person will step up to you and give you a medal.'

'You start your racket again,' said Horace. 'I am simply the one who hasn't croaked yet. It would be more useful if Her Majesty gave me a new set of teeth which fitted. And no, I am not yomping down Whitehall being

253

ogled at, like a bull in a cattle auction. This letter is the very example of why I don't open my mail.'

The girls, left out of the conversation, were tapping the glass to make the goldfish move around.

'Granddad says don't rock the fish tank. You'll knock it over,' said Florence.

'The water has gone all green,' replied Isabelle. 'We can't see the admiral.'

'He has gone into the sunken ship, stupid,' said Florence, tilting her head to try and get a better view of the fish behind the glass.

'Correct, my little pet,' said their grandfather. 'Admiral Farquhar has gone into the Malacca Straits, where HMS Waterwitch sank.'

'And where it stinks,' Florence added.

'Can we get back to Remembrance Sunday, to which Granddad has been invited, please?' Melissa unhooked the long handle of the handbag from her shoulder and plopped the bag down on the imitation Persian carpet.

'It stinks like the dead mouse we found in the garden.'

'The one with the worms on it.'

'It's going to be a big occasion for you, Dad.' Melissa spoke over the girls, which she had learnt to do to still be able to have a conversation with adults. 'I'll let Buckingham Palace know that I will act as your coordinator,' Melissa said to her father.

'Yes, Admiral.' The old man mock-saluted his daughter.

'You'll need a haircut, a new suit, shirt and tie. I will find out from Protocol what colour the tie should be.'

'Strewth,' spluttered Horace. 'While you're launched, why not ask them which side I should wear my pecker in the trousers.'

'Ok, I'll add that to the questions.'

'You what? Don't you dare. Anyway, I won't be doing this circus act.'

'They're counting on you. It is good for British morale. If you don't want to do it for yourself, do it for the men in your unit.'

★

Six o'clock Sunday morning on the thirteenth day of November, Remembrance Day. Melissa woke up tired. One after the other, her daughters had appeared in the bedroom, saying they were scared and needed to sleep with her. At midnight, Lewis, his hair tousled, groggily left for the visitor's room to make space in the bed. In the early hours, Isabelle smacked her mother in the eye in her agitated sleep, and Florence wet the bed.

'It was an accident. An accident. Stop crying, please.'

'Mummy, when can we see Granddad getting the medal?'

'In five hours, I hope.'

Lewis asked whether he could help with anything. He had already laid out breakfast in the kitchen. Bread slices were slotted into the toaster ready for the push. Melissa gave him a slack-mouthed 'thank you' and massaged her nape.

'We need to be at Granddad's at eight-thirty, to bolster his confidence till the official car comes for him at half-past nine. After that, we will have plenty of time to drive into town, park in the hotel's private car park, enjoy the complimentary tea, coffee and croissants, and then taxi to Whitehall for our position in the crowd. That means leaving here in thirty minutes. OK guys, you will find your clothes on the chairs in the kitchen. Isabelle, this side, Florence over here. No dramas today, otherwise the Queen will get very angry with you two.'

'Will she cut off our heads like the Queen of Hearts in Alice in Wonderland?' asked Florence.

No sooner had the girls inspected the clothes to wear than a problem flared up.

'I want to wear my new red dress with the clown on it.'

'If Isabelle is allowed to wear her red dress, I am not wearing this.' Florence lifted up the chosen denim dungarees and dropped them on the floor. 'No way.' She crossed her arms.

'You can't wear a red dress with a clown, because *you* don't have one, *nanana*.'

'That wasn't kind, Isabelle. Please, girls, don't be difficult today.' Melissa shrugged her shoulders in a *I can't cope* gesture. She was leaving the room. 'I have to get dressed, too, and the taupe suit is too tight at the waist. I have nothing else that's appropriate.'

'Yes, I am sure that would be fine,' Lewis said, not having listened. He was focused on Isabelle. Calmly, he asked his daughter, 'Are you a clown?'

'No, Daddy.' The seven-year-old's eyelids flickered nervously in anticipation of being tricked by her father.

'Then draw your own conclusion from this.' Turning back to his wife still at the door, he said, 'Your dad will be on the news, not us.'

'We, as Dad's family, might be singled out by the cameras. You never know. The preparations the Palace have made are thought through, right to the last detail. Pretty impressive. No wonder we won the war in the Falklands. I am actually proud of my Dad. There never has been the right time for me to say it.'

Lewis kept to himself, which was an advisable thing to do.

'I'll go and do my hair.' Melissa disappeared down the corridor.

'Don't take too long,' Lewis shouted after her, tapping his wristwatch. 'We leave in twenty minutes.'

'Shit' was heard, amended to 'sugar' right after.

Isabelle ran out of the kitchen after her mother, tripping over a white Hedwig owl.

'Ouch,' she called out theatrically, hopping on one leg.

'That comes from not putting Lego pieces back into the toy chest.' The way Lewis forked through his thick hair showed that he was up against a big job as a father today. Horace, his father-in-law, may have hopped out of planes for hand-to-hand combat with Argentinians, but he had never put little girls into clothes, brushed their messed hair into ponytails, and endured the 'ouches' without giving up. Today was especially trying. The moment the bows on clips held back the fringes, they were shaken off the head.

'I need to wear a red bow to go with my red dress, Daddy.'

'I thought we decided you wouldn't wear the red dress today?'

'I've changed my mind.' Isabelle tousled her hair to make the point she had her own will. She took off her pyjamas and ran around the kitchen nude. She paused because her foot was hurting. One hand steadying herself against the kitchen table, she lifted it. There was blood. She started to cry quietly but meaningfully.

'Blood,' gasped Florence, who had gone to investigate. 'It is owl blood. You might become magic.'

'It hurts.'

'Don't scream.' Lewis looked at the wound. 'It's just a scratch. We'll find a plaster and you'll be as right as rain.'

'Why is rain right?' asked Florence.

'We can discuss this another time. Right now, we need Mummy to bring a plaster.'

'No. We need magic potion.'

'Melissa!' Lewis yelled into the corridor.

★

Ten minutes later, they were all in the Citroen C5 ready to drive off. Lewis stuck the key into the ignition, depressed the clutch but hesitated. 'You have both been to the loo?' He turned in his seat.

'Oh. I forgot.'

Lewis sighed. Melissa got out of the car and pulled her five-year-old towards the house entrance, with the left hand searching for the house key in the bag hanging from her shoulder.

'Now we're fifteen minutes late,' Lewis complained, before finally driving off.

'It's going to be an important day,' said Melissa to the girls. 'We are driving to Granddad to make sure he is dressed and ready to be fetched by a car paid for by the Queen.'

'Cool,' admired Isabelle.

★

Once they were parked, as a family they walked up to the major's front door.

'What are these sticks in pots?' asked Isabelle.

'We gave some plants to your granddad to make the front garden more cheerful,' replied Melissa.

Both girls looked up at her, expecting more.

'Granddad is too old to water them. They are sleeping. When spring comes, they will bloom again.'

Neither girl believed that.

Using Melissa's spare key, they squeezed into Granddad's house. Down the corridor, prints of warships on the wall, Horace was in the dark kitchen, nudging pills across the kitchen table with a long fingernail.

'I've come to prepare you for your day,' said Melissa loudly.

Horace jumped up and turned, looking startled.

'I've brought Lewis and the girls to help.'

There was a heavy, cold-shouldered silence in the small kitchen.

She sat down at the table; the marks on its top bore witness to many happy and bad moments from her

259

childhood. Melissa held out her hands to her father. He did not react. It was too intimate a move in the chill of the situation. She turned her hands over, open palms towards him. He hesitated. She noticed and was encouraged.

'You're still in your pyjamas.' Melissa checked her smartphone. 'It is a quarter to nine. Yesterday, I came with the new shirt and tie, and laid out what you will wear today on the spare room bed. Dad, I can't force you into your clothes. You have to do this yourself.'

'And I called you on the landline this morning to tell you that I wasn't feeling up to it. My war wound is flaring up.'

'It had better flare down, because your limo will be here at nine-thirty.'

'Once the unit was on the *Seguí*, we had less than five minutes to knock out the Exocet launcher. People think there are mattresses on destroyer decks for us to land on. My broken ribcage. Oooh...' he moaned, and popped the last pill left on the table into his mouth.

'Is that Codeine you're taking still? The one Mum called medicine for your moans and groans?'

'Three hundred were killed in man-to-man combat in one day. Afterwards, many arms and legs were sawn off by the army doctors. For my crushed ribcage, they gave me a prescription for this white pill. That's all that could be done for me.'

'You've told me that before, Dad. Codeine is a painkiller after an injury. The Falklands War was over forty years ago.'

'And see, my injury is still hurting. That's why I have a repeat prescription.'

'Let's get you dressed.' Melissa took off her taupe suit jacket, draped it over the curved chairback and resolutely pushed the sleeves of her blouse up her arms.

'Careful.' Horace warded her off. 'I can't put tight clothes over my chest. It hurts too much.' He eyed his daughter with fright.

'You have lived with this all these years *and* worn clothes.'

'Only because I didn't run to the doctor complaining about pain all these years.' He winced, his face creased.

'You certainly convinced someone in the surgery to still prescribe you Codeine.'

'It keeps me going.'

'Not fast enough. Soon, the courtesy car will be here. Do you want to go in your pyjamas?'

'Oh, my God,' he objected, his head tilted back, his mouth open slack. 'My head, my head. Help! I have such a headache. It's just come on. Migraine. My head is coming off. I told you I threw up this morning, but you don't listen.'

'I listen. I'll make you a cup of tea and you'll take two Paracetamols and everything will be fine.' Melissa dug around in her bag for the packet.

'No, no,' he shouted. 'With Codeine I mustn't take any other medication.'

Lewis, standing quiet near the door, took out his smartphone. After a while tapping, he looked up.

'Anything?' Melissa asked.

'Compatibility between Codeine and Paracetamol is too medically specific to find an answer for online.' Lewis put the phone back. 'Give him Paracetamol. I am sure it'll be all right.'

261

Melissa studied the back of the pill packet. 'Warning. Do not take anything else while taking this medicine.'

Horace gave the tabletop one bash with his large hand. 'You want to inherit this house! I sussed you out the moment you proposed to my daughter.' The major's finger was pointed at his son-in-law.

'I'll call Dad's surgery.' Melissa worked on her mobile before holding it to her ear, listening for a while. 'It's Sunday,' she said in exasperation. 'Nobody there to help us. The recording suggests we call 111 in case of an emergency, which this isn't really.'

'The broken ribs must have perforated something, which has travelled to my brain,' said Horace. 'I have a hell of a headache.'

'Damn it, Melissa,' Lewis said to his wife. 'You have to use some authority with your father. For the whole nation, he is an important person today. We have to deliver him to the Cenotaph in one piece and on time.'

'Spoken like a man,' croaked Horace, 'but a dumb one. I can't go to the Cenotaph, because I am injured and seriously ill.'

Melissa dialled 111. She was answered right away and tried to formulate her question about Codeine interfering with Paracetamol as best she could. She was clearly encouraged to elaborate on this, and then was asked by the operator to give them the address. The conversation was over. She turned to Lewis. 'They don't want to take the risk of making a mistake and are coming here to see the patient.'

'There you have it,' gloated the major. 'I am an emergency and can't go to the Cenotaph.'

'How long will it take them to get here?' asked Lewis anxiously. 'We really haven't got…'

'Sunday, little traffic.'

'Mummy, the flashing light is here.'

A man and a woman in green uniforms entered the house, feet in Swedish clogs. 'I am Helen, and this is Alan. Where is the patient?'

They were shown into the kitchen where Horace sat slumped, his head held in both hands.

'Can he answer questions?' Helen asked.

Melissa nodded.

'If you ask me intelligent questions.' Horace came to life. He noticed Alan was holding a clipboard. 'That's the one writing it all down, is it?'

'Helen and Alan are here to tell us whether you can take Paracetamol with the Codeine you've already taken,' Melissa explained.

'Full name, please,' said Alan.

'Major Horace Stanley Clarkson.'

'Have you lived in this country for the last year?'

'I've served this country since my balls dropped.'

'Are you diabetic?'

'I am mentally healthy.'

Alan was scribbling on his board, his back against the wall.

'Do you live alone in this house?'

'Haven't found another one yet to look after me.'

'Is there anywhere we can examine you lying down?'

'I've only just managed to get up, despite my injuries.'

Helen went to look into the other two rooms and came back to the kitchen. 'No sofa downstairs,' she reported.

263

The two paramedics looked at each other. Helen nodded.

'Give us a minute,' she said, and they both left the kitchen to go outside to their ambulance.

'They're useless,' Horace commented. 'One look at the state of me and they scarper.'

The paramedics soon returned with a folded gurney on wheels. Moving some kitchen chairs out of the way, they opened up the narrow rolling bed by unfolding its legs and clicking them into locks.

'If he hops up on this, we might get a first idea of the problem,' said Helen.

Melissa and Lewis helped the major onto the narrow stretcher.

'He took twenty-five milligrams of Codeine at about eight this morning,' said Melissa. 'And, for his headache, we would like to give him two Paracetamols, if that is chemically safe?'

Helen bent down towards Horace. 'From one to ten, how bad is your headache?'

'Eleven and a half.'

'What do you take Codeine for? Do you know?'

'My ribcage was broken in a commando raid off South Georgia.'

'Gosh,' replied Helen. 'And it still hurts?'

'Evidently.'

Helen stood undecided. 'Twenty-five milligrams of Codeine is an important dose. I am afraid we are not permitted to make any decisions concerning serious previous injuries. We are here to give first aid to accidents on the spot, making the best of the golden hour. I suggest we take you in for further assessment.'

'What? Is that necessary?' Melissa looked shocked. 'Where will you take him?'

'The Chelsea and Westminster Hospital.'

'That is quite close to the Cenotaph. My father has to be in Whitehall by ten-thirty. Latest.'

'Why?'

'The Queen has invited him to participate in the Remembrance Day ceremony, and she will give him a medal at exactly ten-fifty.'

'Gosh,' Helen said again.

They freed the brake and rolled Horace out of his kitchen, not before Helen pointed out that the condition of the aquarium she noticed in the front room could potentially become a health hazard as it might attract mosquitoes.

'In November in East London?' came from the gurney, as they pulled it along. 'I can tell you about swarms of bloodsucking mosquitoes from purulent swamps.'

'I'd rather you didn't.'

Outside, they loaded the patient into the ambulance. Melissa, with the packet of Paracetamol and a small bottle of water, climbed in after her father. The ambulance drove off.

'Why isn't the ambulance making wee wee wee?' asked Isabelle.

'Maybe because it is Sunday morning,' suggested Lewis half-heartedly. 'We'd better go to the hotel, which is open to us from nine to ten. We will later meet up with Mummy and, God willing, your stubborn grandfather.'

'What is a Cenotaph?'

'It is an empty grave for us to remember all those brave soldiers who were killed in wars defending Britain. Every year, the Queen, the royal family, and heads of military units gather for a small ceremony to remember them.'

'Only the heads?'

'Let's go. Loo first.'

★

From the hospital parking lot, help came out of the A&E door.

'So,' said a nurse, watching the gurney with Horace being taken out of the back of the ambulance, 'this is the war hero.'

Horace lay quiet between the white sheets. Melissa smiled into the sun. The ambulance drive and the oxygen into his nostrils had rendered her father considerably more docile.

Stepping as quietly as she could with her high heels on the linoleum floor, Melissa escorted the gurney, her warm hand clasped over her father's, as he looked up at the ceiling passing over him.

'A lot of the bulbs have gone,' he could not help pointing out. 'You've got an inefficient maintenance team.'

'It's just like in your corridor back home, isn't it, Dad?'

'Ouch, my chest,' he wailed, and was moved along faster.

Father and daughter ended up in a curtained-off

cubicle. However, before Helen and Alan could tighten the brakes, they were politely asked to move the patient out again as the cubicle was for an emergency.

'Ruptured appendix,' a nurse explained.

After standing around, Melissa checking and rechecking her mobile for time, they were directed to a lift. Fourth floor. It was exactly nine-thirty.

There was more rolling along speckled linoleum to a clinical investigation ward, and they came to a stop at an empty bed in a bay for four men, the bed closest to the door.

'We'll pop you onto the proper bed,' said the nurse. 'Dr Puranasompop will see you shortly. He specialises in medicine for the elderly.'

'This is all taking so much time.' Melissa sounded despairing, as she watched the paramedics, together with a ward nurse, transfer her father onto a bed.

'I heard,' the nurse said, 'your father is a famous commando. What courage it must take to parachute into a skirmish.'

'Jumping is the easy bit.' Horace had to put a word in. 'The landing is the problem.'

'Here he comes.' There was a special ring of awe to the nurse's voice. The doctor in a white coat sailed into the bay.

'Good of you to come and see me at such short notice, Dr Puranasompop,' said Horace, lifting his head off the pillow.

'You remembered my name,' the doctor smiled, pleased. 'Not many can do that.'

'With the Navy, I've been to the most remote places.

Some of the wogs living there have impossible names. It is a Navy rule to treat them with respect.'

'Dad, remember what we talked about.' Melissa bristled with outraged tension. 'It is a rule in the medical profession to be polite, no matter to whom.'

She sat down in the armchair.

'War wound,' the doctor took up in the manner of a professional, who skips over trivia unrelated to medicine. 'May I?' The nurse uncovered Horace's chest. The doctor touched along the ribcage. 'Tell me if this hurts. That?' he probed. Several times Horace winced, and once he flinched.

'There is obviously some tenderness,' said the doctor, 'but I cannot feel fractures, which does not mean there aren't any. We need an X-ray.'

'Now?' said Melissa in alarm. 'There is no time for that. We just want to know what he can take for his headache while on Codeine.'

'I'll make the major a priority,' replied the doctor. 'Today is a quiet day. I saw no queues at the scanning department on my way here.'

The nurse unlocked the bed brakes. Two patients called out to the doctor, claiming to need him urgently, but the doctor left the bay and kept on walking, despite the men calling after him.

'Why aren't we setting off for the X-ray?' Melissa grabbed the headboard ready to push.

'We have to wait for the hospital porters,' said the nurse. 'Only they are cleared to push beds.'

'My father will not make it to the celebration the way things are going.' Melissa turned to Horace. 'Dad, you are well enough to get out of this bed and come with me now. We'll slip downstairs and grab a taxi.'

'Aye aye, Admiral.'

She peeled back a corner of the blanket and pushed his body towards the edge. She helped him sit up and got one leg out from under the blanket. With slow manoeuvring, Horace managed to get the second leg to join the first. Once he was sitting upright at the side of the bed, she tried to help him to stand, but he snatched back his hands and crossed them over his injured chest.

'My head hurts,' he cried. 'I feel dizzy.'

'What are you doing with our patient?' Matron, for she wore a black uniform with red trim, challenged Melissa.

'He is perfectly able to move about despite his headache, which I strongly suspect is all in his head,' said Melissa. 'I know him better than you do.'

'Headaches are usually all in the head, and I am in charge of the patients on this ward. Please refrain from interfering.'

At that moment, two men in blue scrubs arrived. 'Clarkson,' one said. 'X-ray.'

'Urgent,' said Matron, as if they could only communicate in an abbreviated way.

'Major Clarkson has to come with me,' insisted Melissa. 'Right now, he needs to take two Paracetamol and a taxi.'

'Your father stays here,' replied the Matron firmly. 'Doctor's orders.'

'A Royal Marine outranks a quack.'

'Honestly…' The outraged matron was able to lift

Horace's weighty legs and push them back onto the mattress. At the same time, Melissa grabbed his hands and pulled him back up into a sitting position.

'For God's sake, let go of me, both of you,' cried Horace. 'Two broads fighting over me. I remember a dive in Rangoon…'

His weight was now tilted too much over the edge of the mattress. He fell out of bed, which was not such a distance bearing in mind he had jumped from planes; however, on falling, he hit the side of his head on the corner of the metal bedside table.

Once he was back on the bed, his head wrapped in gauze, the two burly porters pushed the bed out of the bay to take him to the scanning department, while Melissa drafted a text to Protocol in the Palace, informing them that the major was unable to attend. There was no public signal for cell phones inside the hospital, so she opened the window in the bay and, holding the phone in her outstretched arms, she pressed *Send*. She also found that Lewis had left four messages. *Where the hell are you? The Queen has gone up to stand on the balcony. We are in Whitehall and have to take up position. Isabelle is in her red dress – don't ask.*

I'm doing my best, she texted back and told herself to take deep breaths.

The other patients, all three of them, had pushed their emergency buttons. The red light over the ward entrance was flashing. It brought back Matron. The patients demanded the television be switched on.

'The Remembrance Day ceremony is about to start,' one of them spoke for the rest.

'Oh.' Matron checked the upside-down watch pinned to her chest. 'Of course.' She switched the TV on.

Melissa heard the blood rushing in her ears caused by stress, but at least the men in blue returned, pushing her dad and parking him back in his spot. Better even, Dr Puranasompop returned. 'I've had them send the X-ray to the orthopaedic consultant.'

'Much damage to his ribs, I guess?' Melissa ventured.

'I couldn't see without a light box.'

'Hey, doc,' a patient shouted. 'Remembrance Day ceremony has just started.'

The military band approached the Cenotaph, playing a tune heavy on trumpets and trombones. Dr Puranasompop remained looking up at the television, riveted. The bearskins were followed by the Royal Scots Dragoon Guards. *Rule Britannia* was played with intermittent strong cymbal clashes. Following the band came the heads of the three Services. The pipe and drums of the Royal Regiment of Scotland led the civilian services, while Horace retched and announced he was going to throw up, and then did so onto his bedding. The Forces' chaplain marched on, the Lord Bishop of London at his heels. A short, poignant service was held by the bishop, during which all dignitaries bowed their heads. To the side of the road, a red upholstered chair was standing almost forlorn, the one intended for Major Horace Clarkson.

Up on the balcony, the Queen stood, a bunch of poppies pushed into the diamante brooch on her black jacket. Her expression was serene, a softly serious mouth.

The Welsh Guards came next. Alone, Prince Charles bore a red wreath of poppies which he lay in the name of the Queen at the foot of the Cenotaph. The Lord Mayor of London followed suit, and then the Commonwealth ambassadors, all carrying red poppy wreaths and all placing them at the foot of the Cenotaph in an orderly way. Melissa strained to see Lewis and the girls in the crowd filling the pavement.

When the allied troop veterans paraded, Dr Puranasompop stood to attention. 'My father.' He pointed at the TV. 'The man in the wheelchair. He served in the Bihar regiment and became a sergeant. An honour for my family. I have four children. They are out there watching their grandfather.'

Melissa saw an old Sikh being pushed in his chair by a soldier. The old man wore a pale blue turban and had a rug over his legs. His right hand was at his temple, saluting continuously.

'Dad is ninety-seven and received the Meritorious Service Medal from the Queen's hand,' continued Dr Puranasompop. A collection of medals showed on the chest of the white-bearded man. Melissa noticed Dr Puranasompop's tear-glazed eyes.

When the camera panned down Whitehall to give a wider picture of the event, Melissa realised that the red upholstered chair intended for her father had been taken away. Tears burnt in her eyes. Dad's moment was gone.

Melissa returned to her father's bedside. Two nurses were changing his blanket. Matron reported that the orthopaedic consultant was considering operating, as he had a free slot in theatre and was worried about broken bones damaging surrounding internal organs. This could have infected the blood, to cause the severe headache.

'An operation? Now?' Melissa shrieked. 'What operation?'

'Please don't upset yourself.' Matron touched Melissa's forearm. 'They fasten the broken ribs with plates and screws. Almost a routine operation.'

'It's five to eleven,' Melissa said resignedly.

Dr Puranasompop pulled himself away from the television screen. 'Has the consultant been? He will come and have a look at your father before the prepping for the operation.'

'I believe he is on his way now,' put in Matron.

As Big Ben started donging for the two minutes silence, the consultant came into the bay. In silence, Horace was helped out of bed and made to stand next to it. The consultant touched Horace's chest.

'Here.' Horace broke the silence in the room, the hospital, the nation. 'Right here. The broken bone sticking out right here, trying to pierce through my flesh. A serious war wound from the Falklands.'

The last post was played, the bugle touching the most hardened of hearts.

The consultant laughed out loud.

'That,' he spluttered, putting his right hand over the bump on Horace's pale old chest. 'That,' he had problems forming a sentence, 'is your sternum.'

Horace looked dumbfounded.

'The end of your rib plate,' explained the consultant. 'Everyone has a sternum. In men, the sternum is a bit more protruding than in the female skeleton. There is

273

nothing wrong with your ribcage. Nothing at all. Apart from the bump on your head, which can be fixed with two Paracetamols.'

'That brings us back to why we are here in the first place.' Melissa glowered reproachfully, as she poked around her ribs to locate her own sternum.

'I'll write to your GP to make them stop prescribing Codeine as of now,' said the consultant. 'Forty years of opiates paid for by the NHS. If it wasn't for the fact he's in his eighties, I might do more about it,' he muttered, on his way back to wherever his man cave was in the hospital.

Matron switched the television off. A vegetable smell preceded the lunch trolleys being rolled along the speckled flooring. The men in the bay sat up.

★

At the hospital exit, Melissa texted Lewis, before calling an Uber taxi to bring Horace back home.

'Aren't we going to the Cenotaph?' said Horace. 'The Queen wants to give me a medal for my bravery, remember?'

Irritated, Melissa told her father to get it into his head that the Remembrance Day ceremony was over and that everyone had dispersed and was going home.

'But I can't go home. I need to stay in this hospital. My headache, remember?'

'Dad, for the first time in my life, I'm telling you that you are acting like an idiot. You heard the doctor say there is nothing wrong with you. Nothing at all.'

'I feel faint.'

'No, you don't. A taxi is on its way.'

Horace slumped against a pillar and started, ever so slowly, to slide down it, feet guiding the body into a bent position. He slid down further, until he lay flat on the floor, white hair tousled up against the pillar still.

'Dad,' she shouted. 'Enough is enough.'

Paramedics, who saw what had happened, came running with a gurney, onto which they hoisted Horace. An oxygen mask was put over his face. Running, they went back with him to A&E and disappeared from sight.

'This is the day from hell,' Melissa said out loud, following the paramedics back into the building.

In A&E, this time her father was considered urgent enough to be given a curtain-enclosed cubicle. Melissa texted Lewis to explain that Horace had played another trick and was back in the hospital.

'Are you a relative?' a doctor asked, before letting her in to see him. Three figures stood around the bed.

'Can you identify this man?'

'Well, yes. He is my father, Major Horace Stanley Clarkson.' She gave a shoulder shrug.

'We are sorry to have to tell you, but your father has just died.'

'No, he hasn't,' she said.

'Matron, who was the last to be in charge of the patient, reported that he hit his head on the corner of the bedside table during a struggle, in which you were trying to pull him out of bed. A blow to the head can cause a brain bleed, and lead to death in a short time. I am sorry for your loss.'

★

He was a brave man. Afraid of his own humanity, which seemed to him a weakness, he relied on the disciplines trained into him. Encased in his uniform, he felt invincible. Jumping into the void was, each time, a personal suicide, and he landed as a beast, alien to himself. That is the sacrifice men make in wars. They abandon themselves for others. Death is not that big of a deal under those circumstances.

THE ANTHROPOLOGY
STUDENT

'Don't go away,' said Professor Cadogan. 'I have an announcement to make.'

On the benches in the lecture hall, the anthropology students remained seated. They were in their second year and still in the habit of obeying teachers. They did not even start to chat, but waited with anticipation for the professor to go on.

'Google sees the need for a new encyclopaedia of anthropology, which gives access to information about the daily habits of mankind in exposed places on our planet. It will take about three years to put together. The university will be paid for this work. Man's behaviour determines humanity. Geographical location naturally impinges on man's behaviour. We are talking contemporary anthropology. Any questions so far?'

Nobody drew attention to themselves.

'As you know, there is a *practical* planned in your degree. Up to now, it consisted of students mostly doing classical anthropology, digs, or biological anthropology, cataloguing in museums. What I am able to offer you today is to put your names down to live for nine months with humans, observe their personal behaviour in extreme living conditions. The collected data you provide will add up to a comprehensive pool of knowledge accessible to all. The beneficiaries, apart from PhD students, will be the medical profession, the business world, governments, even things as mundane as travel agents, et cetera. Some of you,' with his finger, the professor drew a half-circle over the students, 'will be the ones who can deliver and, at the same time, substantiate your thesis.'

'What kind of extreme living conditions are we talking about?' asked a student.

'Anything.'

'Give us an example, please.'

Peter, sitting next to Alice, said quietly, 'Cadogan is a schmuck. He's the one who gave me a C for my osteology paper.'

Alice pushed her knees together and put her hands on them. Every word the professor now said would be important later. She had to ignore Peter and concentrate.

Cadogan read from a paper. 'One of the assignments was a stay with the Orang Asli in the Malaysian jungle. It has been cancelled. The Orang Asli tribes have been almost completely driven out by deforestation. Another is the igloo life in the Arctic. That is still available.'

'Brrrr,' went Alice. 'Who would want to do that?'

Cadogan continued. 'Here is the list of the places you can go to. I'll leave it on the table over there. On your way out, you can put your name against your choice. That will be a start. Much more will have to be sorted out later. You will have to learn some basics of the language your assigned hosts speak. Once in place, you will almost certainly not have access to wi-fi or any other means of communication. Those who can will send in their monthly observations; the others will keep a detailed journal, ideally with sketches. Yes,' he added, 'this is the way it used to be in the times of Dr Livingstone.'

He paused, then raised his index finger to make another point. 'You are placed alone. That way, you integrate and observe uninfluenced. Do not get emotionally involved with them. Keep in mind you are there to collect habits, foibles and ordinary behaviour, day and night, right down to the nitty gritty. You do not speculate on emotions, religion or life philosophies. You will live nine months as if you had been born into that situation.'

At the table with the list, there was shoving and elbowing. By the time Alice got hold of the pen and the list, many places had names against them.

'Good luck.' Peter tapped her shoulder shortly and threaded himself out of the crowd. Alice saw his name against 'Boat people in Thailand'. She read down the list fast and with fear. No-one had chosen the igloos yet. When she came across 'High Alpine hut, Switzerland', she quickly signed 'Alice Saunders' against it.

By the time she emerged from the building, Peter had vanished. Would she ever see him again? Nine months was a long time. Extreme experiences usually imprinted themselves on the character of people who lived through them. It changed them. Her parents would not be happy with her disappearance up into the Alps. Had they not pushed her to do law and walk in Daddy's footsteps? Too late for that. She texted Peter. *You left without waiting for me. A coffee to talk would have been nice.*

Back came a reply, almost immediately. *Get used to hardship. I did you a favour.*

Pig. She typed, sent it and went home to search on Swiss mountain areas, eating habits and lifestyle. She found little useful information, which confirmed that what the university was asking the anthro students to do was necessary.

*

Three months later, Alice, wearing a plaid shirt, bootleg jeans and leather trekking shoes, was on the platform in Sierre. So far, the Eurostar and TGV had brought her to Geneva, and from there she had taken a train into the Valais. Alice was in high spirits. The trip had been a joy. What she had seen of Switzerland so far was beautiful. September had brought warm colours to the trees. The sun shone; many proud flags fluttered in front of hotels and restaurants. Everything looked crisp and clean, even the windows of the train carriages. She had chosen well. Her thoughts went to Peter who, by now, was probably on a rocking Chinese fishing boat attached to others to form a flotilla. His host was probably already making him fish. Boat people ate fish three times a day. Perhaps a crab here and there to break up the monotony.

A uniformed stationmaster appeared, and a small mountain train arrived at the exact time predicted by the itinerary Alice had been given in Geneva. She picked up her rucksack. What made it so heavy was the large German-English dictionary, as well as the ten bottles of shampoo, the only kind which kept her long hair untangled after a wash. She got onto the train.

Shortly after departure, they gained height by winding up in wide loops. Sierre, far below in the valley, receded and looked toy-like. The train rattled through forest areas and tunnels, and the passengers sat in the dark for a while. They emerged onto the pre-alp, where cattle stood and gaped at the train.

Milk and cheese, Alice thought. *Better than fish.* She tried to contact Peter again, having had no message since arriving at Geneva station. She realised that either he or she had now moved beyond communication. Cell hell felt like stepping off a building into the void. She had to be strong. Peter had said that she had landed a cushy assignment. She knew that this was true; some students would have to eat barbecued howler monkey. Some would have to depend on their body warmth in temperatures of minus 25 Celsius. 'That's when your hot piss comes in handy.' She had not understood.

For her, a Miss Greta Huber was waiting to spend nine months of shared living, two women in an isolated place. If Greta managed to live like that, so could Alice. Besides, it would contribute greatly to her PhD.

'Guten Morgen, Fräulein Huber,' Alice practised. It was, of course, afternoon, but that word she had not yet learnt. The train slowed to engage on a narrow bridge over a deep canyon, several jagged rocks sticking up below them. The passengers looked out of the windows down into it with interest. Alice hid her eyes from the sight.

In Sprieglen, the train came to a stop. Sprieglen was the last stop on Alice's itinerary. She got off the train. She was the only one doing so. The heavy rucksack was on her back. The train snailed away. Alice felt the loss of it, as if it had been a familiar cocoon, familiar because it had linked her to where she had come from – somewhere safer. In Geneva, she had been able to communicate with her parents. Dad insisted he would come and rescue her, whenever needed. According to him, PhDs were achieved with brain and not through physical hardship. *Ridiculous£*, he had texted, mistaking the pound sign for the exclamation mark. *Please come home as soon as you can, Mum speaking.*

Alice walked away from the station towards the sunny expanse in front of it. She was to be picked up by *local transport*.

A peasant pulled a calf behind him, the ring in the soft pink leaky nostril of the animal linked to a chain in the man's hand – that could not possibly be *local transport*.

Alice pulled a writing pad from her rucksack and started to note down the calf, the nose, the setting, when a man in his sixties approached. *He was…* she hesitated with her pen over her pad. What was he? Heidi's grandfather, having fallen on hard times?

'English,' the creature with few teeth in his mouth uttered. 'Come.' Alice picked up the rucksack to follow the man. Limping slightly, he led her to a jeep parked on the verge outside the village.

'Fräulein Huber of the Donnerhorn,' she said, to avoid a misunderstanding.

He nodded his white-haired head and helped her to

climb into the passenger seat, by way of a foot placed onto the hub cab of the jeep.

He drove off along a tarmacked lane. She noticed a loose button dangling on his canvas jacket. Was this a nitty gritty she had to note down?

Heidi's grandfather drove on with élan. To her concern, Alice noticed that the lane had become a narrow, pebbled track. It became steep. Just as she was coping with this, after a bend a sheer mountain wall appeared. Grandfather headed towards it. The track had surely to come to an end, she told herself. But no, it continued. This pathetic excuse for a road seemed to have been glued against the granite wall. Surely this was not drivable? For starters, the jeep was wider than the road, the support unsafe. Alice scraped nail gloss off her thumb with her teeth. The jeep stalled; her heart seemed to have done the same. The silence was sinister, until the drawn-out whistle of a bird of prey disturbed it. The engine did not restart.

The man swore in Swiss German. She looked at him, her front teeth clattering. He brushed over his grey beard almost lovingly.

'What do we do now?' she panted.

To her horror, he stood up in the vehicle, even though they were only hanging onto the mountainside by a thread. He bent over the windshield and, with his fist, hit the bonnet of the jeep, while cursing it, before falling back into his seat. Stones and small rocks drizzled away from underneath the car; she watched them hop down into the abyss, a whole jolly crowd of them. The motor started up.

Grandfather began to sing. It wasn't *Nearer my God to Thee*. It was some *dumbeli bum pum* tune. He was old. He did not care about falling off the road and dying. She asked him to stop the car. She would walk. He smiled at her.

'OK, OK,' he said.

'Don't grin at me. Watch the road. Oh my God!'

She closed her eyes. When she dared open them again, she saw they had made it past the sheer wall and were driving on grassland, heading for a wooded patch. It was steep up again. To her surprise, Grandfather stopped the jeep, shut down the motor and got out of the vehicle. He pulled a few envelopes from his breast pocket and gave them to Alice. The letters were addressed to Greta Huber.

He pointed up the mountain and, on the bonnet of the car, he made his stubby fingers imitate walking legs, until he pulled his hand away and blew at the burn the scalding bonnet over the hot engine had caused him. She had to walk the rest of the way up. That was not printed in her itinerary.

She shrugged her shoulders. 'Which way?' she asked in some panic.

He understood. He limped to a fir tree nearby. On its trunk was a dash of yellow paint. 'OK' and 'OK' and 'OK' meant that she had to follow the yellow paint signs to get her to the Donnerhorn.

'OK?'

They parted. With a mighty exhaust bang, which echoed against the mountain side twice, he turned and drove off back down. She had yellow paint to get her to some safety. When they had said high alps, they had meant high alps. Eventually, there would be the hut, and Greta Huber, who was switched on enough to put her name forward to host an English anthropology student.

Alice entered the wood. The yellow signs were well placed and clear enough. She wondered whether Greta had painted them. Maybe she did not lead a solitary life?

The tall conifers stood close together, which made it dark. Goethe had written about a man with a dead child in his arms riding through the dark woods. She looked around her. What made it odd and threatening was the silence. No birds lived in these trees. No squirrels chased each other. No shafts of sunlight brightened the thick, mossy ground.

Alice walked steadily and regretted having packed the shampoo. Eventually, she would emerge above tree-level and see the dwelling, a welcoming host in front. After that, nine months of interesting observation awaited her.

Alice stopped in fright. Through the trees she had noticed something which should not be there – pale-blue, dangling. She quickened her steps. It was a man hanging from a branch, a noose around his neck. A suicide. She took the rucksack off and ran to the tragic site.

The man was young, an adolescent who had decided to die. But his dangling feet in socks were twitching. He was still alive! A râle came from his throat. The hemp rope around his neck was stiff from dried wax or glue and so rigid that the noose had not tightened enough.

Alice saw the tree trunk which the would-be suicide

had kicked away from underneath him, and she rolled it back to where it had been.

Once safe, she helped him down. Pulling the stiff rope over his head, she noticed how chaffed and bruised his neck was. She also noticed how badly he smelled. Urine had darkened his trousers in patches. Freed of the noose, he sank to the ground, overcome by the enormity of his failed undertaking.

'Greta Huber of the Donnerhorn,' she said to him, sticking to her own survival plan.

He still could not speak. Perhaps the rope had damaged his vocal cords.

'I go,' she said to him. 'OK?' she added, as it seemed to be a widely used word.

She pulled the rucksack onto her back. After a few steps, she noticed that the young man was following her. He kept coughing and rasping. She walked on, from one yellow dash to the next. There had to be an end to this. It became stupidly steep. She had to lean forward while climbing up the rocky path. The young man was still behind her. She heard the struggle he had with his throat. She could also smell him. The trees thinned and the wood came to an end. She was faced with high alp scenery. She knew what it looked like; Google Earth had shown it.

There was a house some distance away, a strange one. It looked like a large book thrown open onto the grass, the book covers being the roof.

★

Greta Huber was not at all what Alice had imagined. She wasn't a feisty maiden with muscular calves and strong arms. She was a rather small and dainty forty-year-old. She rushed out of the open-book house and wrapped her arms around the suicidal adolescent. He tried to unhook her from him, but she clung on. Alice, worn out by travelling, sat down on a rock. Not a word was said. It was clear that Greta was the mother of the boy. Three people would be living in the alpine hut, one of them a suicide candidate. Alice had to adapt her expectations.

'Alice,' she introduced herself.

'Alice,' repeated Greta several times and added, 'Wunderland.'

Observation number twelve. People in this sparsely populated part of the world had a tendency to repeat words, as if they were amazed that they could speak at all. She crossed the last words out – no speculation or interpretation.

When Greta tried to help with the rucksack, she plopped it down again. 'Stones?' she joked.

'Stones is the only thing you have plenty of around here,' replied Alice, and she was not joking.

The women went into the house, Greta calling out 'Rudi' for her son to follow them.

Inside was a low-ceilinged living room, and in the corner stood a sink, or rather trough, into which dribbled water through a pipe from the outside. There was a stove but no cooker, oven or refrigerator. There were ladder-like stairs up to two small bedrooms. Where was the bathroom, the shower? The stairs led on up to a space in the apex of the roof, filled with straw bundles and a sleeping bag. Worn out, Rudi sat down on it; his throat was still rasping.

The tour of the property was clearly not over yet. Greta dragged Alice through the kitchen to the back door.

Alice hiccoughed with fright. A dirty, white goat with pointed horns made moves to charge, but a rope restrained it.

'Gitzi.'

Gitzi could not have touched Alice because of the shortness of the rope attached to a ring in the wall. Basically, the goat was wading around it in its own waste, and had for a long time. It whiffed.

'Milk.' Gerda pointed at the sad animal.

She was a milk-dispenser and nothing else, Alice realised. As if the goat could read her thoughts, she looked up at Alice, who suddenly had to fight back tears. The amber eyes of the animal were beautiful; they revealed a soul. Alice, holding out her hand, approached slowly, holding her breath. One more inch and she could stroke the animal. Head lowered, horns pointed, Gitzi rammed into her belly. Alice jumped back.

Greta could not stop laughing.

When evening came, and it became darker and colder, preparations were made to produce food. Still, mother and son had not said a word to each other. Rudi fed wood through the little door of the cast-iron stove in the living room. On top stood a pan filled with water. When it bubbled, Greta added two large potatoes. The three of them sat close to the stove, the flame of which made it possible for them to see each other. There was no electricity in the house.

The potatoes seemed to take forever to soften. Alice was faint from hunger.

Supper was boiled potato and a beaker of goat's milk. Rudi could not eat anything because his throat still hurt too much. He was now dressed in pyjamas, his trousers hopefully being washed. The milk tasted foul. What made it so rancid was its temperature.

'No refrigerator?' Alice tried to communicate. Mother and son did not understand.

The meal over, Greta sat on a high-backed chair and cross-stitched on a piece of fiddler's cloth, the pattern on her knees. It was a long-term project; many flowers against a busy background. Alice took out her pad and wrote down the experiences of the day. Rudi sat, mouth open, sore throat hurting. *This is going to be difficult*, thought Alice with a growing sense of doom. From outside came the drawn-out bleat of Gitzi. Greta, ready to laugh again, watched the effect it had on Alice.

Greta cross-stitched; Rudi threaded the coloured wool into the eye of the needle for her. It had turned pitch dark outside. Standing at the window, Alice admired the star-filled firmament and the gigantic shape of the mountain near them: the Donnerhorn.

Offered the smaller of the two bedrooms, Alice fell asleep on a mattress filled with straw and a pillowcase, the pillow of it not offered. At least it was clean and smelled fresh. *What have I done?* she asked the wood-planked ceiling above her. Two eyes in the wood and a nose-like shape created an ogre staring down at her. How could she wash her hair with the shampoo she had carried all the way here? There was no running water, only a pipe from a spring out of the rockside through the wall of the house and into a kitchen trough. She would have to cut her hair. Greta had little scissors for her cross-stitch work.

When Alice had needed the loo, Greta had walked her away from the hut to where rocks were piled up. Into the cracks of those had to go their human waste, as simple as that.

Why did mother and son not talk? Greta seemed to have guessed what Rudi had done to himself. Had he done this before? Was life so depressing for him? Perhaps her presence could stimulate him? She heard him rasp in the roof space above her.

The next day, Greta took Alice to show her *Der Kuhlschrank*. The two women walked up towards the Donnerhorn. They had left Rudi behind. He had found Cassell's German-English dictionary and could not tear himself away from it, but Alice had had time to learn that she was to be shown the refrigerator.

Greta's lusty confidence took over. She grabbed Alice by the hand and pulled her along over a bumpy meadow, up and up to the foot of the Donnerhorn. They clambered over rough-edged rocks. They waded through grass which had turned brown and straggly. There were small holes in the ground made by animals. A little further on, Greta cupped her ear with excitement.

'Waterfall.'

Eventually, the women were close enough to see the mass of water pounding down. Anyone caught underneath would be instantly crushed. Spray dotted the air, turning everything white, except for a rainbow that could be seen through it. Closer, when they felt moisture droplets on their skin, Greta made a sharp turn and tapped along a path hacked precariously into the mountainside. At least someone sensible had installed a hand rope. They came to a big hole which led into a cave. It was vaulted and vast. It was also noisy, and not from the waterfall outside. This noise was a deep roar, more like the growling of a large and dangerous monster trapped in the depths.

Greta entered the cave and Alice, who followed, immediately put her hands protectively against her upper arms. The temperature had dropped drastically, and the air changed to dank dampness. The rock's vault and sides glistened with moisture. Almost all of the floor of the cave was taken up by a large natural lake the colour of light-green jade, the water not translucent but milky. This lake was fed by a pair of small cascades, but there was also some underwater activity, causing the surface to bubble up.

'Glacier water,' Greta explained. Alice bent down to touch it but snapped her fingers back from the cold.

What made it difficult to walk around the narrow edge was that the lake had risen higher than the rim of the natural rock basin. Sloshing through a foot of water, Greta insisted on showing Alice the back of the cave. Alice was still nervous to be inside a mountain, fearful of the intermittent roars coming from some hollow depth beneath them.

The end of the pale-green lake was marked by a metal gate, bolted either side into the rock walls. Greta pointed under the water, where the bottom of the gate was a solid metal plate. She took hold of a handle attached to a large winch, around which was wound a chain. The other end of the chain was fixed to the foot of the gate. As she strained to turn the winch, the gate opened slowly and lake water gushed through the gap and plunged down. Alice moved forward to see where the water went and discovered a cavernous gorge, which seemed to go right down into a roaring hell.

The gate acted as a lock. The glacier water kept the cave cold all year round. It was definitely a refrigerator. Greta now took Alice to some wooden shelves fixed against the cave wall. Food was stored in churns, jars, containers, and clingfilm-covered dishes. The cave also provided water. Two metal buckets hung from hooks driven into the rockside.

Greta unhooked a bucket and filled it with lake water. She also took from the shelf a ceramic dish with a lid and gave it to Alice to carry. Then, she went to unloosen the chain around the winch. The gate slowly closed.

The women sloshed back to the entrance of the cave. Turning back, Greta felt the need to communicate more. The water level of the lake had to be watched; the gate had to be closed after each visit.

On the way back, they took turns carrying the burden of the water. Perhaps there was enough of it for Alice to wash her hair today. Her spirits rose, but then she thought the more water she came to fetch, the more she would sweat. The more she sweated, the more she would have to wash herself. Piped water was bliss; she had never thought of it that way. Tonight, after potato with the luxury of butter, Alice would have to write down a lot of new observations.

★

September ended and October started. It was getting dark earlier. Every day was the same, except for the cross-stitching picture, which advanced. Rudi's throat rasped, he milked Gitzi, he went to collect wood that he could chop up for the stove, which acted as hotplate. The only time he became animated was during his sessions with Alice, the two of them reading Cassell's German-English dictionary. Every new word seemed to be a treasure for Rudi. She mimed the meaning of the English word; he mimed the German word for her. Otherwise, he spent the time sitting on the back doorstep, morosely gazing past the goat into space.

Great excitement was caused by the arrival of 'Heidi's grandfather', whose name she learnt was also Rudi. The old man had a big sack of potatoes over his shoulder. A bashed colander he had found somewhere made Greta happy, as if it were a rare and beautiful thing. Alice saw Greta pay him money, which she took from a drawer in the dresser.

On another day, old Rudi returned carrying a handwoven crate. Greta screamed with delight. 'Chickens!'

The youth came running from the house, and the old man put his arm around his shoulders. Alice noticed that their skulls were the same shape. She deduced that they were father and son, as they shared the same name. There

293

was not much choice in men, and Greta must have been healthy and young twenty years ago. Alice could note the observation that male names were handed down through generations – as a means to identify the breed line.

The two hens lived at the back of the house, scratching in the goat shit. They laid eggs and, with potatoes, butter and eggs, the daily meal improved.

October turned into November. Alice shivered in her bed. One of the hens disappeared. The pile of white feathers the next morning showed that the chicken had ventured away from the house and been caught by a fox. To Alice's horror, Rudi fetched his axe and severed a leg of the remaining chicken. Greta was amused by the painful way the bird had to hop along. Now it could not go far and the fox would not get it.

It was Frost Moon. Alice lay under the gaze of the pinewood ogre, her thoughts going to Peter. Had he tired of fish? Tired of soy sauce and Thai shouting? Alice had written several letters to her parents, in the hope of finding a way to post them one day. Her concept of time had changed. The clock did not advance. Small, survival improvements ticked time on. The stiff rope with which Rudi had failed to hang himself served now to attach Gitzi to the wall, allowing the goat even less room to move. The softer rope taken off the goat served to close the potato sack in use, to keep the mice away. After trying unsuccessfully to wash her hair in the bucket of glacier water, Alice had to cut it short. Strand after strand snipped by the little scissors curled at Alice's feet. Luckily, there were no mirrors in the house to show how she now looked.

Then, Christmas was not far off. Alice had done almost four of the nine months and filled several pads with observations. She felt emotional about the thought of Christmas so far from the people she loved. The greatest improvement since her arrival was better communication with Rudi, thanks to the dictionary. However, when Alice asked him how old he was, he did not know for sure.

'School?'

'Not yet.'

Christmas. Yes, Greta would make a Kuchen. There was some tradition. It appeased Alice. Up on this high alp, they would not have problems finding a Christmas tree to decorate; thousands and thousands stood in the silent, dark forest. Greta was saving eggs for the Christmas Kuchen. They were back to potato and goat's milk.

Gathering wood, Rudi found some mushrooms. It was surprisingly exciting to have a new taste to savour. Just after this pleasure, the lone one-legged chicken stopped producing eggs. *It is psychological*, thought Alice. The bird had suffered a terrible injury, a shock to the system. Alice did not attempt to communicate this thought.

Old Rudi was not due for two weeks. At Christmas, they would eat the useless chicken before the Kuchen. It would be great. Greta glowed with purpose. She was a cheerful soul. She laughed a lot at little.

It was Christmas Eve. Greta was beating eggs to make her Kuchen. Rudi stroked over Alice's disastrously uneven shorn hair.

'Not fair,' he said.

Alice fetched Cassell. Page 411. 'Not beautiful, not lovely.'

Around his neck, the scar of the rope still showed. Outside, the weather had taken a turn for the worse, as it could so easily do on Donnerhorn alp. Snow would have been the right thing; instead, it started to thunder, rain and hail. Over the mass of the Donnerhorn, lightning cut into the dark – an apocalyptic sight. Gitzi, at the back of the house, made her fear known by a lament of bleats. Alice shuddered.

'Very good,' announced Greta, coming from the kitchen carrying a cake on a plate. Considering it was not cooked in an oven, it appeared appetising. The cake covering was beaten solid egg-white. A small twig of mistletoe was embedded in it. A thick gold ribbon was wound around it. That ribbon Rudi had once found in the forest and given to his mother as a present. It carried much value for them.

'Solid gold,' Rudi translated with the help of Cassell. Alice shook her head, but not that vigorously.

After the effort of baking, Greta sank onto her high-backed chair. She had excelled herself, but that was not the end of it. The cake had to be kept chilled in the refrigerator until the next day. Alice offered to bring it there, despite the bad weather. Greta was grateful.

Rain washed Alice's face and tickled her scalp between the remaining short tufts of hair. With this wild excess of weather, her shoes would probably give up. The Christmas Kuchen she was holding in front of her was covered by an upside-down plastic bowl, the one

Greta used to soak her feet in hot water. As Alice came closer to the mountain, she heard the increased noise of the swollen waterfall. In Beethoven's Ninth, drumwork produced similar acoustics.

Alice threaded herself along the path against the mountainside, not able to use the rope loops because of the cake. She went in to the mouth of the cave. The lake was so high, jade-coloured ice water licked at the side of the walls. Food, swept off a lower shelf, floated around.

Alice pulled herself together. The Christmas Kuchen had priority. Wading through glacier water with worn shoes didn't hurt so much when one had a goal. Tomorrow was Christmas, Christmas on Donnerhorn alp. In the study of men, Cadogan had taught them some basic principles to work with: the human fate is *to have* or *to be*. To have and be, to have and not be, to be and not have.

On tiptoe, she pushed the plate with the Kuchen onto the top shelf. Behind her, the gruesome beast in the belly of the mountain roared. Emerging from the cave, teeth clenched, she was hit by ferocious rain again. There was something almost personal about the way she was being attacked by enraged nature.

'Bring it on,' she shouted. 'I am a *to be*.' The flame of determination heated her mind for a moment. She continued to talk to nature. 'If I were a *to have*, I would not have chosen anthropology. I would be home, where Daddy would put on ice the caviar his Iranian client had offered him.' No wading through caves. Her parents were *to haves*.

Back at the hut, Gitzi was yanking at the short rope, her head tossing, while crying from fear and despair in goat language. Alice unknotted the stiff rope from the ring in the wall. With Gitzi, she entered the house.

The moment Greta saw them, she shouted, 'Goat out!' and made a sweep with her arm.

Gitzi twisted her head up to Alice, while she was pulled back out under the rain and back to her fate, waiting for death, attached to a wall while being robbed of milk that nature had intended for her progeniture.

'Do not interfere in their habits,' Cadogan had said. 'You study anthropology. You are an onlooker, a classifier. Don't project. Never let your emotions or personal psychological development get involved.'

It was only when the rain finally stopped and the uneventful boiled potato Christmas Eve meal was over, that Alice, on her lumpy straw mattress, started to worry: had she closed the gate before leaving the cave?

Once dawn brushed away the dark thoughts cowering in the corners of Alice's small bedroom, she got up and rubbed wild mint leaves into her teeth. Then she burst into the living room with 'Happy Christmas – Frohe Weihnacht, page 559'.

Rudi was sulking around the room. He was stark naked, and in a dark mood. Greta came in at that moment. Seeing her son, she lifted her arm, her hand in a fist, a threatening gesture. Rudi slunk out; his pink bottom disappeared. What was going on in his mind? All he really did was chop things with the axe and milk the goat. He was deprived of education or guidance to sort out what was going on in himself – a healthy young man with a problem of depression.

Over the treacherous Donnerhorn the sun rose, but stayed low. Alice guessed it to be midday. Christmas lunchtime in many homes of many countries. By now, her father would already be preparing the eggnog, while Maria, the house help, would make sure the traditional Christmas turkey meal with trimmings turned out as successful as the ones the years before. And the dessert would be delivered on the dot by the Italian catering company, as was another of the family's traditions.

In the Donnerhorn alp, the pink, plucked body of the one-legged chicken, its head axed off, was simmering in the boiling water over the cast-iron stove. Time had come to fetch the Christmas Kuchen from the refrigerator. A patterned scarf tied over her head, Greta set off. Rudi took over the high-backed chair. He and Alice were alone. She did not mention the display of his body earlier. Gitzi was silent; a bundle of hay from the loft had been thrown at her feet.

Alice picked up the unfinished cross-stitch work. Finished, it would be a rug depicting a rose garden with a house and mountains in the background. There was a pig in the foreground. Most of the pink of the pig had been done.

By now, the family back home would sit down for the Christmas meal, the presents opened. Here, the boiled chicken body taken out of the pan was getting cold because Greta did not return with her Kuchen. The day dragged on.

When the pale sun was seen to go down behind the Donnerhorn, Alice felt nauseous with guilt. The massive amount of water after the torrential rain must have swept Greta down into the dark, growling hole, because the metal gate had been left open. Alice was responsible for Greta's death. The hungry beast in the belly of the mountain had swallowed her alive. Alice did not want Rudi to go and find out about it.

Great tension hovered in the room. She did not dare look him in the eyes. With slow movements, he put away the knives and forks with which they had planned to eat the Christmas meal. Could he guess or feel what had happened to his mother? He was close to her. Humans living in primitive conditions were known to develop a more intuitive communication, even without speaking to each other. He closed the drawer of the dresser.

'No mother, no Kuchen,' he said and climbed up the ladder to the loft.

There was the sudden, unfamiliar sound of Gitzi repeatedly bashing the back door with her front hooves. Alice, now sitting in the high-backed chair, despite her shaking hands managed to thread a length of wool into the eye of the needle. She picked up the cross-stitch guide, compared it with the work done so far and continued the work on the green border next to the roses. The cold, boiled chicken, one leg out stiff, lay on the table. Simple life had turned into tragedy and she had caused it.

Later that night, Rudi appeared at the door of her small bedroom. He was waiting for an invitation. It had been building up in him – the showing himself naked, the dark moods, the many looks he had given her lately. She had taken from him the only person he was close to – his mother. She rolled to the side on the mattress. He closed the door behind him. He knew what to do, but did it clumsily and roughly. He hurt her, but did not notice. Was this pity sex? When it was over, he went away. Nothing was said between them. Probably, when Greta had had sex with old Rudi, it had gone the same way.

Alice passed the next two days as if in a trance. On the surface, it had the qualities of resignation, hopelessness and suppressed mourning. At the live core of it, however, fear, anger and reproach broiled. Greta did not reappear.

Rudi chopped wood and milked Gitzi. Alice cross-stitched the garden hedge. They ate boiled potatoes and drank goat's milk.

On the third day, Alice found Gitzi in her mess on the floor. The eyes were fixed, and there was no pulse. The milk machine was gone. Alice could not let Rudi chop Gitzi up for bits of her to be boiled on the stove. Instead, she forced him to find a suitable resting place for the dutiful animal. Rudi carried the dead goat over his shoulders up to the foot of the Donnerhorn. Alice followed in an effort to honour the life, the sad life of this goat.

At a chosen moment, Rudi threw the dead animal into a crevasse. *The mountain has been fed with another creature*, Alice thought with bitterness.

Rudi gave Alice the stiff rope off the goat's head. They walked back to the house. The strident call of the circling bird of prey, deprived of a carcass, echoed eerily.

A new calendar year started. Snow came. Alice was surprised how silently it fell, how tenaciously and how thoroughly it covered everything. The temperature dropped. Ice formed on the inside as well as the outside of windows. With Greta gone, during evenings, while the unpredictable flames of wet wood crackled and banged in the stove, Alice worked on the cross-stitch project. Most of the sky was done already. Often, Rudi pulled the cross-stitch blanket away from her to dump the dictionary into her lap to read while the flames still provided light. They had made it to *Pa*, page 350.

'Pantoffel – slipper.' The flames died out; the little fun was over. They sat in a dark room, a room filled with the ghost of the mother who had disappeared under suspicious circumstances.

With every day that passed, the hope of Greta reappearing dwindled. It snowed – a heavy load now covered the wide roof of the open-book-shaped house. Under the light of the moon, the Donnerhorn's top ridge shone silver. Soon it would be February, probably. Alice had to be strong. She wasn't. She felt weak and wept. Rudi patted her spiky hair, which did not grow back. She was lacking vitamins, calcium. She was losing heart.

What Alice had to tell Rudi was that she was expecting a child. His, clearly. Once he had understood, without looking up *pregnant* in Cassell's, he eyed her with suspicion, and then he worked it out.

'Little Rudi,' he finally said, patting her bump.

'A happy Rudi,' she tried to communicate. 'A baby laughing a lot, like your mother did.' *Not one trying to end his life.* 'Maybe we should call him William, like Tell, the Swiss hero.' He did not like this suggestion. She lay her hands protectively over her belly. 'This little Rudi,' she said, 'will not need to hang himself.'

He got up to climb to the loft to masturbate in protest against her. He had understood that her pregnancy was changing things, but he could not fathom its importance. Cassell could not print the implied. A last node banged in the stove. Light dimmed around Alice. *What have I done?* she thought and not for the first time.

'Daddy,' she said into the darkness, 'I am sorry for choosing anthropology. I hope I didn't do it to rebel against you. Honestly, I felt a passionate need to find out where the line was drawn under human beings. I have hit rock bottom and am not curious any longer. You will be a grandfather. How would that work if I came home with little Rudi?'

Several weeks later, Alice felt her baby punching her. Little Rudi was alive and kicking. Some signs of spring should have come by now, but it was still snowing. Alice was so thin, her ribs showed.

Alice had understood that 'Heidi's grandfather' could not make it up to the alp in the snow. With some money from the dresser, Rudi stomped all the way down, through the dark forest, along the rock wall, into Sprieglen. He returned with a bag of potatoes, bananas and a can of tuna fish in brine. He put the fruit and vegetables on the table, but held onto the can, turning it over and over.

'Whoever sold it to you meant well,' Alice said.

'How does it open?' He tapped the metal lid.

'It's protein, for little Rudi to grow strong.'

He liked to hear that and made to go and solve the problem with his axe. She shook her head.

He put the tin into the drawer with the money. He felt hurt, but did not know how to handle the feeling. He picked up the dictionary. She had to finish the cross-stitch picture by the time the baby was born. It would be a play mat for the newborn, who would love the little pig. If only Greta had lived to find out that she had stitched it for her grandson. Alice started to weep.

To cheer her up, Rudi brought the dictionary. 'Unke,' he said out loud and crouched on the floor, making a hop. Expectantly, he looked up at her. She brushed away her tears. They had done the Ps. She turned pages.

'Here,' she said. 'Unke – orange speckled toad.' She heard her own laughter. It was that of Greta.

It was the end of March, surely by now. Snow fell during the night, sneakily silent. It needed force to push open the back door to make it to the rocks to relieve oneself.

Then, to her horror, Alice found the gold ribbon of the Kuchen in the money drawer. Rudi had put it there. Rudi had gone to find his mother. How many times, Alice did not know. She hoped he had closed the gate. The ribbon had come off the cake. Greta had made it to the shelf to fetch the cake and been swept away after that. Alice put the ribbon back where she found it, then went up into her room to cry. Lately, she was doing this increasingly often.

The snow was less deep, but old Rudi had still not come up. Perhaps he was unwell, perhaps the jeep had broken down. Perhaps... better not think about that. There was not much left of the potatoes Rudi had brought up, and the last ones were not just shrivelled; they had turned squashy with blue bruises.

'Dandelions soon,' Rudi tried to console her.

'Do you know how many dandelion leaves I would have to eat to give my growing baby enough food?'

They had their first argument. When he suggested going to look for Gitzi's dead body, in case some of it could still be eaten, she slammed the door. Stomping through short, brown grass, only recently exposed to sunlight after weeks under snow, Alice was shaken by the new thought that she could easily die up here in nowhere alp. And the baby would die with her. There was no help, no way out of it.

She stopped. Was that not what had happened to Rudi's mind, before she had found him hanging from a tree? He had had less to lose than she did. She was born into a house which had heating, a deep freezer, television, computers. And a Waitrose delivery option.

She could go back to that, somehow. On foot, if necessary. Barefoot, as her shoes had fallen apart, and with her baby over her shoulders, like Gitzi on Rudi's. All it needed was determination and a belief that her small life on this big earth mattered.

Feeling better, she turned round and started back. Not far from the backdoor of the house, an animal suddenly shot out of a hole. Her arms flew up in fright. Rudi ran out, chasing the mountain hare, his axe held

305

high. She watched the impossible situation. He stumbled over a rock and twisted his ankle. She helped him back into the house. He was obviously in great pain. It would take time to heal, and he could not go back down to Sprieglen to buy potatoes.

They shared a potato every other day. They sucked on nettle soup. She had to be halfway through her pregnancy by now.

They had made it through the Vs and Ws. They had boiled a mouse and gnawed on its tiny bones. Hunger produced hallucinations in Alice. They were mostly about expensive food on the table. There were so few Xs and Ys, they took only half an hour.

And then came the evening when they made it to the last word in Z.

She continued reading out loud. 'Cassell and Company Limited. Printed in Great Britain by William Clowes and Sons.' She closed the dictionary. There seemed to be nothing left to do except…

She felt it strongly. She went to fetch the soft rope from the pile of folded potato bags. She held it up, just in case she was wrong about it.

'I learnt to love you,' she said to Rudi.

She had guessed right. He took the rope from her. Peace and relief seemed to seep through him. He gave her a sweet, loving smile, one she would never be able to forget. He knotted the rope into a noose as he left the house. Alice envied him.

The hours that followed were torture for her, until the moment when she believed she heard the heartbeat of little Rudi inside her. She owed her son a life. She would go down to Sprieglen. It would take time. There would be blood from torn feet. The passage past the sheer wall, with the rocks rolling down, petrified her the most. Perhaps tomorrow, she decided. Then again, perhaps the day after.

★

A loud noise woke her from her dozing. More unexpected noises followed until the door was flung open, and a familiar, beautifully warm and reassuring voice spoke.

'There you are, Alice, my crazy adventurous girl.'

The Swiss had taken advantage of her father. A short helicopter journey could not possibly have cost as much as they had fleeced him for, even if they had classified it as emergency rescue, with double tariff on a Sunday, and harness-lowering to inclined ground.

ROADKILL

Ever since Hendrik had offered her thirty-five per cent of his company and promoted her to director of marketing, Tina had appreciated the regular meetings in her boss's home. Before that, meetings in GIR's conference room were painful experiences, as employees had strong and unrealistic ideas, which inevitably led to heated disputes. This did not happen in Hendrik's kitchen, with just the two of them to make decisions.

Her young and enthusiastic boss had built up GIR from scratch, together with a university friend who moved on before the company was flying. GIR was an online service to find the right physical location for businesses. The service excluded the US, as the Americans had their own system.

GIR, short for Get It Right, employed analysts to work on availability to buy or lease, foot traffic, parking, competition, site image, and factors as basic as strong wi-fi connection or good sewage services. They would even sniff out undesirable neighbours like a dog rescue home or halfway house.

Once suitable locations were approved, GIR gave the recommendation to go for it. GIR clients who moved in were presented with a luxurious welcoming hamper tailored to the size of their business. *Location, location, location* was part of the logo on the GIR cards, on stationery and in advertising.

Tina liked her job. No case was the same, and she could often travel to give a final site approval. They dealt mostly in the UK, sometimes in Europe, and twice in Singapore, although those plush jobs Hendrik kept to himself. At Christmas, the company was swamped with cards from happy customers, and the company's finances were healthy.

On this Friday morning in Hendrik's kitchen, Tina was sitting on a red Ikea chair, sipping tea he had made. On the table were road atlases, city maps and a pile of ring binders which Hendrik had brought from the office. There was, of course, also Hendrik's large computer screen, giving his face pallor as he sat at it, clicking the personalised mouse.

He obviously spent most of his free time at this table, in the small, terraced house on Waverley Street in Cromer. Apart from the kitchen, which gave access to a narrow east-facing garden, there was the living-cum-dining room. She knew that the narrow stairs led up to two bedrooms and a bathroom. From the front bedroom, if one leant out dangerously, one could catch a glimpse of the North Sea, a demonstration he had given her on her first visit.

She asked herself every time why he did not buy a better house, closer to the sea. Single, he said he had enough space. She assumed that, his father and grandfather having been in the navy, Hendrik must have had a strict upbringing, in which modesty and basic living were considered virtues. At times, even with clients some navy jargon escaped him.

On his living room wall was a display of medals awarded to his father and grandfather for service in the Royal Navy during both World Wars. Hendrik had them beautifully mounted against dark red velvet and was thrilled by them, especially since his mother had given the collection to him and not to his elder brother. Hendrik had not chosen a military career, but had nonetheless inherited precise and rational thinking, and the officer's upright posture. Clients immediately gave Hendrik credit for upper-class breeding, especially when he wore a suit.

Tina envied him his background. She had practised in front of the mirror in her studio flat to achieve some of that. Head up, chin out, shoulders straight, to help her during pitches to potential clients. Perhaps her father, who had owned a corner grocery shop in Norwich, had not given her the genes it needed.

Today, working down their items, they came to a printing company which was searching for ground-floor premises with backroom space, ideally in the centre of a mid-sized market town. She offered to collect information about *possibles* in several towns herself.

'The owner lives in Richmond, London,' Hendrik read off his screen. 'His commuting has to be taken into account.'

'Why the centre of a town with limited parking, when stacks of paper have to be moved, and the weather is what it is?' asked Tina.

'Good point,' he said. 'We'll study the demography of businesses in towns versus industrial compounds, and present it to them.'

She pulled her cardigan off the chair back and shrugged it on.

'You cold? I can turn the heating up.'

'Not necessary,' she replied. 'I know you don't like your house to be overheated. With a name like Hendrik, you must have Scandinavian blood in your veins.' She had finally dared to bring this up. 'All I have retained from school are the stories of a Viking warrior who sailed on the North Sea. He had blond hair just like yours.'

'Roede Orm,' he said. 'A Swedish hero.'

'Is that why you live in Cromer? To look out over the North Sea. Do you sail?'

'Never tried it. Stop fantasising. We have work to do.'

'Let's have a break. Show me your garden.'

'You've already seen the little there is.'

'That was in summer. Now it's winter.'

He got up from the kitchen chair, not that unwillingly. She smiled to herself.

At the open kitchen door, gallantly he let her go out first. She tapped his shoulder lightly in thanks. The cold raw wind went right through her clothes. Her breath created milky patterns in front of her mouth. She started to run down the lawn into the wind towards the small shed.

He took his time, walking with his stiff gait to catch up.

Near the shed was a wintry herb garden. Some herbs,

312

like sage, withstood the cold, as did some determined nettles planning to take over. She bent to pick mint leaves off a stem, the furry leaves she liked to put into tea, when she noticed something most unexpected. A tortoise with a shell the size of an upside-down Chinese wok was squatting in the parsley patch. Its head, in the shape of a hammer, wrapped in green leather, protruded.

She knelt down, and beady eyes focused on her. 'Hello,' she uttered, taken aback by the human expression in the little eyes.

Hendrik caught up. 'Oh no.' He sounded alarmed.

She waited for him to go on.

'It's Eloise, the neighbour's tortoise. She must have borne down on the chicken wire again. Once, the neighbour found her in the front, just about to navigate the road. She is a strong-headed girl, of the oldest land-living species.'

'Not much fun, though,' said Tina. 'All it can do is rock its ugly head and leak milk out of its back end.'

'Diarrhoea.' Hendrik sucked his teeth. 'It has to be the near-frozen parsley. I'll go and fetch the professor. Stay here and make sure Eloise doesn't run away.'

Tina did not understand what he meant and should have said, 'From the Ice Age, a bit of chilled parsley should not be a problem.' The idea of the tortoise running away, also, was ludicrous. This cumbersome clump, the head now hidden, surely only moved at glacial pace.

Hendrik sprinted elegantly back to his small house and disappeared into the kitchen.

She knocked with her knuckle on the tortoise's shell. White indentations separated the hard surface into honeycomb sections; at the centre of each, a dark-blue prevailed.

'Anyone home?'

The head appeared from under the rim of the slightly vaulted carapace.

'Boo.' She tried to scare it into a reaction.

Eloise remained stoical. She opened her clamp-like mouth, tore parsley away at the roots and closed the clamp, before laboriously munching the herb, a protruding green stem twirling in the process.

'Shall I give you a tip?' Tina bent forward. 'Why don't you crawl out from under that stone-hard shell and get a life? Without it, you might even pass for a rabbit – to a drunk, at least.'

Hendrik appeared in the neighbour's garden at a gate in the fence. He was accompanied by an old man. They pushed a large toe sack truck down the garden towards Eloise, with a crate secured to its platform by bungees.

The moment he saw his tortoise, the old man smiled broadly. 'There you are, bad girl,' he said to his pet. 'You're grounded. No television for a week.'

The tortoise blinked a reptile blink. After the telling-off came the task of getting Eloise into the crate, which was custom-made from thick MDF board, and had windows cut in three of its sides in the shape of hearts.

Tina drew breath, ready to mock, but decided against it. The old man, until now absorbed by his pet, noticed her.

Hendrik introduced them both. 'This is Christina, my colleague from work. Actually, she is co-owner of my company.'

'Is that so?'

'Tina, this is my good neighbour, Professor Griffiths, professor of zoology.'

'If you introduce someone you should do it correctly,' the professor grumbled. He held out his gnarly old hand to Tina. 'Call me Benedict. I have a professorate in wildlife studies, speciality herpetology, narrowed down to testudines. I am also on the board of the local palaeontology society. There. Now I should be clear to you.'

Tina smiled at the tall and thin man, bending slightly to her.

'Help us get Eloise into her travelling box, will you?' said Benedict.

'I don't think I can lift her up,' replied Tina.

'God, no,' he said. 'She weighs close to thirty kilos. However, compared to the giants from whom she is descended and who can weigh seventy-five kilos and live over one hundred years easily, she is a mere bonsai. You have to tease her up the ramp, like this.' With his thumbnail, Benedict clipped a dead branch of thyme. 'Tap it gently against her backside and she'll get the message.'

The professor frowned at the tortoise's backside and then looked anxiously at Tina. 'Dear, oh dear. Either it has been too emotional for her, or she ate something bad. Her bowels are loose. Poor baby.'

Tina and Hendrik exchanged looks.

'I'll make you acorn tea when we get home.'

Eloise was not in the mood to go into the box. A sea-fret came in off the North Sea, wrapping the garden in grey mist. The temperature dropped.

Benedict decided he would hold the trolley steady, while Hendrik and Tina pushed the tortoise up the ramp.

'Come on, darling,' the old man coaxed. He reached into his cord trouser pocket and produced a pink plastic ball, which he fed through a window into the box where they could hear it bounce. 'Go and get it.'

Tina rationalised that there was no reason why, in the Ice Age, animals would not have liked toddlers' toys. She pressed her lips together to prevent herself from saying something disparaging.

'Naughty, naughty.' Benedict's breaking voice showed that he was cold and worn out. He produced from his other pocket a metal hook fixed to a wire, and hooked it through a small hole which had been drilled into the carapace over the head of the reptile.

It worked. The tortoise, feeling the pull, put one courageous foot in front of the other and disappeared into the box.

'Watch your tail.' The professor closed the hinged back wall of the crate, secured it and then pulled the trolley back through the gate to his garden. Luckily, there was only one narrow step to surmount to the house.

In the professor's kitchen, Eloise was released. Tina turned her head away from the soiled newspapers covering the tiled floor, the blobs of limp half-chewed vegetables, a rubber ball to play with and a bowl of water standing in a puddle.

On the back of the door hung a small piece of wood on which was carved *Eloise's room,* with daisies surrounding the words. Chafed green wellies stood near the door. Perhaps Eloise was not just a messy pet, but also an ankle-biter, or clipper.

Benedict invited the young people into his living room, which had the same layout as Hendrik's and the same wood-carved fireplace surround. Through the window, Tina saw that the unified stretch of concrete car parking in front of the terraced houses was broken, in the professor's case, by a two-seater garden bench.

She was invited to make herself comfortable in a brown velour easy chair and decided to decline any food offered. From the unhygienic kitchen came the noise of repeated banging.

'Eloise does *not* like to be transported,' said Benedict. 'She hates coming with me to lectures. The airlines try their best to pretend there is a dog in the box. On trains, I have a whole set of other problems. Lately, I have been hiring a man with a van, for the UK at least.'

There was another thump. 'Ignore her,' said Benedict. 'She'll tire herself out banging around in the kitchen.' He opened a drop-lid cabinet. 'I have brandy, whisky, or gin and tonic. Don't look so surprised. Even old fossils like me are up to date with booze.'

However, having dropped the can of tonic water, he still opened it immediately. The liquid foamed over, and spilled down his waistcoat and the front of his trousers.

'Professor Griffiths gives lectures all over the world. Cheers!' Hendrik raised his glass of whisky to distract from the clumsiness.

'Cheers.' Benedict toasted with his drink in return. 'In many countries, they toast to health. In Britain, we need to be encouraged to cheer up.'

In the kitchen, the tortoise still hadn't tired herself out.

Tina got up to take the glass of almost-neat gin, and paced around the unfamiliar room. Through the window, she noticed the fret had thickened, nebulosity erasing from sight the narrow strip of garden identical in size to Hendrik's. The chill seemed to seep through the single-glazed window. Turning her back to the cold, she contemplated the room. On the wall, over the fireplace, hung an enlarged grainy picture of giant tortoises in the Galapagos, Benedict standing close to one of the giants, his hand on the animal's shell. The mantelpiece was garnished by a row of what appeared to be random stones.

She crossed over a threadbare patch of carpet, perhaps where Eloise did exercises, to a chunky over-ornate bookcase, the dark wood dominating the few books that fitted into it. *Evolutionary History Riding on Giants*, Benedict Griffiths. *Living with the Descendant of a Fifty-Million-Year-Old Reptile.* The professor was an author. Tina pulled one out. The book sleeve had a photograph of a younger Benedict, kneeling on sand with small, recently hatched turtles around him. She opened it at random and read '...*the honeycombed shapes on the shell are each air-chambers, so the carapace is in fact not the heaviest part of the animal...*' From the pages came the scent of musty sawdust. This book was not often read. She put it back. Against the street-facing wall, a hammer balanced on a hook.

'It's a rock pick,' said Benedict, following her gaze, 'for fossil-hunting. With the sharp point, one can crack open even flint stones.'

She was not listening, shocked by the discovery, in the corner of the room, of another tortoise. Or perhaps Eloise had found a way to escape from the kitchen, and ended up here. Why didn't Benedict react? His foot was close to the creature, hiding under its shell.

Worse still, once he noticed that she had discovered the animal, he gave it a kick with his foot. She checked her drink; she had drunk little so far. The unreal nature of this day hovered in the grey light of the room, along with the dust particles.

'You think I have another Eloise, don't you?' He kicked the shell again.

'It's a Conesus turtle stone.' He laughed, revealing the neglected teeth of someone who drank a lot of tea. 'With its turtleshell pattern, it is a pseudo-fossil. One of the largest ever found, dating from the Ice Age. Mud heaps turned into rock heaps, the honeycomb shapes were separated by angular cracks of crystallised minerals created by the seepage of water. An extraordinary coincidence of nature, almost as miraculous as the finding of the complete skeleton of a mammoth from the Pleistocene epoch at the foot of the cliffs, a few hundred metres from where we are now.'

Tina admired the geological specimen on the floor. This was more than perfect camouflage. It was nature's timeless plan for trickery.

'There are many things I don't know,' she admitted.

'I agree with Tina,' contributed Hendrik. 'I watched them pry the skeleton out of the cliff. Some of the million-year-old bones were as tall as I am. Such a time span is incomprehensible to the brain.'

'Oh no,' Benedict objected. 'Galapagos tortoises emerged fifty-five million years ago; the turtle rock only two and a half million – practically yesterday.'

'Is that what your lectures are about?' asked Tina.

'It's part of it, naturally, so I take Eloise and the rock with me as props.'

Who would believe that, in one of the terraced houses on Waverley Street in Cromer, lived a famous professor, with a living sample of the world's oldest creature, and the rarest pseudo-fossil ever found in America?

'For you, young lady, special friend of my neighbour Hendrik.' Benedict picked a stone from the mantelpiece. It was a small turtle stone, the size of a hot cross bun. 'I found this one myself near Lakeville.' He placed it into her hand. 'A souvenir of your visit today, and for your bravery in putting up with the cold in my house. I've never installed central heating. I moved here forty-two years ago, and I guess I like it the way it is. If it's cold outside, it's winter. But I have to confess, when it gets below zero, I have recourse to a hot water bottle.'

'Understandably!' Tina laughed. In the tall, narrow fireplace, obviously the only source of heat, was a pile of salt-bleached driftwood. The door to the room was held ajar by a cuttlefish bone wedged under it.

'All is quiet in the kitchen. A bad sign.' Benedict sighed and left to check on Eloise.

'Gone to sleep,' he reported, coming back carrying a cake tin lid with custard cream biscuits on the silver side of it, as if it were a silver tray. Tina declined. He did not offer it to Hendrik. He sat back on the seat next to the bookshelf.

320

'Do stop walking around,' he said to Tina. 'You're wearing out my poor carpet.'

'I like walking around and looking at things.'

'Sit and tell me what you are working at. Hendrik said you were colleagues in his company.'

'We work online, mostly. We don't do anything which has lasting value.'

'You are his secretary?'

'No. I am co-director of the company.'

'Couldn't Hendrik find a man to do that? He is a lucky fellow to have found you. It wasn't right for a young fellow like him to live without a woman for so long.'

'I am a businesswoman.'

'That depends on what business we're talking about, hey? Nudge nudge.'

'No nudge nudge.' She was irritated. 'I part-own and direct a company with an eight-million-a-year turnover. There is nothing personal between Hendrik and me. There never will be.'

'You just have to try a little harder to excite him,' said Benedict. 'You've got the looks.'

She sighed deeply and then approached the door. 'I'm off. Say bye to Eloise for me. Take care.' Resolutely, she grabbed the door handle.

'Hold your horses,' called Benedict. 'I understand.'

'Yes?'

'You're one of those Amazonians – a woman warrior.'

She left the house. At the door of Hendrik's house, he caught up with her.

'You won't be able to change him,' he said.

'His species got stuck fifty-five million years ago. Clearly.'

'We can have our next meeting at your place, if you prefer.'

'That would be boring without Ice Age creatures,' said Tina. 'And I include the professor in those.'

'Benedict is internationally famous. Look him up.' Having a thought, Hendrik offered to drive her home. 'The fret is still thick.'

'I want to take the bus and be slowly driven out of this unreal situation, back into Norwich and my normal life,' she said. 'And then I will go to bed early and single.'

'If I were not your boss, I would kiss you now. You are hot, Benedict is right about that. But we'd better keep things professional.'

'We'd better.' She put her hand briefly to his cheek.

★

A month later, on a Saturday, the printing company, which had moved into the premises GIR had found for them, came back with problems. The director pestered Hendrik on the phone. A Brazilian dance studio had opened on the first floor, even though they had been told it was leased to a computer game designer. The whiff of marijuana hung in the entrance and all the way up the staircase, to which were added thumping music and loud yelling. Not to mention coke-heads hanging around. Apparently, the police had come to clean up the place twice during the first week they had moved in.

Hendrik, for whom order and regulation were

paramount, was upset by this news. It could also harm the reputation of his company, especially if someone picked it up and posted it online. Something had to be done, but what? He called Tina to tell her that they had to decide on immediate action. He suggested they met in the office, and reminded her to bring the keys.

If this went viral... His mind came up with a YouTube video. A frontless house; on the ground floor were printing activities, silent and serious; on the floor above, fiesta, dancing and loud music. A topless woman bending over the floor rim, throwing a rose to the grey man at the printing machine. The printers starting to dance; the music spreading. *Bring more rhythm and joy into your everyday work. Trust GIR to find you cool spots.*

Hendrik was frightening himself as he got into his car on the concrete in front of the house. The motor did not start. He cursed and then, bracing himself and controlling his trembling hand, tried the key again. The motor ignited.

'All right.'

Perhaps they could find new premises for the printers. Perhaps they could find a flaw in the dance studio's lease and force them to move out. Whatever, something had to be done fast in order to avert the worst. He yanked the gearstick back, and twisted his head over his left shoulder to reverse. There was a sudden bump, and the car rocked on its suspension.

'Idiot,' he said to himself. He had rammed into Benedict's garden bench. Checking in the rear mirror, he was puzzled to see that the bench was intact and clear of his car. What, then, had he hit?

He turned off the engine and got out. Behind one of the back wheels lay Eloise, her shell rim touching the ground all round. Oh God! He had driven over her and the soft body was now squashed.

'Eloise, come on, get up,' he almost wept.

There was no sign of life. A dark, oily substance seeped from under the tortoise. The substance was on the animal's shell, as well. Was blood from the Ice Age that dark? He had destroyed one of the last creatures from which knowledge could be gleaned about how life on Planet Earth had evolved. He felt congested by high blood pressure. The GP had warned him the last time it was checked.

Hendrik looked around him, as if crazed. With a modern car, he had squashed a descendant of the oldest creature ever to have lived on the planet – he, a little man dwelling in a small house on Waverley Street in Cromer. Finally, he knelt down on the concrete, gasping for breath. In pain or death, Eloise had concealed herself under her shell.

How could he tell the professor about this tragedy? It might do more to him than raise his tension; the horror of it could easily kill him on the spot. In that scenario, he, Hendrik of no importance, would have killed two pillars vital to mankind. In Viking Roede Orm's veins had pulsed courageous blood; he became a legend. Hendrik's father and grandfather had risked their lives to defend Britain and been decorated by the Queen, while he, Hendrik, drove a car backwards without checking first what was in the way. And the car was only a humble Hyundai 1.2.

What should he do now? What could he do? Even if he found a vet, he needed a man with a van, and a ramp. Exactly the type of complications that resulted from spontaneous behaviour he most abhorred. He, and he alone, could be blamed. Had it not already started to go down the hatch with GIR's mistake with the printing company? And now he faced a dead, or half-dead, perhaps suffering, tortoise. What had brought him onto the wrong track? Had the professor's allusions to Tina and him being intimate, and not just work colleagues, affected him subconsciously? Now shaken, he admitted to himself that the few fleeting touches Tina had offered him, like the quick brush of her fingers against his cheek, had meant more to him than he had admitted to himself. They were no more than butterfly wing caresses. The tickling of her hair, her scent when she sat next to him at the computer. He shivered in memory of it.

He advertised the benefits of living a single life, but every one of those superficial touches had shot right down into the core of him – a depth in which swirled passion and a fevered desire to erupt, reach out, grab her and cash in on those teases.

At his feet now, Eloise was suffering silently under her carapace. Tina would never accept affection from him, not after what he had done to this innocent animal. He had to hide Eloise and hope she would recover without medical help. Fifty-five million years of survival of her species might come in handy right now.

Hendrik strode into his house and came out with the table prolongation leaf, just as it started to rain silent tears. Each drop diluted the dark blood which had run from under the damaged reptile.

Bravely, he started to push the plank under the

squashed tortoise. He had to use force, probably because the animal's flattened body was in the way, perhaps her chin. When he was all the way under her, the light came on in the professor's front room. He might come out. Hendrik had to work faster.

It was raining properly now, desolately. He went to fetch a hammer and two large nails, and then started up the Hyundai's engine, to let it idle. Not loud enough. He brought Alexa close to the front door, and requested rock music. He turned it up.

A group of young people passed the house, talking loudly, the girls giggling. They did not identify the clump on the ground as a tortoise. In the professor's front room, the curtain twitched. Hendrik drove one nail into a corner of the table leaf. The wind rose, the rain started to drum on the car, and he thanked the heavens for it. He hammered the other nail in the opposite corner. Benedict's hearing was clearly bad.

Eloise still gave no sign of life. Hendrik ran into his house again and emerged with a ball of string, which he threaded round the nails, joining the ends with knots.

Grabbing the middle of the loop, he started to pull the load across the concrete. A lorry rattled past, and Hendrik took advantage of the noise to drag the board to his entrance door. If only he had a side gate to the back, but terraced houses didn't have these.

Eloise listed on the plank as he dragged her over the metal sill, but did not slide off. Hendrik repositioned her in the middle, before the journey went on along the corridor to the kitchen, through it and out through the back door into the wet, glistening grass of the garden.

Hendrik's Nordic hair was plastered to his head. There was no light in any of the rooms of the professor's house facing the garden. Luck was on Hendrik's side. He tilted the table leaf at the parsley patch. The heavy load of Eloise slid into the herbs she loved to munch.

'Sorry, my dear,' he said, before returning to the house with the blood-soiled board. The moment he finally settled at the kitchen table, his mobile beeped. Tina wanted to know why he had not appeared in the office to discuss the printing company problem.

'Hi,' he said casually, brushing sweat and rain off his forehead with his sleeve. 'Do you know whether it rained two and a half million years ago?' he asked her.

'Probably not,' she said. 'Icicles fell, more like.'

'Did I ever tell you that you are beautiful as well as clever?'

'No, and don't start now. What's the matter with you?' A pause. 'Are you drunk? What did you take?'

'No, and nothing.'

'What did you do?'

'I crushed Eloise. With the back tyre of my car. Reversed over her by mistake.'

'Roadkill?'

'You can call it that,' said Hendrik. 'She is resting in peace in my parsley patch.'

'Does the professor know about this?'

'Not yet.'

'Bad boy,' she said, but cutely.

★

It was close enough to Christmas for the shops to be heaped with Christmas-related objects. From his upstairs bedroom window, Hendrik checked his herb garden. Eloise had not moved, was slowly decomposing with the wet weather. Hendrik did not have the courage to go down the garden to check. He also avoided meeting the professor, who had come several times ringing at the door and whom he had seen pacing through his garden morosely, head hanging, on several occasions.

Hendrik spent time avoiding confrontation with his own thoughts. Pushed by Tina, he visited the Brazilian dance studio on the floor above the printing firm, to threaten them with eviction based on disturbing the peace and possible drug trafficking. A salsa blasted; an exotic woman sashayed her haunches. Breasts danced before him, and he had to dare to look. The rhythm pulsed. He felt heat drizzle through veins he did not know he had. He agreed that this was hotter than printing pamphlets, when she grabbed his hips with both hands and brought his pelvis against hers with carnal brutality.

*

Eventually, a note was pushed through the brass letterbox in Hendrik's door. *You may have something that belongs to me. Could you please return it? Benedict.*

Hendrik drank a whole bottle of gluhwein he had grabbed in Aldi, without heating it. Dizzy, he drove to work and begged Tina to help him get over this glitch in his life, but she made it clear that she did not want to get involved with the decomposing tortoise, the heartbroken professor, or the Brazilian dance teacher. She sent him home, declaring him useless.

Hendrik realised he was on his own. It felt familiar. The North Sea fret pushed into Cromer. He thought of Roede Orm, statuesque in the bow of his boat. He sat at the kitchen table without moving, while the dark gathered around him. Why had he chosen such a life?

'I don't know,' he said and again. 'I don't know.'

After a while, he looked up. 'You do know. You must know.' Had he started up a company finding the right places for others because he, himself, did not fit in anywhere? He definitely had not fitted into a woman's life, and now he had undermined a professor's teaching.

It was time.

He rang the professor's doorbell.

'It's Christmas,' he said to Benedict. 'And I have come to confess.'

'Ah, so it was you,' said the professor. 'Did you really think you could get away with it? You have no idea how rare it is, and how much it means to me. Where did you put it?'

'Please, don't get mad at me. I understand what you are going through. In my parsley patch.'

'Strange move.'

'She liked my parsley. Broke through the fence to get at it. I will do everything in my power to make it up to you, I promise. I am already punished for my mistake. Christina will not forgive me for what I have done. She is the one who runs the company. She, the one who makes things happen. Poor Eloise. The voices of dinosaurs were memories in her genes and I, a mere nothing...'

'Stop whinging. What happened was clear.' Benedict pulled the hat off his head. 'Theft happened. Back from Durham after my lecture, the driver unloaded Eloise's crate and wheeled it into the kitchen. But then, the stupid man just left the turtle rock in the front, when I had given specific instructions. Anybody could have taken it, but I did wonder if it was you. Do you want to come in for a cup of tea?'

'Can I take a rain check? Right now, I just want to go home and scream.'